AN INCH OF TIME

AN INCH OF TIME

A Chris Honeysett Mystery

Peter Helton

CRÈME de la CRIME

This first world edition published 2012
in Great Britain and the USA by
Crème de la Crime, an imprint of
SEVERN HOUSE PUBLISHERS LTD.

British Library Cataloguing in Publication Data

Helton, Peter.
  An inch of time.
  1. Honeysett, Chris (Fictitious character)–Fiction.
  2. Corfu Island (Greece)–Fiction. 3. Detective and
  mystery stories.
  I. Title
  823.9'2-dc23

ISBN-13: 978-1-78029-031-7 (cased)

All Severn House titles are printed on acid-free paper.

Severn House Publishers support The Forest Stewardship Council [FSC],
the leading international forest certification organisation. All our titles that
are printed on Greenpeace-approved FSC-certified paper carry the FSC logo.

Typeset by Palimpsest Book Production Ltd.,
Falkirk, Stirlingshire, Scotland.
Printed and bound in Great Britain by
MPG Books Ltd., Bodmin, Cornwall.

ACKNOWLEDGEMENTS

Many thanks to Juliet and to James for my welcome to Severn House. Thanks also to Jess for the alarm message: *Time to get up and write those books*. No thanks to Asbo the cat for walking over my keyboard and inserting the message *knuggl dreqqq* into the final draft.

ONE

'No, Chris, it's spring now,' Annis pronounced from inside the six layers of clothing she was wearing under her painting sweater. I had counted each one with regret as she put them on that morning.

'You're delirious with cold. It's winter. Deepest winter.'

'Well, *officially* it's spring now.'

'*Officially*, it's bloody freezing. Two paces away from this stove you'd perish in this *perishing* cold within minutes.'

'How would you know? You haven't moved away from that stove all morning.'

'It's only because I've been feeding it so diligently that your brush hasn't frozen to your canvas yet.'

'We'll get warmer weather soon; can't be long now.'

My own easel was empty since I was between paintings. Also between investigation jobs and between cheques from Simon Paris Fine Art, which was the reason for me trying to keep the wood burner in the studio going with any object that would burn. I fed another chair leg into the stove. We'd run out of logs days ago and I'd been burning oil rags, old paintings and broken furniture. Also furniture I had freshly declared broken that morning. 'Warmer weather soon is what you said last week. We've had snow showers since then. Actually, I'd prefer snow to this muck.' What had looked like morning mist had turned out to be a stubborn fog. Mill House and its ramshackle outbuildings lay at the bottom of the valley and it was often visited by lingering mists and miasmas, as though the place wasn't damp enough with the mill race hugging the house. Our studio – or rather the leaky, draughty barn we used for painting in – sat at the top end of the meadow, no more than sixty yards from the house, yet right then you wouldn't have known it. I walked across to the grimy windows we had bodged into the side of the barn to give us that Rembrandtish gloom Annis and I preferred for painting. Outbuildings and yard were hidden in mist except for a vague loom of dark in the damp greyness. 'It's like trying to paint inside a bottle of milk,' I complained. 'Semi-skimmed.' She ignored me and got on with her work – a large, complex canvas she had started the day before. From where she drew the inspiration for her mysteriously glowing canvases she never revealed, and over the years I had asked often.

It was five years ago now that Annis, then still a student, had somehow managed to squirrel her way first into my studio, then into the rest of my life. She helped with the private eye business if I asked nicely. She was good at it too, but much preferred to spend her time in the studio. Apart from studio, house and occasionally work, we also shared a bed, though this arrangement wasn't one to be taken for granted, since there was also Tim. Of whom more later.

For a while I stood and watched Annis watch paint dry. You'd probably need to be a painter to appreciate this pastime. For a painter, an unfinished canvas will always hold more fascination than a completed one. In fact, a finished painting is a bit like a good meal you had last week – a pleasant memory but offering no sustenance. Yet each time I finish a painting I slip into this limbo, like a man who is hungry but can't decide what he feels like eating.

Annis pulled her bobble hat deeper over her strawberry curls. 'Honeysett, I can hear you thinking; it's most distracting. Why don't you go and make soup or something?'

I brightened up instantly. 'Soup! Good idea. What colour?'

'Oh, any. Something big and cheerful that'll take you a long time to do.'

'I'll give it a go.'

Big I could do; I wasn't so sure about cheerful. The winter seemed to drag on for ever this time, and this wasn't the cold, clear and crisp season of the north but the dark, damp and dreary winter of the west of England. Outside, the air was saturated with moisture that settled in my hair. The rush of the mill race was muffled with mist, the vegetation sketched damp streaks across my jeans and the smell of wood smoke, normally so cheerful, filled my head with wintry darkness. More than anything, it was the lack of light that had finally got to me as it spread grey melancholy like botrytis across my life with months of low cloud and lingering mists. I could just about make out where the sun was trying to burn down through this murk, but reckoned it would be hours yet.

The postman had at last found his way down here. The cheque from the gallery I was waiting for wasn't among the pile of mail he had left on the hall table. Apart from a vet bill, it was all junk; I chucked it into the fireplace where it could do some good.

Right, then: soup, she'd said. I checked the larder, vegetable basket and fridge. Something big, she'd said. Well, you couldn't get much bigger than minestrone. What made a soup minestrone? Haricot beans, smoked bacon, tomatoes and tiny pasta shells. For the rest, you use whatever is around.

I shoved my biggest cauldron on the stove, glugged in enough overpriced extra virgin to turn the bottom green and set to. In went garlic, chopped onion and bacon. I yanked open a couple of tins of chopped tomatoes and tipped them in. Easy-peasy, this. A good squirt of tomato purée, a couple of pints of stock from the fridge and the phone rings. Far, far away in the attic office.

The fact that I had hidden my office up there gives some indication of just how committed and organized I was about running a serious business as a private investigator. And how successful it was in financial terms. Aqua Investigations was really a Yellow Pages listing, an answerphone in the attic and a grumpy painter who had forgotten what on earth made him start this detective lark in the first place. Too many black-and-white movies at too tender an age, I suspect.

Normally, I'd have ignored the call, let it go to the answerphone, then checked it later, but, in the hope of thus keeping the rest of my furniture out of the fireplace, I took the stairs three steps at a time and snatched up the phone at the fifth ring. Unfortunately, by then I didn't really have enough breath left to answer it.

'Aqua . . . Investigations,' I panted.

'Good morning. Is that Chris Honeysett?'

'It is,' I wheezed.

He sounded doubtful. 'OK . . . Is everything all right there? Is this a bad time for you?'

'No, everything's fine. I've been running . . . bit out of breath, that's all. How can I help?'

'Keeping fit – important in your line of work, I expect. Now, my name is John Morton, and we would like to hire you to deal with a little matter for us.'

The royal 'we'? 'And who might "we" be, if you don't mind telling me?'

Here Mr Morton mentioned the name of a large British supermarket. Very large. Even I shopped there. Of course, if I'd had any sense, I'd have hung up immediately and gone and buried my loyalty card in the garden. And then built a garage on top of it just to make sure.

Instead, my stomach rumbled thinking of all that food. Perhaps they could pay me in smoked salmon and quince jam . . . 'Don't you have store detectives for that kind of thing?' I asked, already distracted.

'This is different, Mr Honeysett; it's not an in-store matter. You do come highly recommended.'

Oh, really? That kind of talk usually meant they'd asked another agency and been told they wouldn't touch it. When pressed, they then mentioned my name in a sentence that also contained expressions like 'exorbitant rates', 'mad enough' and 'last resort'.

'I'd like to discuss this face to face,' he continued, 'but I'm told you don't keep an office in town. I'm staying at the Queensberry. Join me for lunch downstairs in the restaurant. It's eleven twenty now; let's say twelve thirty at the Olive Tree. You *do* know it?'

'I do indeed.' Only chronic shortage of funds meant I wasn't spending a lot of time eating there.

'Twelve thirty, then.' Morton hung up. Not that the man was at all pushy. At no point had I agreed to anything, but for some reason he seemed sure I'd be there. Perhaps he could hear my stomach rumble.

The kitchen had steamed up when I got back and already smelled promising. Close-quarter knife-work now. There were potatoes, carrots, a red pepper, some celery and cabbage; all were finely chopped and committed to the deep. Some parsley clinging to life in a pot on the window sill went in next (omitting the pot), together with some seriously depressed-looking thyme from our little herb garden outside the kitchen door. I shoved the cauldron to the back of the stove where it could bubble away for an hour or so. Annis would have to finish this off. I left pasta shapes and tins of beans in a prominent place and went to give her the good news.

'Perhaps they can pay you in Colombian coffee and croissants,' she suggested.

'Fresh turbot and asparagus.'

'Pinot Noir and Vacherin cheese.'

'Pilsner Urquell and Stilton.'

Painters hardly ever discuss art. They talk about money and the food they'd buy with it if they had any.

'And you have no idea what they want you for?'

'"A little matter", I think, was the expression he used.'

'I see.' Annis nodded sagely. 'Another one of those. And you're meeting at the Olive Tree? Who's a lucky Honeypot, then? But don't go there on the Norton; the goggles leave rings round your eyes. Take the Landy.'

'Ta, I will.'

Offering me the use of her fiercely loved 1960s Land Rover was a measure of just how much she wanted me to get the assignment and out of her hair. After the sad and sudden demise of my old Citroën DS 21, I had taken to two wheels. What had started as an emergency matter had turned into affectionate attachment to the ancient bike, despite its ludicrous credentials as a PI vehicle. Strictly speaking, the Norton too belonged to Annis, only she'd gone off riding bikes after crashing hers into a bridge over the canal due to a mysterious and complete absence of brakes. It's a long story.

Remembering that, unlike a motorcycle, you couldn't park a car just wherever you felt like it, I made sure I got into Bath with what I thought was plenty of time. I was wrong. It took so long to find a parking space within walking distance of the Queensberry Hotel that I only just made it in time and was once more out of breath when I was shown to a reserved table for two in a quiet corner.

From the outside, the Queensberry was Georgian, this being the predominant idiom in Bath; inside, however, the decor was contemporary simplicity. The restaurant was moderately busy. Large, cool abstract canvases punctuated the walls in the restaurant. Uncharitably, I concluded they had been chosen for their unobtrusive blandness so as not to distract the diners from the food.

John Morton didn't give me much time to contemplate the decor, however. He appeared at my table with a speed and energy that made the Olive Tree's first-class waiters look like sleepwalkers. He was about fifty, with close-cropped blue-black hair, and moved his six-foot-two and eighteen-stone body as though recently shot from a cannon. We shook hands and he took his seat opposite me. Immediately, a single menu arrived, together with bottles of mineral water and one of Pilsner Urquell. The glass that came with the lager was chilled.

'I have very little time since I have a plane to catch at Filton Airport, which is why I took the appalling liberty of ordering starters for both of us. I could have let someone else handle this but I prefer the personal touch; that way I'm spared many disappointments.' His big expensive voice ran over me irresistibly like the tide. The starters arrived after a further minute. 'I know you like fish, Mr Honeysett, so that is what I ordered; you are naturally free to order whatever you like as a main course. I myself can only join you for the first course. Regrettably, I'll have to complete my lunch over the Atlantic,' Morton said without any hint of regret. If he was flying from Filton Airport, then he'd most likely be using a private jet and I was pretty sure his food wouldn't arrive cut into squares or in a plastic tray. He took a sip of water, then tucked into his starter of pigeon breast and beetroot. His teeth were preternaturally white and his whole appearance so well groomed and slick that the few spare stone of gastronomic weight he carried were all but invisible. My own dish had been announced as pan-fried monkfish with lemon butter and I tried not to fall on it like a starved street urchin. 'So what's this little matter you would like me to look into?' I said fool-ishly, while thinking *I wonder who told him to feed me fish?*

My host had perfected the art of talking while eating delicately. And fast. 'I want you to find someone for us. An employee of ours went missing and you know what the police are like, overstretched trying to deal with crime. Naturally, we're concerned and want you to make *discreet* enquiries as to her present whereabouts.'

'Tell me what you know already.'

'Her name is Kyla Biggs, she's thirty-three years of age, a valued member of our British team and she's based in Bath. She disappeared on holiday. She was travelling by herself. Should have returned eight days ago but didn't.'

'Where did she holiday?'

'Greece. Corfu, to be exact, but that's all we know. Find out what happened to her. We got little help from the British police and no joy at all from their Greek counterparts. The Corfu police appeared to be suggesting that she did a "Shirley Valentine", as they put it.' His eyebrows lifted briefly in dismissal.

'Did a what?'

'A cinematic reference, I believe. "Run off with a Greek waiter" is what they were trying to imply.'

Corfu. They want me to go to Greece. Somewhere warm. 'You think that's out of the question? Is she single?'

Morton shook his head in exasperation. 'Kyla Biggs has a great future with our company and knows it. Even on her present salary, she could *commute* from Corfu if she'd fallen in love with someone there. She's also a highly responsible and considerate person. So, no, I don't believe she ran off with a local Adonis.'

'Do we know who she booked her holiday with?'

'Flight only.'

'So we don't know where she was staying?'

'I'm afraid not. The Greek police drew a blank.'

This could take some time. *Especially if it was sunny.* 'Corfu was a big island, last time I looked. But I do have a contact there who can assist me,' I exaggerated. Actually, I'd never been there, though an old college friend had made Corfu her home. I hadn't heard from her for years.

'Go and find Miss Biggs for us. We chose you because we're told you speak fluent Greek.'

I nodded. Turkish, actually, but I didn't feel this was the moment to split hairs. Why cloud the issue? This was a terrific starter and the lemon butter worked well with the monkfish, so I'd be fine. 'And whoever told you that also mentioned I liked fish?'

Morton had finished his starter, sipped water and smiled indulgently. 'They didn't have to; we knew that already. I know quite a bit about you. You do eat a lot of fish, drink Pilsner Urquell, live with a lady and ride a motorcycle. You're also broke.'

You can go off people so quickly sometimes. 'You don't need a detective, after all.'

'You shop at our store, remember? You pay with plastic, so we know about every item you've ever bought. Our computers work this up into a customer profile. You also buy petrol from us and the amounts suggest you ride a motorcycle. You buy items of female hygiene and the rest is self-explanatory. Lately, you have spent more money on special offers and less on luxuries, suggesting you are feeling the pinch. Many do right now.' He had reached into his pocket and extracted a thick business envelope bearing my name in typescript. 'You'll find a photograph of Miss Biggs and contact numbers inside, as well as a thousand pounds to speed you on your way.' He set it delicately next to my beer glass.

I parried his move by extricating a slightly crumpled sheet of densely printed A4 from my jacket pocket. 'Standard contract; sign at the bottom.'

'Of course.' He produced a Mont Blanc ballpoint pen and made a squiggle on the bottom without reading a line of it. 'I'm afraid I must leave you to your main course; I have a car waiting. Please contact us as soon as you know anything at all.' He stood up to leave.

I rose too but hesitated when he offered to shake hands. 'There's just one thing I should perhaps mention: I don't fly. I never use planes. Ever.'

Morton's expression changed from businesslike to mild amusement. He grabbed my hand and shook it. 'Then I suggest you don't linger over dessert. Goodbye, Mr Honeysett.'

Ten seconds later he had disappeared and been replaced by one waiter who cleared away the plates and another who asked if I was ready to order my main course. I fingered the sealed envelope by my beer glass. Could this be an elaborate hoax? If this was full of bits of newspaper, then I would get a chance to put my considerable experience as washer-upper to good use. I dismissed the thought. Morton had judged me correctly: I was the performing seal of the private eye world and he had thrown me a fish.

'Yes, I'm ready.' There was Cornish turbot on the menu, surely worth a shift of washing-up in any man's life. The food arrived so soon I wondered if the kitchen too had known what I would order. Only when the waiter had placed the dish in front of me and had retired did I run a casual fingernail along the length of the envelope exposing the joyous pink of a wad of fifties. The sight made me breathe more easily. I extracted the three-and-a-half-by-five-inch photograph of my quarry and propped it against a water bottle from where Miss Biggs watched me eat in black-and-white aloofness. The turbot was cooked to perfection; the herb risotto was sheer bliss.

In her head-and-shoulders picture Kyla Biggs wore short and stylish hair, a business suit and fashionable glasses. She looked as if she knew where she was going and the gaze she directed at the camera was one of energetic confidence. Shacked-up with some hairy Greek waiter she wasn't, unless she had suffered a breakdown due to a moussaka overdose.

I attracted my own waiter's attention – not at all difficult – and asked for the bill. 'That has been taken care of,' he informed me neutrally. Did I care to peruse the dessert menu?

It was painful, but Morton's advice on not lingering seemed sound since I had a trip to plan which I'd find difficult with a dessert spoon in my hand. I managed an almost decent tip without having to pull out a wad of fifty-pound notes and walked back to the car feeling quite the *bon viveur* and at one with the world. They were *paying* me to go to where the sun was hiding, I thought jubilantly; just how good was that?

And they say fish is good for the brain.

TWO

'Greece? Even jammier.' Annis stirred the cauldron of soup I had left on the stove and tested the pasta for *doneness*, which, according to her, *was* a word. 'Of course it's a word, I just used it, and anyway, it's done, so there.' She heaved a steaming ladleful into a shallow bowl, broke a hunk of bread off a crusty loaf and smothered it in Somerset butter. Real *Good Life* stuff. I followed her example.

'You unbelievable glutton – you just had lunch at the Olive Tree.'

'I deliberately skipped dessert to leave room for this.'

'And they pay you to go to Corfu. I can't believe it. I went there, years ago; it was brilliant. So that's your prayers answered; what about mine?'

'Perhaps we're praying to different deities.' I shrugged. 'Come with me, of course.'

'How? What with? Your thousand pounds won't last us long.' She shook her head, but with a certain reluctance. 'Anyway, I've just started a painting. If I leave it now, it'll never happen.'

'True. But the cheque from Simon Paris would do it. You could always get a cheap flight out when it comes.'

'It's an idea, anyway. Perhaps once I've finished the painting, but by that time you'd long be on your way back, wouldn't you?'

'All depends on what I'll find when I get there.'

'Are you going to look up your old painting pal while you're down there? Does she still live there?'

'Morva? As far as I know. I haven't heard from her for a couple of years. I'll see if I've still got a phone number for her. She might be able to help. Especially if she's learnt a bit of Greek. Someone told Morton and Co. I spoke Greek.'

'Did you tell them you didn't?'

'Forgot to mention it.'

'Wise move. Did you mention your fear of flying? And the fact you haven't – still haven't – any transport of your own? How are you going to get down there, then?'

'Good question. First I thought train, but that would leave me without transport once I arrive.'

'You could rent a car or a bike down there, but they'll charge tourist rates. It's bound to cost you a bomb, especially if it takes a while to find her. Unless they'll forward you more money, you could be in trouble there.'

Driving down was the obvious answer, yet neither of our antique conveyances would make it that far.

There was always Tim, of course. Tim Bigwood was the third leg in the shaky tripod that propped up Aqua Investigations. He helped with all things locked, anything to do with computers or gizmos, since I'm useless with those. (I can just about fiddle a lock open but I always make sure to take sandwiches.) A reformed – or so he said – safe-breaker and now IT specialist in the employ of Bath University, he completed our triangle in more ways than one. It was about three years ago now that Tim and I found we shared more than just an interest in strange ways of making a living, when we discovered that Annis bestowed her favours on us in more or less equal measure. For reasons that may have less to do with our broad-mindedness than with her persuasiveness, this triangle still survived intact. Since Annis lived with me at Mill House, it was hardly an equilateral one, so I wasn't complaining. Much. And it did seem to work, most of the time.

I called Tim at work. His shiny black Audi TT would, of course, make short work of the journey to Greece. Tim made short work of my delusions. 'There's a really good reason why you haven't got any transport, Chris, and that's because anything you drive tends to disintegrate beneath you.'

'That's only because they're usually ancient to begin with.'

'True. But if anyone can turn a three-year-old Audi into something ancient, it's you. You didn't really expect to borrow the TT, did you?'

'Not really. You don't fancy a trip to Corfu, then?'

'Not on what you're paying me. Only kidding. But I do have a real job, you know? The bill-paying kind. And I can't take a holiday for another age now. Can't you try Jake again?' he suggested fatefully. 'He can usually come up with something.'

Tim was right: Jake was the obvious answer, though I probably owed the man so many favours by now that I might one day have to start working for him. Should I call him? I decided on a visit. Why give him the chance to hang up on me?

A fine mist of moisture drifted on the wind as I kick-started the Norton. There were so many layers under my leathers that had I come off the bike I might have just bounced along the road. This illusion of protection wore off less than three miles into the journey. My face was frozen by the stinging rain, my fingers went numb and the rain had found its way under my jacket.

Jake owned a smallholding a few miles outside Bath towards Chippenham, where he had originally tried to make a go of breeding ponies. The business had failed, so, with a little lateral thinking, he switched from pony power to horse power and turned his hobby – restoring classic British cars – into a business. It took off and is still flying. Jake had looked after a succession of automotive ancients for me that, according to him, could only be described as classics in the sense of 'classic mistake'.

By the time I got there I was frozen numb. Wind and rain were much wilder up here. I was relieved to see the bright light spilling from the workshop doors and hear the sound of growling power tools. Jake's place looked even more ramshackle than my own, though appearances were deceptive. Unlike me, he had a complete mental map of where was what and could always lay his hands on what he needed. At least, that's what he tells me. Every available outbuilding was crammed with cars – some complete, some quietly rusting, awaiting attention. The perished concrete of the yard was littered with cars and car parts, under tarpaulin or seemingly abandoned to the elements. By now I felt pretty abandoned to the elements myself. I parked the Norton under the eaves of a corrugated iron shed and walked into the workshop. The warmth from an enormous space-heater instantly steamed up my goggles.

Jake looked up from where he was grinding showers of sparks off some car part or other, held in a vice. 'Ha, look, it's Biggles. Sorry, we stopped doing biplanes. You can't get the parts, you know?' One of Jake's mechanics, a factotum with electric hair, nodded at me from under the bonnet of a curvaceous Bristol car and went back to work. I ignored both of them and stood in front of the roaring space-heater until I was once more in command of a full set of limbs.

By that time Jake had made tea and handed me a mug. 'You still running round on the Norton? In this weather? You must be madder than I thought. Or are you in fact here because you have come to your senses?'

'Well, it is and it isn't. I've got a job on and the Norton just isn't up to it.'

'I always said a classic bike's no transport for a private eye. It's hardly inconspicuous, is it? And far too noisy.'

'It's not even that. I don't think the bike's going to get me there. The job's in Greece.'

'Nice work if you can get it. Better off on four wheels, then, I agree, but I still think a classic car isn't a good idea . . . oh, I get it. What was I thinking? You don't want to buy a classic car.'

'Not really.'

'You mean you want to borrow one. To go to Greece? You must be kidding.'

'A woman went missing in Corfu and they want me to find her. Naturally, I want to help but, as you know . . .'

'You don't fly – yes, I know. Also can't stand heights and you're scared of dogs. You're lucky mine have enough sense to stay indoors in this weather. So it's the usual: you're broke and need transport. When will you manage to hold on to enough money to buy a decent motor?'

'Don't know, but this could be the one. Big corporate client.'

'Anyone we know?'

'Can't tell you; it's confidential.'

'Yeah, right.'

So I told him. I was always going to anyway.

Jake approved. 'Hey, nice one. Perhaps they can pay you in roast beef and vintage cider.'

Each to his own. 'Would that get me transport to Greece?'

Jake slid the grimy baseball cap off his bald head and

scratched at a welding scar. 'It just might. Times are hard and getting harder. There's quite a few people who are mothballing their classics because they've turned into indefensible luxuries. Fortunately, not all of my customers think so. But everyone's struggling. Remember my mate Charlie, the builder-stroke-brickie-stroke-handyman? He's never been out of work since he was sixteen. Well, he is now.'

I made sympathetic noises. Whenever the economy takes a dive, sales of my paintings go down and the detective business picks up. More divorces for a start, and half of all divorces involve private detectives.

Jake brightened up. 'But roast beef gave me an idea. An idea that means you can avoid having to eat all that foreign muck on the way, too. Follow me.'

I didn't bother telling him that I considered foreign muck a definite bonus of this job and that my main worry wasn't how to avoid it but how much of it I'd be able to snaffle on my meagre budget. Jake led me out of the workshop, back into the rain, across the yard and past several outbuildings. We skipped puddles in the crumbling concrete hardstanding between them until we reached what might once have been a milking shed. In its lee stood a mobile home. At least, it did if you used your imagination.

'You can certainly borrow this. I took it in part exchange last year. It'll be ideal for the job, don't you think?'

Did I? The vehicle in question was a large Ford motorhome and had probably seen better days in the last century. It was whitish with broad brown stripes running around the body. 'Does it go?'

'Of course it *goes*. I wouldn't be offering it to you, knowing what you're like as a mechanic. In fact, the engine is sweet; I worked on it last year. Yeah, we even took her to the Lake District last autumn.'

There was a definite 'but' in his voice. 'But?'

'Sally hated it. Her idea of getting away from it all apparently doesn't include taking the kitchen with her. It also rained and we trod on each other's toes a lot, being stuck in the van. I'd never get her to do it again.' He opened the side door for me. 'Which is why I never finished doing up the inside.'

That was patently obvious. Inside, the van had everything; only the fittings had not worn well. Gift horses being what they are, I didn't quibble. I thought it had potential. As a death trap.

'It's basically all here. You've got your bed that converts into the table and benches you see there. There's a shower in there, quite nifty –' he slid open a narrow door – 'which I admit is a bit small for a grown woman like Sally, if you know what I mean.' He opened the cupboard next to it. 'I installed that myself – the Fretford Porta Potti Three. Actually, I'm not sure I ever emptied it.' He hastily shut the door on it. 'This is the fridge, which is new, and the cooker with oven and grill. Gas bottle down here. It's all there, basically.'

The cooker proudly proclaimed its pedigree on the front of the grill: The Leisure Princess 6. I pulled out the grill pan and hastily returned it. 'It's great, Jake. You think this will take me to Greece?'

'No problem. Once you put some wheels on it.'

Which is what I did in the squelching wet for the next freezing hour. Jake helped me with the last bit, getting her off the bricks. The van looked more of a viable proposition now with a wheel at each corner. Under Jake's ministrations, the engine coughed and backfired once, then ran smoothly, sounding normal. As I started to familiarize myself with the controls, an unusually cheerful Sally turned up. Never had her eyes looked so friendly upon me. The prospect of seeing the back of the motorhome – with my track record, possibly for good – had brought her out into the rain, frizzy dark hair stuffed under a plastic hat, carrying a large cardboard box full of camping gear.

'You'll want this,' she said, shoving it under the table with a gleeful expression. She didn't hang around. 'Say "*iássu*" to the Greek islands for me, Chris. Have a good trip,' she called as she walked back to the house, with a definite *rather-you-than-me* inflection to her voice.

Jake had already stowed a cardboard box under the bench with the words 'Bits and bobs you might need – spare bulbs and stuff', and now he handed over the papers. I called the classic insurance people and insured the van for a laughable sum against third party, fire and theft – the most likely being fire, considering the state of the grill pan – then stashed the Norton in the back and drove home a happy camper. I had never driven a motorhome and found that it took a lot of gas pedal, gear shifting and thoughtful cornering, but by the time I got it to Mill House I had warmed to the thing, though not literally; it was perishingly cold and I couldn't get the heater to work. On the passenger side the seal around the windscreen appeared to be leaking, which explained the miniature lawn of algae spreading across the dash in that corner.

As I was parking the van in the yard near the kitchen door, for some reason I decided to call her Matilda. I didn't know at the time that the name meant 'strength in battle'. With a little more foresight, I'd have chosen a different name, perhaps one that meant 'not so good uphill' or 'what are you laughing at?'

Annis stood in the kitchen door and laughed for longer than I considered polite. Derringer, the resident feline villain, appeared beside her, eyeing the new arrival with suspicion.

I felt protective towards my new charge. 'There's nothing much wrong with her; the engine is sound and the rest is cosmetic. Tax exempt, too.'

This brought on a fresh wave of mirth. She grabbed a raincoat off the hook by the door and ventured out for an inspection. 'Tax exempt! It should be drawing a pension. There's classic vehicles and there's . . . this. I bet you a fiver it won't make it to Dover harbour on its own wheels.' She gave one of them a speculative kick. 'Tyres look new,' she grumbled, then tried the passenger door.

'That's stuck,' I admitted. 'The driver side works, though.'

'That's always handy.' She opened the side door. It groaned reluctantly on its hinges. 'We could use it as a shed, I suppose. Go park it by the barn. We'll keep chickens in it.'

I rolled the Norton out of the back with the aid of a plank of wood. 'It's going to Greece. Tomorrow.' I followed Annis's meaningful gaze around the interior. 'The day after,' I amended. 'I'll have this fixed up in no time.'

'But of course.' A second after Annis left, Derringer jumped in. I climbed in after him, closed the door against the wet and cold, and when I turned around the cat had disappeared. I opened cupboards and lifted lids but found no trace of him. 'Nice trick,' I admitted. Especially in a space that small.

The gas cooker worked, despite the historical strata of gunk that covered the top. I found the fridge was a lightless hole in which something forensically challenging had perished a long time back. The shower discharged a dribble, and Jake had been right about the toilet.

When, hours later, Tim's immaculate Audi rolled into the yard, I was too deep in soap suds and Marigolds to notice until he came and stuck his woolly head through the door. 'Ah. Was it me who suggested going to Jake's for transport? I'm so sorry.'

'Another doubting Thomas. Annis is cooking supper. We can have coffee in here in style afterwards. In the meantime, can you see what you can find on Kyla Biggs?'

'Is she the damsel in distress you are hired to find?' He ran a speculative finger over a sill, examined it, then wiped it on the back of the driver's seat. Tim lived in a clinically clean ultra-contemporary flat in Northampton Street.

'She's the one. They gave me a name and a photograph and nothing else.'

'And a thousand quid, I hear.'

'Petrol money.'

'You still owe me for the last job we did.'

'Send me an invoice.'

'I did.'

'Damn. How much?'

'Call it a hundred for cash.' He held out a broad hand.

I still had the envelope in my jacket and handed over a couple of crisp notes which disappeared into his jeans pocket.

'I'll see what I can do, then.'

'You can use my computer,' I offered.

'No thanks, I'm not a field archaeologist. I've got my notebook in the car.'

An hour later I stepped back to admire my work and thought Matilda's interior looked worn but acceptable – at least by my standards, which admittedly have been called 'bohemian' by some. 'Appalling' by others. As I turned around, Derringer materialized from thin air on the table opposite the cooker. Some of his other tricks, besides appearing out of nowhere, were being able to smell if you thought of eating fish and the knack of opening doors by hanging from the door handle. 'I know there's no point in asking. Let's go; must be feeding time.'

It took me only a few minutes of fiendishly tricky detective work to find Morva Lennox's phone number in Corfu in the back of an ancient diary. Morva's work had always sold well enough to keep her in near starvation and teaching jobs. A few years ago, she and her husband, who was some sort of consultant, upped sticks and moved to Corfu where they bought a flat in the capital. Year after year I promised to take her up on the open invitation to come and visit, but now I couldn't even remember when I had last written to her. I dialled the extremely long number with excuses at the ready. The phone was snatched up after the second ring and a forceful female voice barked something in Greek at me. I asked for Morva Lennox, repeating the name several times without appearing to provoke even a glimmer of recognition. The woman simply poured more Greek into my ear and hung up. Had Morva moved? I had the address, so I'd find out in a couple of days.

When I came down from my shower, the kitchen radio was tuned to Planet Rock, a Tim Bigwood trademark. I briefly paused in the door frame. Tim and Annis were standing by the Rayburn talking while Annis checked on her cooking. She leant across and planted a laughing kiss on his neck. There was nothing unusual in this, yet I couldn't help noticing how much like a couple they looked. Any outsider observing the scene might have assumed I was the visitor. I blinked the thought away and walked in.

Annis heaved a black iron pan on to the table and lifted the lid. The smells of seaside, wine and garlic-charged steam rose from a multitude of mussels, Indian yellow in their slate-blue jackets. 'Perfect timing, Chris.'

'The smell alone takes me halfway through France.'

'Yes.' Tim sniffed the aroma. 'La Rochelle or thereabouts, I think.'

We gathered round the pot and were soon slurping away over our individual bowls of moules marinière.

'Ah yes, your Miss Biggs.' Tim pointed a mussel shell and sprayed garlic sauce over a sheaf of A4. 'I printed those out on the Gutenberg press in your office, hence the streakiness. I didn't find much on her. Owns a flat in Marlborough Buildings, which means they pay her well.'

'What's this?' I pulled the printouts towards me.

'That's a press release, couple of years old now. It's not about her – it's really about food – but it mentions she was employee of the year. There's a picture.'

'Right, I'll have a look at it later. What do you think is the best route to Corfu? Left or right?'

'Oh, you don't want to go through the Balkans; that'll be slow going. I'd go all the way down Italy and take the ferry from Brindisi, smack opposite Corfu. You can book the ferry tickets in advance online.'

'You can?' I pleaded. 'Dover to Calais, too?'

'No sweat. I'll do it for you in a minute.'

After the meal I issued my invitation. 'Coffee in Matilda. Dress casual. And for warmth.' The box that Sally had donated to the van contained sets of cooking gear and crockery, all lightweight and curiously reduced in size, which had rekindled my playing-house instincts from deepest childhood. Tim and Annis indulged me by sitting expectantly in their jackets and scarves at the little table while I prepared coffee, using a dented whistling kettle on the two-ring Leisure Princess. The rain was drumming on the roof and I discovered little leaks here and there. And there.

'It could be quite cosy in here once you reach warmer climes, but at the moment it's little better than sitting outside,' Tim complained.

'Yes, hurry up with that coffee,' Annis agreed.

The kettle began to hum. 'Any minute now.' The gas flames shrank, spattered and went out. The bottle was empty. We all traipsed back indoors to have grown-up coffee in front of the fire.

THREE

'Come and say goodbye again,' Annis murmured suggestively from inside a tangle of hair between the pillows.

I ran a thirsty tongue the length of her spine, tasting the salt of her sweat. 'I think I'd better; otherwise, you might forget me the moment I've crossed the channel.' A scrabbling noise at the door followed by a slight draught told me that Derringer had opened the bedroom door by swinging on the door handle. A moment later he walked on to my back and after a minute of sniffing settled between my shoulder blades, making me the filling in a girl-and-cat sandwich. 'I think you should at least look at me while I say goodbye to you,' I complained to Annis.

Her half-asleep moan could have meant anything, but she dutifully wriggled around, eyes still closed, and wrapped her arms around me – and the cat. 'Oh my god, that's so weird,' she said, eyes wide open now. Derringer stood up and dug his claws into my shoulders. 'That's like an illustration from a children's book; all we need now is a cockerel on top of *him*. That's too weird; goodbye, Christopher.' She kissed me wildly for three seconds, then slithered from under me and made for the shower.

I subsided into the empty space and shrugged off Derringer. 'Now look what you've done. I'll make sure to return the compliment one day.'

Despite taking my time over breakfast, the world was still dripping darkly with fog when I stepped into the yard. I had packed and loaded Matilda the night before and would buy more provisions on the way.

Annis kept up her encouragement. 'Just as well the Landy's got a tow bar. Give me a call when she rolls to a stop and I'll come and fetch you home. This side of the channel only, mind.'

'Oh ye of little faith. I do wish you were coming with me.'

'I might join you later. If the cheque from Simon Paris comes. If my painting is finished. And if you're still there. Then I'll get a cheap flight from Bristol.'

I cheered up. 'Great, we'll have a holiday in the sun.'

'And it'll take me *three hours* to get there,' she said with heavy stress on 'three hours'. 'You're completely mad, Honeypot. There's still time to change your mind and get on a plane like a normal person. You could be there in less time than it takes to drive this piece of junk to Dover.'

'You'd have to shoot me with a tranquillizer dart first.'

'Tempting, but we still haven't paid the last vet bill.'

We kissed again through the open window, then looked each other in the eye for a quiet minute while the crows stirred in the trees by the millpond. I started the engine. Annis waved a melancholy goodbye as I drove out of the yard and bumped Matilda up the narrow unmade track to the road. The madness had started.

Tim had not only booked my tickets but had also printed out a route map and itinerary for me and I had my trusted road atlas on the passenger seat. It was ten years out of date but I was working on the assumption that the basic features like the Channel, the Alps and the Med would still be where they were when it went to print.

I had sobered up a little since the first excitement of being paid to escape this gloomy tail end of the British winter and a few tiny doubts had begun to creep in. What I had said to John Morton was true: Corfu was a large island. I'd looked at a map of it and found it had lakes, rivers, mountains and hundreds of villages. I didn't speak a word of Greek and knew absolutely nothing about the place.

And less about Kyla Biggs. The information Morton had given me was sparse and the picture he had furnished me with represented my only real knowledge of the woman. I needed to get more of a feel for who I was trying to find, yet the only thing I had was the address Tim had found for me, so that was where I headed first.

Marlborough Buildings was a row of grand Georgian town houses, many converted into flats, with views front and back across the fifty or so acres of Victoria Park. The first floors of most of the houses were graced by narrow wrought-iron balconies and it turned out, according to the name on the bell, that Kyla Biggs owned a first-floor flat in the middle of the row, with a view not just of the park but also of the Royal Crescent. I shuddered to think what the mortgage on a recession-proof place like this must cost. I idly pressed the bell button, for no other reason than that *you never know.*

'Can I help you at all?' The voice emanated not from the intercom but from an elderly woman behind me, clutching a large leather handbag and a bunch of keys like weapons. She eyed me with distaste or suspicion, a reaction the sight of men with long hair and leather jackets can easily provoke in elderly strangers. I'm really quite harmless and most people quickly realize that.

'My name is Chris Honeysett. I'm a private investigator and I've been asked to find Miss Kyla Biggs.' I managed to find a slightly scuffed card in the lining of my leather jacket and handed it over.

Her expression had already changed from suspicion to concerned interest. 'Oh yes? I have never met a private detective before.' She even managed the hint of a smile as she reappraised my appearance. 'I suppose you're in disguise. Well, you won't find her here. Kyla went on holiday to Greece and hasn't returned. If you really want to find her, and I wish someone would, you'd have to go to Corfu, I fear.'

'I'm on my way there,' I assured her, 'but I thought coming here might give me more of an idea who it is I'm looking for. I've not been told much.'

'Who hired you, if I may inquire?'

'Her employers did.'

'Oh, did they? Well –' she reached past me and unlocked the door – 'in that case, you'd better come in, hadn't you? I'm Mrs Walden. I live on the ground floor.' I followed her inside her flat through a door with highly polished brass fittings. 'Please sit down while I make tea. You will have a cup of tea, of course.'

I said I would. I knew that there was no need to call 'milk, no sugar' after her as she disappeared towards her kitchen. Even though it was obvious that Mrs Walden had sold every piece of furniture she could bear to live without and I could see lighter patches on the wall where paintings had once hung, I knew tea would arrive on a tray with milk jug and sugar pot. I was sure Mrs Walden had standards. Two unmatched armchairs either side of a polished mahogany coffee table in front of the fireplace and a dark dresser in a corner were the only furniture left in this large, high-windowed room. The grate contained an unlit coal-effect gas fire. On the mantelpiece, between a radio and a stopped clock, stood a row of library books, all of them detective novels, which probably explained how I had made it through the door.

'So, you are working on the case of Kyla's mysterious disappearance?' she asked, pouring tea into flowery china cups. 'Would you like the fire on? You may find it a bit chilly in here. I don't usually have it on until the evening.'

'Oh, it's fine,' I protested. The temperature in the room was just this side of hypothermia and I regretted having turned down her offer since she looked a little disappointed at having been denied an opportunity to indulge in the extravagance of early warmth. There was more disappointment when she realized that I knew next to nothing about what I sincerely hoped would not turn out to be a *case*. 'How well do you know her?' I asked.

'Reasonably well. Kyla is a kind, caring sort of person. She works for the supermarket but not on the shop floor; she is educated. Though, of course, that's no longer a guarantee of a good job these days, is it? She brings me things sometimes – items of food, things she gets for free, even a bottle of wine once in a while. Very neighbourly. So it's such a shame and so unfair to have her flat broken into while she is missing.'

'Broken into?'

'Three . . . yes, three days ago. Didn't you know that?'

I could see that in Mrs Walden's eyes I compared badly with the detectives on the mantelpiece. 'No one mentioned it. I'm not sure even her employers knew, but then why would they? How did they get in?'

'Through the basement, then they jemmied open her front door. They were very quiet, I give them that; I'm quite a light sleeper and I didn't hear a thing.'

'Was much taken?'

'Well, it was hard to tell. The police asked me to take a look around, see if I noticed anything obviously missing, but I couldn't tell. She has a laptop computer and it was not there, but she might have taken that with her on holiday, of course. I told the police that I don't think this was an ordinary burglary. There were valuable things that any self-respecting burglar would have taken.'

'That's certainly curious.' If it was true. Some burglars specialized, and if they found the jewellery box, the car keys or some money, they might leave other valuables untouched. 'Does Miss Biggs have a car?'

'Yes, that's still in her garage across the road; the officers checked for that. Are you going to Corfu to find her? The police are clueless, you know; they seem to think she ran off with a Greek waiter. Ridiculous.'

'Talking of which, did Miss Biggs have a boyfriend, fiancé . . .?'

Mrs Walden lifted her chin and shook her head just twice. 'Nothing of the sort. She is a sensible young woman and wastes no time on boyfriends. That's what makes the Greek waiter theory so unlikely.'

'I don't suppose she told you where in Corfu she was going, where she was staying?'

'No, but perhaps this might provide a clue. Just a minute.' She left the room and returned with a postcard. 'This came only yesterday.'

I quickly read the few lines Kyla had written: 'Not much sun today and we had a terrific thunderstorm last night but sea and sand are plentiful. Back before you receive this, I'm sure. Love, Kyla.' I turned it over. The picture was of a restaurant with tables shaded by vines, near a stretch of water. The handwritten sign over the door spelled 'Niko's Taverna'.

'This could be useful,' I admitted.

'You may keep it.'

She wished me good luck as she let me out by the front door. 'Go and find Kyla, Mr Honeysett. And Godspeed.'

I'd left the van parked nearby in the avenue that ran through the park. Before I could set off, however, there were one or two things I needed. First stop was the McBooks in Milsom Street. The language section in the basement had several Delude Yourself packs for Greek, but each cost a fortune and required a CD player, while all Matilda could offer was an ancient radio-cassette combo. The nearby library had just what I needed – a *Greek Made Easy* language course with a book and cassettes. It looked to be of an age with the van. By the time I'd get there I was sure I'd have a working knowledge of the language. If small children in Greece could speak it, then how difficult could it be? I got my ticket blipped and returned to Matilda. At the petrol station I bought a replacement for the empty propane bottle, and, with a full tank of fuel, headed for Dover.

The van behaved impeccably. I was used to driving classic and/or rickety machinery around and soon found that the optimum speed for Matilda was fifty-four mph. Below that, it felt like riding a pregnant hippo, and going faster soon resulted in the kind of vibrations that made my hands go numb on the steering wheel, blurred the mirrors and had the crockery singing in the cupboards.

It was the off-season for passenger travel from Dover and I had an open ticket for whatever SeaFrance ferry was available. SeaFrance used the Eastern Docks Ferry Port. The signposts were big and unequivocal, and even the greatest confusenik would have had problems getting lost (as the lorry driver I asked for directions kindly pointed out).

In August the place would be overrun with coaches and holidaymakers; now I simply rolled up to Frontier Control, had my papers checked and fifteen minutes later, with Matilda parked in the fume-laden hold of the ferry *Berlioz*, I stood on deck enjoying the sea air for about ten seconds. Then a hard, uncompromising wind blew straight out of the east and swept me inside and into the warmth.

There were few people about. Having driven non-stop to get there by lunchtime, I made straight for the brasserie which was named Le Brasserie, in case you were harbouring any doubts. The place had a confused ambience, perhaps resulting from the mixture of white tablecloths and polypropylene chairs, and was half empty, which guaranteed me a table near the window from where I watched England recede into greying mists. I happily bade the waiter '*bonjour*', which more or less depleted my non-culinary French. He took his revenge by handing me a French menu. I stared at it in alarm.

Nuggets de Poulet accompagnés de purée ou frites . . .?
Glace ou Mousse au Chocolat . . .?
Coca-Cola . . .?

I blinked, then the penny dropped. *La Table des Enfants* – I had the children's menu. I turned it over and my stomach stopped rebelling, despite a slight rolling as we left the harbour for choppier water.

As a farewell gesture to both Blighty and the east wind blowing from the Urals, I started with smoked salmon and blinis, but for the main course I steered straight for the Mediterranean with red mullet and marinated vegetable kebab *accompagné* by surely the smallest bottle of beer ever to sail the seas.

Because of the time of year and since it was the middle of the week, there was a marked absence of *nuggets de poulet*-munching children in the restaurant. My closest neighbours were a middle-aged couple who argued in flat, resigned voices about something they had probably argued over for years. It didn't seem to impair their appetite, however, nor their impeccable politeness as they passed the salt and poured more wine for each other. There were several men eating alone like me; some looked like lorry drivers, some middle-income businessmen. A man with a square face and severe haircut contemplated his mobile phone with intense concentration while eating chips in a distracted fashion, and a woman with bleached hair at a table by the window dissected a steak while reading a book she had propped against her bread basket.

My red mullet turned out to be a scrawny creature who had probably travelled far, and I consoled myself with the thought that every hour brought me closer to a big pond full of his fatter cousins.

The same stiff easterly breeze that had so quickly driven me inside slowed our journey, so that it was over two hours before I finally rolled off the *Berlioz* and on to French tarmac at Calais. Having completed the formalities, I couldn't wait to put a few miles between me and the dispiriting roundabouts and hoardings of the harbour. I had twelve hundred miles ahead of me, nearly exactly two thousand kilometres. The temperatures here were no improvement on what I had hoped to leave behind, but at least it wasn't raining. The only thing to do now was drive south until the sun came out. A hundred yards in front of me, a loud blaring of French (car) horns reminded a dreamy British driver which side of the road they preferred to drive on in France. It took me a while to get on to the motorway, but once on the A26 I simply slotted into the slow lane, pointed Matilda's nose towards the Alps and drove for hours.

French lorry drivers are much the same as anywhere else; if they think their rig can go one mile per hour faster than whatever is in front of them, then they will overtake it even if it takes them all day. Which meant that for much of this leg of the journey I had articulated lorries in front, behind and to my left, all of us munching miles as best we could. The turbulence some of those massive rigs produced while surging past meant I had to keep a tight grip on the steering wheel. It was late afternoon and at just such a moment that I heard a small sound behind me which ought not to have been there, only I couldn't possibly turn around right then. The van produced so many noises I wasn't used to yet and the old Ford engine in front made such a racket that I forgot about it for another mile until I heard the sound again, this time close up. 'Tell me I'm imagining this. Please tell me that's not you, Derringer.'

This was answered by an unequivocal *meow* of the 'feed-me-now' variety that I had long come to recognize as a prelude to Derringer's much worse 'no-one-around-here-*ever*-feeds-me' yowl.

'Do you have any idea of the price of cat food in France?' Silence. 'Or the fine for taking a cat across European borders without a pet passport?' No comment. Derringer jumped on the backrest of the passenger seat. I cleared the maps off the seat and he sat next to me, completely ignoring the traffic, just staring at me. 'Yeah, very clever. There isn't a crumb of cat food in this wreck, so you'll have to wait until I get off the motorway and to a supermarket.' He was not impressed by the arrangements. Fifty miles later I stopped at a motorway service station. Derringer wanted out, but there was no way I was going to go cat-herding on the motorway, so I slammed the door in the rogue's face and went in search of food. The only vaguely suitable thing I could find was a rubberized ham sandwich for which I handed over an astonishing number of euros. While Derringer polished off the ham, I dispatched the oddly bouncy bread and decided to leave the motorway soon, find some shops and stock up with provisions.

It was dark by the time I finally drew up in front of a shabby-looking *supermarché* in a tiny town called Bar-le-Duc. On the inside, the supermarket was drab but well stocked with most of what I needed, including all the Camembert you could carry, but, mysteriously, not a single can of cat food. I bought cans of tuna instead. Derringer might have to share. Apart from the supermarket, Bar-le-Duc didn't look like a bad little town to spend an evening in. I found a place to park near a bridge over the fast-flowing waters of the Ornain river. Derringer laid wordlessly into some tuna while I cooked myself a cheese omelette on the Leisure Princess, fully intending to find a bar, preferably one with an open fire, and test the local wine. I woke up at one in the morning, shivering and with a crick in my neck. It took me ten minutes to rig up the bed and fall asleep again.

A persistent knocking sound woke me from heavy-goods-vehicle dreams. It was a policeman clicking a beringed finger against the side window. I opened the driver window to find out what he wanted, but still had a crick in my neck so gave him a sideways look. The *gendarme* informed me in fluent French that I couldn't park my van here and should move off sharpish. The only word I understood was *le camping* which he pronounced with all the disgust it deserves. I said *bon*, *oui*, *merci* and started the engine. It was then that I noticed the blue Toyota with the British plates for the first time, or rather noticed that I had seen it before, at the motorway service station. It was parked on the opposite side of the road and I could see the number plate because the car in front had just been driven away. As soon as I pulled off into the thin early morning traffic along the river I forgot all about it. I stopped at the first *boulangerie* for a couple of still-warm baguettes and left Bar-le-Duc, which looked picturesque despite the greyness of the hour, by a southern route. From here on I travelled on minor roads, away from the rush and crush of lorry traffic. A few miles out of town, when it felt as rural as France can suddenly get, I stopped by the side of the road, brewed coffee and tore into baguettes, slathered with oozing Camembert. By the time I'd finished my breakfast Derringer was nosing an empty can of tuna along the floor and my maps were richly globuled with cheese.

I drove all day. While the slowly changing landscape of France rolled by and became ever more mountainous, I sought to remedy my woeful ignorance of Greek language and custom. I shoved the first cassette into the tape player.

Welcome to your Greek-Made-Easy language course. Introduction . . .

The voice on the tape spoke in measured, soothing tones of how easy I would find the language, how much more enjoyable my holiday or business trip was going to be and how I was going to gain confidence by repeating expressions and whole phrases in the exercises. So far I was coping admirably.

Modern Greece is a country of eight million inhabitants and roughly the size of England. One sixth of the area consists of some two thousand islands . . .

Wait a second: two thousand? It couldn't be. I wondered how many islands the British Isles consisted of, yet two thousand seemed a preposterous number. All I could hope was that Kyla Biggs had stayed put in Corfu and not decided to go island hopping. I could never hope to find her if she had left the island of Corfu to explore the other one thousand nine hundred and ninety-nine.

No part of Greece is more than eighty miles from the sea and eighty per cent of the land is mountainous.

I shifted down as the road rose steeply through pine-forested hills that began to look more and more like mountains and Matilda slowed as the labouring Ford engine hauled us towards Switzerland. I hoped that Kyla was the sea-and-sand type and had stayed on the flat.

It was late evening and dark by the time I approached the Swiss border at Goumois. I pulled over and stopped within sight of the sodium-lit border post.

'Derringer? Time to do that disappearing trick you do so . . . well?' I turned on the feeble light in the back and saw no sign of him. For a moment I panicked. We had both enjoyed several *al fresco* toilet breaks on the way . . . no, I remembered closing the door with the cat inside. He was here somewhere, in the woodwork, and hopefully had the sense not to make a sudden appearance during the border formalities.

I had my passport checked twice and was wished *bon voyage* by both the French and the Swiss border guard when I stated my destination – Brindisi, Italy.

A sign told me that I was now in the district of Franches-Montagnes, which to my un-French ears sounded a bit like 'French mountains', and that the elevation was 1,617 feet. I drove on into the night which closed in on me in the rattling Matilda once the lights of Goumois disappeared behind us. The headlights on the van were feeble by modern standards and the night seemed vast and cold. As soon as I could I pulled off the road into what looked like a forester's track under the dark loom of tall pines.

With the engine turned off and the lights killed, I sat in the ticking, creaking darkness, feeling as though I was still driving along an after-image of rolling tarmac into nowhere. The headlights of a following car swept by, choreographing the fringe of the forest into a jumping band of shadow men. When darkness returned, I made the bed and crawled under the clammy duvet.

The next morning Derringer woke me by pummelling my chest, complaining about the cold and wafting stale tuna smells into my face. It was so cold up here his breath waved little white flags of surrender. The windows were steamed up; boiling the kettle made it worse. Outside, a mist obscured all but the immediate surroundings. I'd been driving south for two days, yet the weather was colder than ever. After some scrambled eggs that were homesick for their coriander leaf and brinjal pickle, I backed into the road and set off.

Yes – ne. No – ochi. Hello – yiá soo. How are you? – ti kánete? I like it – moo arési. I don't like it – then moo arési.

My memories of Switzerland are steeped in clichés: it was clean and multilingual, expensive, and looked disapprovingly upon scruffy long-haired private eyes, while they in turn stared unbelievingly at the price of a litre of milk in roadside shops. *Then moo arési.* It also left me with the impression that there wasn't an acre of flat ground in the country. Matilda made hard work of the endless climbs, but I drove on relentlessly, having convinced myself – and frequently promised Derringer – that we would emerge from the St Gotthard tunnel into the warm, sun-drenched south. I warmed myself with thoughts of Greek tavernas by the sea.

Eating out will surely be one of the great pleasures of your stay in Greece. You will enjoy it even more once you have memorized a few simple phrases. In this chapter you will learn all you need to know to order meals and drinks and ask for the bill.

Waiter! – garçon! A bottle of wine – ena boukáli krassí. One beer, please – mia bíra, parakaló. Two beers, please – dio bíres, parakaló. One Coke – mia Coca-cola . . .

Only the drenched part of my sun-drenched prediction came true. It was midnight by the time I had managed the endless climb to the pass, and on the other side was southern rain, indistinguishable from its northern cousin. I stayed on the motorway and drove through the night, chasing a similar delusion about the weather in Italy.

In this chapter you will learn to find your way around by asking questions. Where is . . .? – Poo íne . . .? Where is the baker's? – Poo íne o foornos? Where is the post office? – Poo íne to tachidroméeo? I finally crossed the border at Chiasso in the early hours, yet not too early for the lorries which were much in evidence once more. 'You can come out now,' I called to Derringer who, perhaps picking up on my nervousness as I approached the border, had disappeared into his hidey-hole again in a rare display of cooperation. He remained wherever he had curled up. 'I know; so much for Italian spring sunshine. It's all a swindle.' A few minutes later I left the main route and moved gladly on to a B road.

One thing improved immediately. In Switzerland I had been moved on by traffic police almost as soon as I stopped anywhere – it appeared the Swiss did not approve of parking – but I knew that Italians parked anywhere they liked any time they liked.

I pulled into a muddy lay-by, toasted country number three with a very large bottle of folksily labelled Swiss wheat beer and fell asleep as soon as I closed my eyes.

FOUR

I awoke to piercing rays of sunlight. Derringer lay asleep at the bottom of the bunk in a patch of *bona fide* Italian sunshine, exposing his golden belly fur to the warmth steaming through the window. For a long moment I just lay there, enjoying the unusual sensation of sunlight that I could feel as well as see, something I hadn't experienced since last autumn. Yet soon my stomach let me know what it thought of a supper of wheat beer on a load of nothing, and Derringer took a break from sunbathing to wind up his feed-me whine.

I had parked on quite a busy country road. While the traffic barrelled past the window, I broke my fast on excellent rye bread, Gruyère cheese and coffee and counted my euros. I had spent a hair-raising amount, most of it on fuel. How could one van drink that much juice? Answer: easily. It was ancient and all I seemed to have done so far was to grind up and down endless hills and mountains. I consulted my map and looked at the long shaft of Italy's boot and decided there was only one answer: live on sandwiches and stick to the motorway.

How much is that? – Pósso káni aftó? One kilo tomatoes – ena kiló domátes. Do you have any eggs? – Meepos échete avgá? One melon – éna pepóni. Two melons . . .

I'll spare you the tedium of that journey and try not to think of the sights I missed. I lived on oozing slices of sizzling takeaway pizza, bags of bread rolls and impossibly thin wafers of salami, and cursed the time I was wasting simply to avoid three hours of hyperventilation on a charter flight. For all I knew, Kyla Biggs had by now turned up and safely returned to her flat in Bath.

Unbelievably, it was early morning of the fourth day when I pulled Matilda's wobbly handbrake near my embarkation point in the harbour of Brindisi, her nose pointing at Greece on the other side of the Ionian Sea. A classic Mediterranean sunrise set the Adriatic ablaze, compensating me for the two-thousand-kilometre slog I had just completed.

Despite a mug of strong black coffee and the noise of the harbour all around me, I fell asleep, then woke in a panic. A quick check confirmed that it was high time for embarkation. The port was a lot busier now. Several car ferries had docked, their rusting iron jaws wide open. As I joined the queue to drive into the bowels of my ferry, the *Ikarus Palace,* my eye was drawn by a glint of sunlight on car metal to a blue Toyota some two hundred yards to my left. It was the last car to negotiate its way up the ramp of the *Ionian Sky*, a rival ferry of the Agoudinos Lines. It was impossible to make out the driver, though I could just guess at very fair or even white hair. Then, just as the big car disappeared, I glimpsed a flash of yellow at the back – the number plate was definitely British.

I told myself that I had probably spent too many days talking to the cat and that at any one time there had to be more than one blue Toyota with British plates driving around Europe. Yet if it was the same car, as the hair at the back of my neck seemed to think, then it was a rare coincidence, and I've never been a great fan of those. Should the Toyota's destination turn out to be also Corfu – the ferries continued on to the Greek mainland – then I was going to challenge the driver, but my best chance of doing that was to get there before him. Unfortunately, it was the *Ionian Sky* that left first. I stood on deck and watched as she cleared the breakwater, gaining a considerable head start. I silently urged on my captain, whoever he was, to pull his finger out, wherever that was. At last, with much vibration and a groan, the *Ikarus Palace* pulled itself away from the quay. By now the *Ionian Sky* had shrunk to the size of my thumb, ahead and to the north of us. There was nothing I could do about that, so went in search of lunch.

Considering the earliness of the season, the *Ikarus Palace* was carrying a surprising number of foot passengers, many of them encumbered by rucksacks. Most had had the foresight to buy food in Brindisi rather than fall hostage to the phantasmagorical prices charged in the, admittedly snazzy, self-service restaurant. I ended up with a less than imaginative cheese-and-tomato toasted sandwich and a bottle of water in order to save my finances.

I took both up on deck. The wind had picked up but there was hardly a cloud in the sky now, and I greedily drank in the sight of so much glittering blue sea, so different from the English Channel of four days ago. We appeared to be gaining on the *Ionian Sky* but were just that moment ourselves overtaken by a foot-passenger-only hydrofoil, sweeping past with an impressive bow-wave as it bounced its way east across the water. The spectacle provided enough distraction for me to have missed the fact that a man had joined me at the guard rail. 'They'll get there in half the time. Twice as seasick, naturally,' he assured me, with more than a hint of a German accent. He was a tall, tanned forty-year-old with no-nonsense grey hair and a two-day salt-and-pepper stubble. His jacket was tightly zipped up against the wind. Around his neck he carried a large pair of Zeiss binoculars as well as a Nikon camera encased in rubber armour.

'Not much chance of seasickness on a day like this.'

He seemed to weigh up this rash statement of mine before answering. 'Perhaps not. Kerkyra?'

'Pardon?'

'Sorry, I mean Corfu. Kerkyra is what the Greeks call it. Are you going there or on to Igoumenitsa?' The fact that the names rolled so easily off his tongue probably meant this wasn't his first trip.

'No, just Corfu.'

'Your first visit?'

'Yes. Never been to Greece, even.'

'*Really*?' His tone suggested this was most unusual. 'I watched you drive your motorhome aboard. It must be very old.'

'Ancient.'

He seemed happy with this exchange and strolled away. I sipped my water and wandered around the deck myself. Some brave souls, desperate to squeeze every shade of possible suntan from their holiday, were lying half naked on deckchairs, despite the cool breeze. Others wandered about with that

aimless how-to-kill-six-hours expression that doubtlessly I
would soon wear myself.

It wasn't until several hours later, after much purposeless
drifting across upper and lower decks and another sandwich,
that I noticed a hazy line appear on the horizon – the Albanian
coast – and somewhere in front of that haze, as yet indistinguishable, lay the island of Corfu. For a while now we had been
sailing quite close to the *Ionian Sky*, still gaining on her. In the
absence of anything else to do, I had fixed my eyes on her,
wondering what earthly reason anyone could have for following
me across most of Europe. It was then that Mr Zeiss once more
joined me at the port-side guard-rail. 'So, will you spend much
time on Kerkyra? You are on holiday, yes?'

'Erm, yes. I'm hoping to visit a friend who moved out here
a few years ago.'

'Hoping?'

'I'm not sure she still lives at the address I have.' Why was
I telling him this? Why didn't I just say that I came for a
week's holiday? Boredom, probably.

'A little adventure for you, then.'

I changed the subject. 'Looks like we'll be overtaking the
Ionian Sky any minute now.' We had nearly drawn level with
the rival ferry.

'No, we won't.' I gave him a look that invited him to
elaborate. 'Just a bit of Greek showmanship, to let everyone
know we are the faster ship. But the *Ionian* always docks first.'
He strolled off once more. True to his prediction, we fell
behind again until the other ship was once more far ahead.

Corfu had lifted its dramatic outline clear of the haze. We
were now following dead astern of the *Ionian Sky*, with the
darkly wooded slopes of the island's mountains to starboard.
Every inch of it appeared to be covered in vegetation, so
different from the arid image of the archetypal Greek island
I had held in my mind. We passed bays and beaches that
looked inaccessible from the land, with villages clinging to
the hillsides above them. And here too was something I had
only ever read about and had assumed to be fiction: the smell
of the land. Through the fierce sharpness of the sea's ozone
drifted the moist, verdant smell of land, mixed with the aroma

of wood and charcoal smoke. It conjured mysterious little yearnings in my soul for things I couldn't have put a name to. I became even more impatient to get off this windy boat and on to warm, dry land.

Soon we entered the narrow channel between the mainland and the east coast of the island and not long after that the capital, Kerkyra, came into view. The approach was dominated by a large and ancient fortification perched on a high rock. Below it lay a surprisingly small harbour with the usual collection of drive-through buildings, customs sheds, car parks and lines of waiting vehicles. The *Ionian Sky* had already docked and was disgorging its cargo, mainly cars, vans and a solitary motorcycle packed so high with luggage that only the helmeted head of the rider was visible among it. I looked for the Toyota but saw no sign of it. The *Ikarus Palace* prepared to dock. It was time to descend to the car deck and get ready to drive on to Greek soil. Or at least Greek concrete.

Mr Zeiss, who had been using his binoculars, came and stretched out a steady hand. I shook it. 'What address do you have for your friend? Is it in town?' he asked.

'Yes. Hang on.' I fumbled my notebook from my jacket and showed him the address.

'I know it. It's in the Old Town. Do you see the broad street over there with the huge yellow car rental sign at the corner? Follow that until you get to a square with a little greenery in the centre and mad traffic all round. Take a left at the top corner and drive down Theotoki for a couple of hundred yards and park wherever you can. Somewhere on the left you'll find a large bookshop, Lykoudis. It's the second or third little street on the left after that.'

'Thanks. You know the place well, then.'

'Reasonably.' He paused, as if sizing me up. Below us, men were lashing thick ship's ropes to bollards on the quay and their shouts gave me my first real experience of the Greek language. It sounded nothing like it had on the tapes. 'My name's Kladders, by the way.'

'Honeysett,' I offered automatically.

'Well, Mr Honeysett . . . I don't know who you are, and your story is none of my business . . . but I think you should

know that you are being followed. Had you noticed?' He
stretched out a hand and pointed to a gap between two long
customs sheds at the edge of the fenced-in harbour area. On
the strip of tarmac visible in the gap, I could make out a flash
of blue. He unslung his binoculars and offered them to me.
Through their startling magnification I could make out part of
the blue Toyota. From the driver's window someone was
returning the compliment by pointing a pair of binoculars in
our direction. I couldn't make out a face in the deeply shaded
interior of the car but thought I could see a spark of silver
hair again. After a few seconds the binoculars were withdrawn
and the window slid up. Seconds later the car moved off.

I handed back the bins. 'Thanks. I had noticed the car
before.'

'Do you know who's following you?'

'Nope.'

'Or why?'

'Not the foggiest,' I admitted.

'In that case, take great care, Mr Honeysett.' He raised one
eyebrow at me, shook his head and walked briskly off. I
pondered this for a minute and was left with one question:
how did *he* know I was being followed? If I saw him again,
I'd ask, but there was no sign of him when I got to the car
deck and I had no idea what kind of vehicle he drove.

Predictably, the van smelled of cat, but Derringer was out
of sight.

FIVE

There was no sign of the Toyota when I finally cleared customs and rolled out on to the busy coastal road. It was a dusty place. Lining the noisy road were empty cafes, restaurants and car rental places. Immediately outside the customs building, rows of taxis were competing with carriages drawn by straw-hatted little horses and porters with handcarts offering their services to foot passengers. I found the road Kladders had mentioned and followed it. This too was lined with modern concrete houses, mostly two or three storeys high, car and motorcycle rentals, booking offices and hardware stores, billboards and signposts. I had no time to look. The traffic was intense. This was the off-season? Lorries, vans, buses and coaches seemed hell-bent on eliminating the weaker opposition, such as cars, motorbikes, scooters, pedestrians and dogs. Soon the concrete horrors gave way to more elegant, older houses, until eventually I arrived at a bustling square. All the bustle was concentrated in the streets framing an island on which benches, statuary, flower beds and bits of lawn failed to attract many visitors this evening. Despite having learnt Mediterranean driving in Turkey and having just taken a refresher course in Italy, the Greek style of locomotion took some getting used to. Cars and motorbikes had a habit of coming at me from unusual angles and Matilda's tiny mirrors were no match for this chaos. Several times I had to break hard, which brought Derringer out in protest.

'We're stopping in a minute – in fact, as soon as I can find somewhere to abandon this thing.' What I wanted most of all was to stop moving. I followed Kladders's description along a broad street lined on one side with trees and found a space to park under one of them. I turned off the engine and let go of the steering wheel. Three hours. Had I travelled by plane, a three-hour flight and a short taxi ride would have got me to exactly this point. Derringer's disgruntled mewing

reminded me that, of course, I wouldn't have a cat to keep
me company, and I also realized that I might never have
spotted that someone was following me. I emptied the last
can of Italian pet food into a cat bowl I had bought near
Bologna and got out into the street. Naturally, since I had
no idea what my shadow looked like, apart from the possibility of very light hair, there was little chance of spotting
them once they got out of their car.

Corfu Town did not look Greek to me. Most of its old
buildings looked as Italian as anything I had seen in Italy. I
later found out that most of these tall houses, with their
frail-looking wrought-iron balconies, shuttered windows and
pantiled roofs, were in fact a legacy of the Venetian occupation
of the island.

There didn't seem to be many tourists. The season hadn't
really started yet – this being the first week of April – and the
majority of people in the street looked like locals. What struck
me most as I stood on the wide pavement and tried to get my
bearings were the smells. Despite the traffic in the street, here
under the trees the predominant aroma travelling on the cooling
air was that of freshly roasted coffee. I soon found the reason
for this: there were three coffee roasters on this street alone,
pumping their seductive smells on to the evening air. A little
further along, a street vendor was roasting chestnuts, while
next to him a man sold pasties from a heated glass box. I
pointed, paid and in return received a triangular pasty on a
piece of brown paper. It was hot, crumbly and delicious, filled
with cheese and spinach, and didn't last long. So I went back
and bought another.

Most of the traffic disappeared to the left, but I walked
straight on, leaving the noise behind. Following the worn
pavement, I found Lykoudis bookshop. The assistant spoke good
English and sold me a map of the island, with a plan of the
town on the reverse side. Nearby I found a cafe that seemed to
consist of a narrow doorway and three tiny zinc tables on the
pavement. Two of them were occupied by three men in their
late sixties, wearing grey trousers and grey jackets over knitted
jumpers, despite the heat. They sat with their backs to the wall
and studied me as I sank on to a chair at the third table,

profoundly grateful for the fact that I was no longer in motion across Europe. The man closest to the door called something over his shoulder and a skinny boy with a faintly stained shirt emerged and said: '*Oríste, ti thélete?*'

'*Énan kafé,*' I told him.

'*Pos ton thélete?*'

'*Skéto.*'

'*Amésos.*' He disappeared inside.

The whole exchange went so quickly I had to pinch myself: did I really just order a coffee in Greek? It appeared so, since the man closest to my table fired a sentence at me, obviously believing that I spoke the language. I didn't understand even a single word of what he said, which put my four-day crash course of the language back into its proper perspective. I threw up my hands in an apologetic gesture and he turned back to his friends, his suspicions confirmed – *xénos*, a foreigner. Why else would he carry a map of the island?

My *kafé* – a lighter version of Turkish coffee – arrived in a small white cup, together with a glass of very cold water. I slurped at the tiny bubbles on the surface; its taste fulfilled the promise of its fragrance. As I began to relax and stretched out my legs, I realized that it would probably take a bathtub of the stuff to keep me awake for much longer. The thought of another night in the van held little allure now and I was hoping for a bed. A decent shower, not the lukewarm dribble which was all Matilda could offer, and fresh sheets were what I was after. I reached into my jacket for my notebook and Morva's address.

It wasn't there. I went through all the pockets – nothing. I felt along the lining where things often ended up if I forgot which pockets were sound. Still nothing. I was certain I hadn't left it in the van. The last time I had taken it out had been to hand it to Kladders so he could read the address. But surely I had taken it back? I was wide awake now. One gulp finished the coffee. I paid what seemed like not very much at all and made my way back to the van where five minutes of furious searching under the disapproving eyes of the cat produced nothing. I tried to visualize the address. Morva Lennox, number fourteen *Odos* something. Something Street wasn't going to help, but Kladders had said turn left after the bookshop. I'd find it.

I bought the cat's silence with another tin of tuna and walked back. Something Street, when I found it, was a narrow lane, bridged by lines of washing stretched between the houses. It was too narrow for cars but had enough space for a mad scooter rider who beeped me impatiently out of the way. Number fourteen was a tall and ancient-looking house with peeling plaster and louvred shutters at the windows. There was a row of bells, none of which displayed any names. I pushed at the door; it was on the latch. The air inside smelled damp; the scuffed marble floor tiles were wet. On a landing above the first flight of steps, a woman with steel-grey hair twisted a mop inside a zinc bucket. She wore a drab black outfit and had bandaged calves above swollen ankles and gave me a resigned look as I walked towards her across the freshly mopped floor.

I remembered another two words from the chapter called *Asking Directions and Saying What You Want*. '*Poo íne* Morva Lennox?'

She gave me a long answer from the chapter *Well, You Did Ask, Dear*. This time I understood at least one word: Lennox. She obviously knew the name. I told her I spoke very little Greek. She didn't stop talking, only now it was more to herself, as she came painfully down the stairs and beckoned me to follow her by making a curious clawing motion with one hand. She led me outside and along the lane to the nearest corner and made me follow her into a souvenir shop that had everything apart from customers: bundles of sandals hanging by the door frame, cassettes and CDs of Greek music, miniature replicas of classic statuary, including some extremely priapic examples, printed tee shirts, beach paraphernalia, sunhats and sunglasses. My guide called loudly for the proprietor, whose name appeared to be Alexiiiiiiii. When he materialized, she handed me over with a single sentence that contained the name Morva, then disappeared before I remembered the Greek for 'thank you'.

The proprietor was a short man in his late twenties, with soft pale skin and nicotine-stained fingers. I introduced myself and we shook hands.

'I am Alexis. Welcome to Corfu, Chris.' He pronounced my name 'Crease'. 'You are looking for Morva? She is here no more. She is moved in the country. You are a friend?'

'Yes, an old friend. That was the last address I had for her. When did she move away?'

'Two years.' He shrugged. 'Maybe more.'

'You wouldn't have her new address?'

He waggled a vague hand, then pointed to the map I was still holding. 'I can show where.'

He unfolded the map and smoothed it out on the glass counter above a display of Rolex replicas. He waggled his head disapprovingly. 'This map, it is shit map, it is very old.'

'I bought it today.'

'OK, is new shit. All Corfu maps are like this. They show you where they want you to go, not where you want to go. Here.' His finger followed the red ribbon of a road across to the other side of the island, then south to where it turned into a much thinner white ribbon that stopped at the edge of a brown patch indicating a small mountain. He pointed at the brown patch, half an inch beyond which the road ended in nothing. He picked up a biro. 'I write in, OK?' He added a squiggle to the tail of the white road and marked the end with a cross. 'Here. Ano Makriá. Here you find Morva Lennox. You rent a car?'

'I brought my own.'

He pulled a painful face. 'OK, pity. Drive careful.' He handed back the folded map and guided me out the door. 'Tell her Alexis say "*iássu*".'

He closed the door behind me. I heard him turn the key twice.

Not even the outskirts of Corfu managed to be all that unlovely, and as the traffic thinned I had more time to look about. Predictably, tourism seemed to be the main occupation here, though once the road detached itself from the resorts by the sea and climbed into the hilly interior it also seemed to leave most of the tourist industry behind.

Corfu was an island of trees. I had no idea how many were cut down to make way for roads, tourist villas and hotels, but

there seemed to be several million left. Terrace after terrace
of olive trees flew by and the sea of greenness was pierced
over and over by the lances of the cypress trees. The quiet
villages I drove through looked as if nothing much had changed
here for decades. Most of the houses were small and simple,
often whitewashed, with painted wooden or wrought-iron
doors. Flowers grew in profusion, many planted into large feta
tins that lined the walls. Bougainvillea framed entrances; fig
trees shaded courtyards. Whatever the size of the village, there
never appeared to be more than one narrow road that was
negotiable by motor vehicles. I saw no tourist cars, only small
tractors, well-worn pickup trucks and bikes and scooters being
ridden by helmetless riders. Even though I constantly checked
my mirrors, there seemed to be no sign of the blue Toyota.

Darkness crept up on me in the hills. The next two finger-
posts, written in Greek with the English spelling underneath,
didn't correspond to anything on my map. I had been steadily
climbing on a narrow tarmacked road, with the winking lights
of villages taunting me from across the mountainside above,
but I never seemed to arrive anywhere. Here, away from the
tourist traffic, the roads had been allowed to deteriorate. I
drove carefully around the potholes to give the ancient
suspension a chance. During the next half-hour of driving
around I met only two other cars, both going in the opposite
direction at twice my speed. I passed small stone dwellings
that looked unlived-in and appeared to be attached to the many
orchards around here, consisting mainly of orange and lemon
groves. The road snaked steadily up the tree-clad mountain
without ever seeming to lead anywhere. At the next turn, I
stopped at a road sign. It had its English translation obscured
with angry streaks of red spray paint, but the Greek writing
seemed near enough to what I was looking at on my map. I
took the turn. The potholed road narrowed and dipped back
towards sea level, then suddenly the van's wheels hummed
happily on a short stretch of smooth black tarmac. Lights
appeared ahead and a moment later I entered the village of
Neo Makriá. Derringer was complaining at me from the back
of the van; his patience with the constant movement, irregular
toilet breaks and erratic feeding had run out. A minute later

the engine started to cough, Matilda having run out of fuel. I had plain forgotten that I had changed to 'reserve' as I drove off the ferry. When I rattled on to the village square, the engine ran on fumes and Matilda rolled to a stop next to a young palm tree. Derringer, Matilda and I had all come to the same conclusion: enough was enough.

Neo Makriá looked as though it prospered without the aid of the tourist euro. All its houses looked freshly painted. At the edge of the square stood a bright yellow kiosk, illuminated by a crown of coloured light bulbs. The *kafénion*, a traditionally men-only cafe, as I had learned on my language tape, had three men sitting at tiny tables outside, their backs to the wall. They looked very convincingly like the three from the cafe in town, down to the knitted tops and worry beads sliding through their fingers. Only these three were drinking *ouzo*, a clear aniseed spirit that goes cloudy when mixed with water.

It was a mild evening. Children on tiny bicycles chased each other round the square, lapping a hopelessly outpaced kid pedalling furiously on a tricycle. At one end of the square some kind of ball game was in progress. Adults were going about their business, strolling, chatting in small groups and, above all, watching me.

I made for the *kafénion*. The proprietor, Dimitris, an energetic thirty-year-old with a moustache and a five o'clock shadow, spoke English.

First things first. Was there any food? He could rustle up some bread, cheese and olives. Otherwise, why didn't I try the *psistaría*? He even took me the hundred yards to the establishment.

'Is there a guest house in the village where I can get a room for tonight?' was my next question.

'How long do you want the room for?'

'Just for one night. I'm going a bit further tomorrow but I have had enough of driving for today and, besides, the van's run out of fuel.'

'We have a room. I tell my wife. Come back to the *kafénion* after your meal.'

The *psistaría* – the grill – was a simple affair with yellow Formica tables and those chairs made from painted iron hoops and multicoloured plastic bands; it was run by two young men. They were doing good trade over their battered counter in front of a long charcoal grill on which rows of tiny pork kebabs on wooden skewers were being basted and thick metal skewers held sizzling pieces of highly seasoned lamb. I knew they were highly seasoned because I watched one of the men throw extraordinary amounts of pepper and salt at them. I ordered a couple of *souvlaki pittes* and sat down at one of the yellow tables outside with a large bottle of Henninger beer and felt myself relax a little. For a while I simply sat and enjoyed the village scene in front of me, the smells of the charcoal grill, the simple flavour of the beer; stationary pleasures. The food arrived soon, morsels of grilled pork with tomatoes, onions, parsley, yoghurt and a dollop of spicy sauce, all wrapped in soft pitta bread, held together with greaseproof paper and a napkin. As soon as I had finished the first I ordered two more.

While I tackled my second lot of souvlakis, one other foreigner arrived at the grill: a broad-shouldered, silver-haired man in his fifties with a fleshy, richly veined nose.

He stopped at my table on his way in. 'Are you here for the birds?' He had a surprisingly high voice for a man his size.

'The birds? You mean birdwatching?'

'Yes,' he said impatiently. 'Aren't you? Most people who come this early are twitchers. But you're not?'

'Not really, no.'

He gave a resigned nod. 'That's a shame. I was going to ask you if you had seen any Egyptian vultures yet. I haven't seen one yet this year and I'm getting a bit worried. No use asking the locals; they don't seem to be interested at all.' He snorted with disapproval and disappeared inside. When he came out again with a bottle of fizzy orange, he chose a table well away from me; obviously, we had exhausted our conversational potential.

Neo Makriá, I noticed on my way back to the van, had invested in crazy paving in a big way. Every little alley I could see had been freshly paved, in dizzying 1970s fashion. I checked on Derringer inside the motorhome. He briefly looked at me from the bench where he lay curled up, then settled back to sleep. 'You and me both.' I grabbed my bag and headed towards my bed.

At the *kafénion* Dimitris insisted I drank an ouzo 'for welcome' before he led me the five steps to the house next door. His wife, Irini, spoke little English, so it was Dimitris who showed me to my room. It was a small attic room with irregular, whitewashed walls; woodwork and floorboards were painted blue. It had a single bed, a chair, a chest of drawers and smelled of fly spray.

I hoped no one else in the house wanted a shower that night because I stood under the blessed stream of hot water for a very long time, trying to iron out some of the aches and kinks I had acquired on my journey. I finished towelling my hair in my room while looking out of the small window at the square. The village had quietened down now. I could see the van from here. Just then the birdwatcher strolled up to it. He stopped, looked around him, then peered through the side windows at the interior, shading his eyes with both hands against the glass to do so. Then he quickly walked out of sight.

Dimitris assured me that Greeks didn't go in for breakfast much; a coffee first thing in the morning had to suffice for most. Despite this, he managed to find freshly baked bread, butter, thick slices of mortadella, yoghurt and honey, as well as cups of instant coffee for me. While I turned my attention to these offerings in a patch of early morning sunshine at a table outside his cafe, a boy on a scooter was dispatched to the nearest petrol station to fetch a couple of gallons of fuel in a jerry can. Dimitris was a quiet man in the morning and didn't ask me any more questions. Last night I had finally had the sense to get my story straight: I was on a two-week holiday. What could be simpler than that? Now I unfolded my map and showed him where I was heading: the end of Alexis's inch-long biro squiggle.

'Ano Makriá?' He looked surprised, but his frown was quickly replaced by a smile. 'Ah, you like to be painter, yes?'

'Erm, yes, very much,' I said truthfully.

'Ano Makriá.' Dimitris gave a knowing shake of the head

and scratched his already stubbled chin. 'Is not a good place, I think. There is no nothing there, no . . . fertilities?'

'Facilities?'

'Yes, that word. Bad road in winter. Much rain and then perhaps no road in winter. Is crazy there. You can be a painter somewhere elsewhere. With facilities.'

'OK, I'll bear that in mind. So how do I get there?'

Dimitris sighed as though I had defeated him in serious negotiations, grabbed my map and folded it impatiently. Then he walked off, eventually disappearing between two houses. He returned two minutes later with a seven- or eight-year-old boy on a small bicycle who would be my guide.

Derringer looked even grumpier than usual, despite the can of baked squid I had bought for him at the grocer's. 'Cheer up, cat; this is the last leg, nearly there.'

The Greek kid was very excited by his appointment and sped away along the narrow road, pedalling frantically. I followed at a careful distance in the van, since the boy looked over his shoulder every five seconds, each time wobbling dangerously. Not far beyond the last houses of the village we turned off on to a rutted dirt track between terraced olive groves. For a while the track remained level as it twisted between the dense groves of tall, ancient trees, then began to rise into the hills. The kid still pedalled like mad, but when the track rose more steeply, he had enough. He stopped and let me overtake him. As a farewell, he gestured up the track with a fishtailing gesture, said something incomprehensible and turned his bicycle around.

'*Evcharistó* – thank you' was all I managed before the kid hurtled back down the track through the dust cloud the van's wheels had kicked up.

The track climbed first up, then down again and wound itself around the mountain just above sea level. To my left, the turquoise of the Mediterranean came into view, quite close now, but I was concentrating hard on the potholes and the crumbling verge that was all that stood between me and the rocky shore below. The well-tended olive groves had fallen behind and been replaced by unloved-looking trees, badly maintained terraces, fallen walls, the odd roofless stone hut and the remnants of wooden shelters and lean-tos. Here and there the winter rains had washed out the ruts worn by vehicles and filled them with grit. I had little confidence in finding Morva or anything much at the end of this track. What if it simply petered out somewhere without the space to turn around? Just as I began to wonder whether it was possible to reverse all the way back to Neo Makriá, the track took a sharp turn and the view opened out into the sun-baked dead end of a narrow valley, not much more than a notch in the mountainside.

The terraced groves of olives that rose up its sides looked sunken and neglected and were profusely overgrown. Among the wild vegetation that had claimed the valley stood a deserted, half-ruined hamlet. There was a church to my right, its open tower without a bell. I could see about ten or twelve houses with their outbuildings, all showing varying degrees of decay. Only two or three were wholly without roofs; the others looked like complete houses while giving a definite impression of desolation. There was no doubt that the village was uninhabited, abandoned, deserted.

Not wholly deserted, though. Just then I heard the unmistakable bragging of a cockerel and, turning in that direction, discovered a thin twirl of smoke rising from the chimney of a low but sprawling farmhouse. It stood on the edge of this ruination, surrounded by terraces that looked marginally less wild than the rest of the place.

Of course, another indication that there was life in the place was the moped, the small Honda motorbike and the little Ford parked at the end of the track. Here it turned into what had once been a cobbled village road, now a ruinous sea of stones that couldn't be negotiated by any type of vehicle other than a tank. Beside it, a narrow footpath had been trodden through the wild grass and flowers.

Matilda bounced unhappily over the bumpy terrain under the stand of unruly holly oaks, where I left her next to the car. Journey's end. As I got out, Derringer shot through the door and disappeared at a gallop into the high grass.

For a moment I stood at the start of the ruined cobble-road and looked with a painter's eye, adjusting my palette. With my back to the cars, I could see no evidence that the industrial revolution had ever happened. There were no telegraph poles, cables or electric lanterns, not even an old radio aerial left on a roof. The houses were built of dust-grey stone, the roofs tiled with terracotta weathered to the palest ochre. The wood of the sheds and outbuildings had bleached to silver like bones in the sun. But that didn't mean I would have no need of brighter colours on my palette because an astonishing profusion of wild flowers in every shade of yellow, pink, blue and purple drifted through the unchecked growth that covered the ground between the many trees.

A half-hearted call after Derringer produced no results. I could hardly blame him for wanting to escape from what for him had become practically a prison van. I took the goat path towards the house with the smoking chimney. It stood on the far side of the church in its own compound of crumbling walls, towered over by a venerable mulberry and shaded by fig and walnut trees. Nearly all the other trees in sight were olives. As I entered the courtyard, a few chickens scooted into the lee of a wall among piles of new bricks and sacks of cement half-heartedly covered with tarpaulin. The house itself, consisting only of ground and first floor, looked solid and was definitely lived in. Near the front door stood a long wooden table shaded by vines and the fleshy foliage of an enormous fig tree. A multitude of oil and feta tins with their backs to the wall had been planted up with bright herbs and electric geraniums. The open door was nothing but a black rectangle in the strong morning sun.

'Hello the house!' Nothing happened; not even the hen pecking crumbs off the table reacted. I stood in the door, letting my eyes adjust to the low light within the building. What I feared most at this point, of course, was a Greek guard dog that would jump out and, in the absence of its owner, consider it his job to thoroughly savage me.

The door led straight into a whitewashed room. Its windows were small – to keep the heat out in summer and in during winter – and its main feature, apart from two spartan sofas and a few bookshelves, was a large black wood burner with ten feet of convoluted stovepipe that disappeared into the wall between a small painting and an oil lamp. A few faded rugs dotted the uneven stone floor. The rest was the type of I'm-a-busy-painter clutter I recognized from home.

The door to the next room was ajar; a faint scratching noise came from there.

'Hello?' I gingerly pushed the door open and found myself looking into a small painting studio. I was pretty sure I was in the right place now, though the few examples of work on the walls, mostly watercolour sketches of nature subjects, didn't look like her work. One wall was entirely taken up by shelves crammed with enough drawing and painting materials to equip an art shop. The scratching sound came from a small brown hen pecking persistently at half a biscuit among some empty mugs on top of a plan chest. A door on the far side led into a kitchen. I went to investigate. It's what PIs are supposed to do.

It looked as if it had survived intact from the 1930s: a small solid-fuel oven, presumably the source of the smoke I'd seen rising from the chimney, a three-ring hob running on bottled gas and a large stone basin with a cast-iron water pump. I pushed on the handle of the pump; it gave a faint gurgle.

'In Greece it's considered polite to ask first.' Morva's voice, full of schoolmistress disapproval, made me turn guiltily. She had drawn herself up to her full five foot two and was standing in the door brandishing a billhook. 'Oh my god, it's you. It's *you*! Chris, what are you doing here?' We hugged by the sink. 'I can't believe you finally got yourself down here. I can't believe you *found* me.'

'Were you lost?'

'Oh . . . well, you know . . .' She made a vague gesture with the billhook, which looked old but sharp. 'It can feel a bit remote sometimes, yes. It isn't really. Well . . . I still can't believe you're here, and just when . . . And you've still got the long hair and everything.'

I wasn't sure what 'everything' meant, but apparently I still had it. Morva looked as if she still had everything too, though she had acquired enough lines in her face to prove she'd been busy while hanging on to it. She wore her hair long and a bit wild and had allowed the grey to take over.

I pointed at the billhook she was holding. 'Were you on your way to a peasant revolt or did you intend to prod me with it?'

'Oh that.' She dismissed it with a shrug and leant the murderous-looking object in a corner of the nearest window. 'You know the kind of thing: speak softly but carry a big stick.' She took a small long-handled saucepan off a hook above the cooker, spooned coffee and a little sugar into it, then added water from a fire-blackened kettle. 'So, tell me all. What brought you down here now? What time did you land?'

'I drove down, through Italy, in an ancient motorhome.'

She set the pot on to the gas stove, opened the valve on the tall red gas cylinder and lit the ring. The gas caught with a low bark. 'Really? Dan and I did that all those years ago when we first moved down. We broke down in every country on the way.'

'Is he around?'

'Sweet Daniel? Ran off with an Australian waitress half his age. Half my age, more importantly, I suppose. Shacked-up Down Under now. Three years ago.'

'Not so long, then.'

'I think I'm over it. But that's how I ended up in this weird corner. Here comes Margarita, my latest acquisition.'

A girl pushed through the door, sideways because of the two enormous jute bags she was carrying. She was just over twenty, I guessed, and had startlingly thick black eyebrows that knitted together in the middle. She heaved the bags, which emitted an earthy root-smell, on to the table and the two women immediately started a conversation in Greek from which I was excluded until Morva made a quick introduction. 'I just hired Margarita yesterday, from the village down the hill. She'll cook and has agreed to help around the house, too. Long may it last.'

'You must be doing well if you can afford a cook.'

'Ha! On the contrary. I'm practically ruined and need the cook to give me time to earn the money to pay her. Things are a bit tricky at the moment. I think I leapt before I looked when I bought this place.' Eyebrows lifted high, wide eyes momentarily staring hard at nothing.

'It does seem a bit . . . out of the way, I must say. How come you moved here of all places? It's one hell of a trek if you find you forgot the milk.'

'It's one hell of a trek if you remembered it.' She set the little coffee pot and two tiny cups on to a small tray. 'Let's have it outside and give Margarita some space. And then I'll tell you all about it.'

Outside, the day was hotting up, yet in the dappled shade of the courtyard it seemed everything a refugee from an English winter could hope for. All around us the fresh leaf on the trees and the intense colour of the flowers made me forget winter ever happened.

There was nothing at all unusual in Morva's tale of middle-aged marital break-up until she said, 'And then I met a rich Greek-American with a rambling old farmhouse to sell. I'd been getting quite desperate. I just couldn't find enough work, any work, and I wasn't selling nearly enough paintings to survive much longer. So I thought I'd run painting classes. I soon found that the kind that pay you a living I just couldn't run from the place I had in Corfu Town. And then I got talking to this bored-looking guy at a local exhibition in town. Giorgos, except he preferred to be called George. His parents had emigrated to the States; his father had made a lot of money – he didn't say how – but they still owned this.' She nodded the back of her head at the house. 'And he'd come back to see what should be done with it and probably to look for his roots, as they do. Only, of course, everyone else from this village had long moved away, too. No one has lived here for a quarter of a century. The government refused to cough up the money for a real road – not enough households to justify the expense – and without it – well, you saw. The nearest school is too far away and, anyway, there's practically no water here. I don't think George had ever been out of New York before. He took one look at the place and found that what his dad had described as an idyll was a ghost village with zero tourist potential. He sold it to me so cheaply that at first I thought it was a joke, but it was all above board. I now own a half-ruined farmhouse and about a hundred neglected olive trees in an otherwise deserted village halfway round a mountain.'

'Can you make money from the olive trees?'

'One day, perhaps. The trees have been neglected and become unproductive. It would mean an awful lot of work and I don't know enough about it. There's an olive oil cooperative just down the road. I went down there one day to ask about what I could do with my trees and they wouldn't even let me past the gate – not interested.'

'And you run classes from here?' Talk about making your life difficult.

'That's the idea. I know what you're thinking, but it is quite idyllic here, you have to admit. If you're any kind of painter. I only have three students at the moment – you'll meet them in a minute; they're out sketching up there. Only two are staying here all the time. But I'll be starting to run proper residential courses in a couple of months. Or would be if I could get that –' she pointed at a single storey wing of the farmhouse that formed one side of the courtyard – 'turned into acceptable accommodation. Only the second lot of builders have now run out on me without explanation. At least the last lot didn't rip me off. Just never came back, simply disappeared – got an easier job elsewhere, no doubt. My problem is I'd got the bookings and taken deposits off people. If I have to cancel and refund the money, I'll be in trouble. The three students I have now are all that stands between me and bankruptcy really. And here they come. That's the beautiful Helen, always the first to arrive.'

I could hear a female voice coming closer, singing a lazy da-di-da version of a Beatles song. 'So, what do you teach them?'

'Drawing and painting, oils and watercolour. Landscape, flowers, trees, goats, chickens, each other – you'll never run out of subjects.'

'And you put them up here?'

'Two of them stay here. Helen and Rob. There's three bedrooms in the house. Sophie actually lives on the island and goes home some nights but often falls asleep on the sofa. Especially when she's had a few. So most nights, really. And all of them get all their meals. Hi, Helen.'

The woman entering the courtyard pulled a straw hat from

her head and fanned her face with it. 'It's getting quite hot up there now at midday.'

Morva rose. 'Helen, meet Chris, an old friend of mine from art school days. Just arrived out of the blue.'

Helen scrutinized me over the rim of her sunglasses. 'Another painter, I hope?'

'Oh yes,' I assured her.

'What can I get you to cool you down, Helen?'

'Red wine spritzer?'

'Coming up. For you, Chris?'

'I'll have the same if I may. D'you want a hand?'

'Oh no, you stay and get acquainted.'

Helen dispensed with her sunglasses. Her cool grey eyes narrowed. 'Have you come to join our select band of hopeless daubers?'

'Not quite. I came to see Morva, really. We first met at art college.'

'Are you a professional painter, then?'

'For my sins.'

'You lucky man. I never made it to art college myself.'

'It's not obligatory. I'm not even sure it's the best way to learn.'

'Really?' Her eyes widened and she leant forward. 'What makes you say that?'

Helen started quizzing me with such energetic inquisitiveness that it was a relief when the other two students turned into the courtyard and more introductions interrupted the interrogation.

Rob was a wiry man in his sixties. His straw hat displayed a pattern of painterly fingerprints that gave clues to his preferred palette and to the fact that he worked in oils. As he dropped his hat on to the table, he revealed a near bald pate where a few strands of hair were cruelly made to do the work of many. Rob appeared to move at a set speed that never varied, whether walking, talking, sitting down or lifting a glass, as though he had left the handbrake on.

The third student who sat down at the table provided a sharp contrast. Sophie gave the impression of surplus energy stored just below the surface of her evenly tanned skin. She was at

least twenty years younger than Rob. Despite the fact they
had been chatting amicably as they arrived, she didn't sit next
to him. Instead, she chose a chair near the end of the long
table, a little apart from all of us, creating space around herself.

They were two days into their painting course and full of
chatter about art. Morva came and went with carafes of wine,
pitchers of water and bottles of beer. The lunch prepared by
Margarita arrived *meze* style on small dishes: stuffed vine
leaves, a bean salad, small spicy meatballs, fresh crusty bread,
olives, pickled chillies and feta cheese. Picking at all this was
no barrier to conversation, and before long I had been dragged
into a good-natured argument about oil paints versus
watercolours in landscape painting, where I found myself
unexpectedly on the side of the watercolourists. I mean, who
wants to lug half a stone of oil paints across the scenery?
Morva, as the host, wisely kept out of the fray. Several times
during lunch I found her eyes resting thoughtfully on me, as
though she had never seen me before or was trying to remember
just who I was.

Siesta was well observed in Ano Makriá, much helped by
the wine. Helen and Rob withdrew to their respective rooms
upstairs in the main house, while Sophie let herself fall on to
one of the sofas in the main room downstairs, though the three
large bottles of beer she had guzzled over lunch had no visible
affect on her. Margarita got busy clearing our mess away.

'I'll take my siesta in the van,' I said to Morva, though I
didn't feel in the least bit drowsy.

'You can't; it'll be like an oven in there. No need to, either.
The first lot of builders finished one room in the annex, or as
near as. It's spartan, but it's got a bed in it. I'll show you.'

The room she showed me was small with whitewashed
walls, a blue wooden door leading straight on to the courtyard
and a small window opposite that looked into the shade of the
olive grove behind. One bed, a small table and a straight-backed
chair with a cane seat were the only furnishings, giving it a
monastic air Van Gogh would have approved of. This was the
only completed room of five in the long, low building that for
centuries had done service as anything from goat shed to
storage room and became much more dilapidated further along.

'It's perfect.'

'I'm aiming for quintessential Greek island dream. A chest, lamp and a rug and we're there.'

'Can I stay here tonight?'

'Please do. I'll bring you an oil lamp later.' She fixed me with the same kind of look she had given me during lunch, except that close up it was more unnerving.

'I don't think I need a siesta,' I admitted.

'OK, let's walk for a bit. And then you can tell me what the hell you're really doing here.'

SIX

'Did you really drive that thing all the way down here? I'm surprised you made it.' Morva sniffed suspiciously at Matilda's interior.

'So am I, tell you the truth. Here, that's the woman I'm looking for.' I had dug out the photograph of Kyla Biggs for her.

'Yes, I do remember that; it was only a few weeks back. It was in the paper. But I'm afraid that really does happen all the time. It's a very seductive place, this. Usually it's kids on their gap year or someone who suddenly decides to make a fresh start without leaving a forwarding address.'

'Not usually people with a well-paid job and property in England. I have a feeling that if Kyla Biggs wanted to move to Corfu, she'd do it properly.'

'Most likely. Though there's always the possibility of mental breakdown,' Morva said, looking back towards the house and catching her lower lip between her teeth.

As we walked back along the goat track into the empty village, a few cicadas started up, unseen in the long grass. 'Is that your car back there?'

'Yes, the poor little thing. The moped with the holy medals is Margarita's. The little motorbike, what's left of it, belongs to Sophie. She rides it everywhere, flat out, without a helmet. Probably with her eyes closed.'

We were walking now on what had once been a well-used cart track traversing the village. Most of the houses had a generous amount of land around them, except near the church where several low buildings huddled together as though leaning against each other for support. There were few sounds beyond the rasp of the cicadas and the gentle breeze from the direction of the nearby sea.

'Are you still living with that girl? Alice?' she asked abruptly.

'Annis. Yes, she's still there, miraculously, painting away as we speak, no doubt. Which reminds me, I'll have to call her and tell her I've arrived. She didn't think I'd make it. Bet me a fiver I'd never make Dover, in fact. My mobile won't work here. I don't suppose you've got a phone?'

'There's no mobile coverage around here and I can only dream of a phone line. Or anything else, for that matter. There's a kiosk with a phone in Neo Makriá but even that doesn't always work. Not for me, anyway.'

'Would it be so difficult to have a phone line laid?'

'You wouldn't have thought so, would you? First they made some positive noises, then I was told categorically no. Same with electricity and water. First I was told yes, then they dragged their feet, then I was told it was out of the question.'

'You've got no electricity at all?'

A slow resigned shake of the head. 'Not as much as two milliamps' worth. I can't afford the solar panels and I definitely can't afford a generator. I might one day. No, you've landed smack in the eighteenth century.'

We walked on. 'This is your eighteenth-century realm, then.' I still found it hard to believe that anyone, but especially a woman on her own, had looked at this spooky hamlet full of rustling ghosts and thought *Hey, this is the place where I want to live.*

'You think I was mad to buy the house, admit it.'

'I thought Mill House back in Somerset was a bit out of the way, but this is in a different league. It makes me think of Prospero and his cell.'

'That's a thought. I could do with a spirit like Ariel. Do you want the job?'

'No, thanks. I'm a water sign. I think what you really need is a Caliban or two to finish your building work.'

'Yeah, that too.' She hugged herself as though suddenly feeling cold. 'I'm not very clued up on Shakespeare, Chris. Remind me, how does it all pan out in *The Tempest*?'

'Happily ever after.'

'That's all right, then.'

'So what happened to all the people who used to live here?'

'A lot of them emigrated but some of them moved further round the mountain to what is now Neo Makriá, new Makriá. You must have come through it to get here.'

'And do they ever come up here?'

'Not really. Not in daylight they don't.'

'What do you mean? They come up at night?'

She screwed up her face into a mask of doubt. 'I think so.'

'You *think* so?'

'Oh, I don't know. I never actually see anybody, not really. Not that I go out looking – I'm not completely mad. It stopped more or less in the winter but it started up again this spring. I sometimes hear things at night.'

'What kind of things?'

'Like people walking around the place in the dark. Trying to be quiet. Once or twice I thought I saw a light – you know, like torchlight – even right in the courtyard. When I opened the window, it was gone. Could be children from Neo Makriá, but apparently they're all too scared of ghosts and spirits to come this way. Even the grown-ups are all superstitious here. But it could be a dare for the kids, I suppose. Anyway, it's nearly an hour's walk out here from the village.'

'Could they be from a different village?'

'They would have to come through Neo Makriá. This is a dead end unless you're a mountain goat or come by sea and scramble up the cliff. Ah, look, there's Rob's easel.'

'Where?' My eyes were too busy trying to make sense of the overgrown jumble of crumbling houses and sheds to have noticed it standing in the shade of a twisted olive tree that was leaning heavily on a low, crumbling wall. Next to the easel stood a large plastic art box, and on an upturned wooden crate rested his palette. We walked around to inspect the work in progress. Rob's painting was of the ruined house we had just passed, methodically rendered in flat, passionless dabs of oil paint.

I probably made some inappropriate sound because Morva felt moved to defend the painting. 'Rob's not that bad, really, it's just that it's all so . . . oh, OK, it's bad. I'm not sure where to begin with him. But he enjoys it, that's the main thing.'

'Is it?'

'Well, you know what I mean. It's a painting holiday, and in his case, well, the emphasis should perhaps be on holiday. Chris, that's very naughty of you.'

I had flipped open Rob's big art box and pulled open the

hinged tiers of drawers. 'I'm a painter *and* a detective, so what do you expect? Aren't you fascinated by how other painters arrange their stuff? I think it's very revealing.' In Rob's case, it conformed to my first impression of him. Everything was neatly laid out. Apart from his tubes of paints and brushes, there were compartments full of pencils, erasers, a viewing frame and small bottles of solvents, as well as miscellaneous items – a clip-on torch, candle stubs, canvas clips and drawing pins and a pair of oil-stained leather gloves. I carefully closed the box again. I felt I knew Rob a lot better now.

'The other two put their easels up near the old olive press, if you want to inspect their—'

That's when we heard the scream and both froze for a second, Morva with her arm still pointing. A woman's voice. The scream wasn't repeated.

'That came from the house,' she called, already running.

I ran after her. 'Whose voice was that?'

'I couldn't tell.'

The vegetation and rubble didn't make an ideal sprinting track, but Morva skipped through it like a mountain goat. I followed closely in her tracks and even so cracked my ankle twice on rocks hidden in the grass. As we tore into the yard, we could hear agitated voices from inside the house, all female.

We found Sophie, Helen and Margarita at the foot of the stairs, all talking at once, Margarita in a full flood of Greek with enough hand gestures for the three of them. Helen, wearing only snow-white bra and knickers, looked palest.

'Who . . . screamed?' I asked, out of breath.

'Me,' said Helen, raising a hand as though in class. 'So would you if you found a snake sharing your bed.'

'Quite possibly,' I admitted. 'Where is it now?'

'Up there,' said Helen and Sophie in unison and pointing unnecessarily at the only *up* there was: the narrow wooden stairs.

'Where's Rob?' Morva wanted to know.

'He must be out,' Sophie said, 'unless he's one hell of a deep sleeper.'

Morva called loudly for him without result. 'Well, someone will have to go and deal with it,' she said, not moving. I looked at her. 'Don't look at me,' she said. 'I can't do snakes. Absolutely not.'

'I'm not going up there until that snake's gone,' agreed Sophie.

'Me neither,' vowed Helen.

Margarita disappeared towards the kitchen, muttering to herself.

'You go,' Morva decided, giving me an encouraging push. 'I really, *really* can't do snakes, Chris,' she added firmly. 'Spiders and lizards, yes. Not snakes.'

Great. I climbed the stairs full of doubt. Could I do snakes? And since when? I turned round at the top and looked back. Three women looked up at me, making my-hero faces. 'What did it look like?' I asked, stalling.

'Like a snake. You'll recognize it when you see it,' Helen promised. 'My room's the second along.'

The door was open. There was a bed sheet and clothing strewn on the floor and a couple of pill containers and a glass, unbroken, swept off the bedside table in a panic. What did I know about snakes? Not a lot. They didn't jump – I was grateful for that; I never liked things that jumped. Snakes don't jump. *They strike.* I couldn't hear any slithering or hissing, which was nice. What else did I know? Snakes curled up neatly in folds of bed sheet just by the pillow and went to sleep. I knew that because that's what this one had done. It had stripes all along its body and was probably forty or fifty inches long. Now what? In my limited experience of legless reptiles, gleaned long ago in Turkey and from a more comfortable distance, snakes, when startled, slithered off to hide somewhere. This was fine outside, but just what I was trying to avoid in here, since I'd end up chasing it all over the house. While wishing for a net or at least a pair of leather gloves, I slowly crept up on it, sending up little prayers to whatever Greek Orthodox saint was in charge of creaking floorboards. When I reached the bed, the floorboard under my left foot creaked. I held my breath. No reaction. I had seen crazy wildlife people on telly handle poisonous snakes and saying how lovely they were; only just now I thought this one looked rather uncuddly. Well, it was no use standing there until the thing woke up. I'd just have to be quick. I'd simply grab it behind the head and get a firm grip. On the count of three: one . . . two . . . three . . .

Four . . . five. *Don't be such a coward.* I reached forward, saw my hand tremble, took a deep breath and grabbed the snake. It came alive with all its writhing and wriggling powers intact. Its mouth gaped open, its curved, glistening fangs mesmerizing. The snake's body writhed and curled up my forearm.

'I've got it – get out of the way!' I carried the struggling reptile downstairs past the 'well dones' and 'yuks' of the three women and out into the forecourt. My next worry was how to disengage myself from the disgruntled beastie without it biting me in revenge.

Morva and Sophie followed me outside. 'Don't let it go here; it might come straight back in,' Morva warned.

'Oh, OK, you want me to take it for a walk, do you?'

'Well, chuck it somewhere under that clump of olive trees over there.'

Just then Rob appeared from the afternoon shadows under that very clump of trees. 'What have you got there?' he asked as he walked up.

'Snake,' I said. 'Found it in Helen's bed.'

Rob's eyebrows shot up.

'I mean Helen did. Not sure how to let it go now.'

'Ah yes, a four-lined snake. Just put it down and it'll disappear into the grass.'

'Is it dangerous?'

'What? No. Totally harmless. I'm parched. Any chance of a cup of tea, Morva?'

I put the snake down and let go. The treacherous thing disappeared into the shadows, taking my new-found hero status with it.

That evening I learnt some more of what living in the eighteenth century entailed. Water had to be drawn for cooking and washing. There was a well with a wooden cover in the courtyard for drinking water, and a dark and ancient cistern fifty yards away at the back of the shuttered ruin of a farmhouse which yielded water for washing and laundry. After three trips to the cistern, each time lugging back a big yellow container of water, eighteenth-century Greece was in danger of losing some of its romance.

Yet in the courtyard at dusk, as Margarita served supper, with paraffin lamps, candle lanterns and mosquito coils lit and the wine flowing once more, it all began to make sense again, feeding some deep-rooted yearning for a simpler life that never was. The enthusiasm of Morva's three students for talking about the afternoon's work, of artists they admired and paintings they had seen seemed inexhaustible. After a few glasses of rough local red and a meal of pot-roast lamb, I felt that the past was perhaps not such a bad place to be.

I had withdrawn to my monkish cell just after midnight and fallen asleep the moment I dropped on to the bed. What woke me in the middle of the night I couldn't tell; my brain was too busy trying to work out where it was. I was glad when I remembered. Unfortunately, as I sat up in the dark, my brain also remembered all the wine I had drunk. Sensing more than seeing them, I found the matches and lit the paraffin lamp by the bed, then opened the door to the night. In the courtyard, I found nothing but starlight and the clean fragrance of the night.

I was about to turn back when I saw it, on the far side of the ghostly hamlet: a light. For less than a second it illuminated the side of a ruined building, then vanished, leaving nothing but a doubtful trace on my retina. Behind me the house stood dark apart from the light falling from my door. For a few minutes I stood at the entrance of the courtyard, staring into the darkness, listening. All I heard was the call of a distant owl, and when no more light appeared, I began to think I had imagined it.

I turned around to go back to bed and stopped in my tracks. Through the half-open door of my room I saw a distorted shadow move across the wall. I had a visitor. Walking carefully beside the narrow shaft of light that fell across the ground, I managed to get to the house without making too much noise. Breathing as quietly as I could, I stopped by the door and listened. All I could see through the narrow opening were my bags against the bare wall opposite the bed, but I thought I could hear tiny noises. I swung the door wide and stepped inside. Briefly, Derringer looked up from the patch of the bed I had vacated, sighed and closed his eyes again. It took me a long while to get back to sleep.

SEVEN

I was glad to see that Derringer ignored Morva's chickens, since I was enjoying my breakfast eggs and didn't want the supply interrupted. The chickens in turn seemed to have delegated a black hen to keep an eye on him while the rest scratched in the yard. The students had trooped off to their easels, leaving Morva and me alone at the long table.

'Am I making more coffee?' she offered.

'No, it's time I started to work for my money.' *Before it runs out completely*, I added mentally.

'How are you planning to go about it?'

I shrugged. 'The usual way. I'll stick my nose in where it isn't wanted, ask a lot of questions and make a nuisance of myself. Except I've never had to do it in a foreign language before.'

I could hear the laboured prattle of a moped engine in the distance. A couple of minutes later Margarita arrived, carrying more shopping bags. Morva exchanged a few words with her, among which I recognized my name. For a long second Margarita looked at me with something like horror, an expression Morva missed as just then Derringer jumped on her lap. Margarita muttered a few words, lifted her shopping bags off the table and disappeared inside.

'What did you just tell her?' I asked Morva who had turned her attention to the cat.

'Mm? Oh, I told her you weren't just a painter but a private detective as well. She'll be chuffed; she watches all the cop shows on telly.'

Chuffed was not how I would have described Margarita's expression. 'She gave me a very strange look. What's private detective in Greek, then?'

'*Astinomikós idiotikós.*'

'Really?' It didn't sound all that clever.

A minute later Margarita reappeared, rushing past us, calling something over her shoulder.

Morva shrugged. 'Says she forgot the garlic; she's popping back to the village. I could have sworn we had strings of the stuff. But Margarita is so superstitious, I don't think she'd feel quite *safe* without a crate of the stuff.'

'Vampires?'

'Vampires. Also water spirits by the wells, imps in the kitchen, goblins in the groves, ghosts in the churchyard and the evil eye. The list is endless. Her moped is encrusted with amulets for protection. But, of course, she wouldn't dream of wearing a helmet.'

Eventually, Morva walked me to her car, which she had offered to lend me. A rust-red Ford Fiesta from the last century, it looked only marginally better appointed than the van but would be a lot easier to drive around the island's twisting roads. Not to mention cheaper. On closer inspection, the colour of the thing had been an inspired choice. I stuck my finger through a rusted hole in the door.

'You've no idea how wet Corfu gets in winter,' she said guiltily. 'Now, a word of warning, Mr Shamus: be discreet. And stay away from the police.'

'I usually try to. But I was hoping they might be able to tell me at least what the timescale was. And perhaps they've found out by now where she stayed.'

'Read my lips, Chris. Stay away from them. In fact, if you see one, scram. They don't like competition from PIs anyway, that's well known, but if they find a foreigner asking people questions, they can get downright nasty.'

'I'll bear that in mind.'

'The police here are famous for being corrupt. Unless you have a lot of money to spend on bribes, don't get into a situation where you might have to. You'd better have some kind of cover story, just in case.'

'I'm just looking for a friend, that's all.' Who could possibly object to that?

'I hope you're a good liar.' Morva waved me off with a doubtful look on her face. 'Drive carefully – the roads are crap.'

I had noticed. Though a crap road would have been a definite improvement on the track connecting old and new Makriá. In the village I parked as before by the palm tree. The grill that had been so busy before was shut. Dimitris's *kafénion* was open, however, and I was being keenly eyed by the three characters sitting with their backs against the wall at the little tables outside. They watched my every move as though they were expected to sit an exam on the subject. I made a mental note to ask Morva if there was some arcane rule in Corfu that all *kafénions* had to have three old geezers sitting with their backs against the wall.

It was the yellow kiosk at the edge of the square I was after. I had noticed these in town. Fulfilling the functions of a corner shop combined with post office and telephone exchange, they seemed to cram an extraordinary variety of goods into the tiny space, leaving just enough room for one surly proprietor to sit on a stool in the centre and mop his cabin-fevered brow. Whatever didn't fit inside the hut hung from the outside: scarves, hats, sunglasses, kitchen utensils, plastic toys. A fridge and an ice cream freezer completed the set-up.

As I walked towards it, I noticed just how quiet the village was. My footsteps on the hard ground seemed the noisiest event around. It wasn't that there was nothing happening here – two boys were straining to load half a pig into the back of a van, a woman was sweeping her doorstep, an old man was checking a burden of sacks on a donkey – only it was all happening very quietly. The pace also appeared wrong, like a film run on slightly reduced speed, or as though everyone in the village had his mind on other things.

The man inside the kiosk looked soft-skinned and pale against a backdrop of cigarette packets and Greek paperbacks. I butchered sufficient Greek to make myself understood and was told to go round the side, where, on a waist-high shelf, sat a large red telephone from which I called Annis at Mill House.

'Rubbish, you're in a lay-by off the A2 – admit it.' Her voice sounded very far away.

'No, I'm actually standing in the square of a . . .' I nearly said 'strange Greek village', but since I wanted her to join me here, left it at 'Greek village'.

'You haven't found her yet?'

'Kyla Biggs? Give me a break, I only got here yesterday. I found Morva, though; it's where I'm staying.' I gave her a quick description of the place. 'Did the cheque arrive?'

'Yesterday. I banked it. That's the good news. I have some rather bad news, though.'

'Out with it, then.'

'Derringer is missing.'

'Oh no, he's not. He's run away to Greece. As a stowaway.'

'The little swine! Everyone's on holiday except me.'

'Are you coming down, then?'

'I might. Only not yet, hon, not until I've finished this painting. But go on, tempt me. What's the weather like?'

'Warm, dazzling sunshine. What's yours like?'

'Hard to tell with this fog.'

'I'm so glad.'

I paid for the call and a pair of cheap sunglasses that had taken my fancy. 'Foggy in England?' the kiosk owner asked. It was a rhetorical question. If you were in the habit of using the village phone, then presumably the entire village got to share your happy news.

Dodging potholes and constantly stopping to guess the way meant I made slow progress. Someone harbouring an anti-Anglo grudge had used a spray-can to obscure the English translations on road signs for miles around, and one thing you don't learn while listening to language tapes is how to read a foreign alphabet. Fortunately, some of it was sufficiently similar for me to make an educated guess, enough to get me eventually on to the main road south.

Spring was well advanced wherever I looked. The hard heat of summer had not yet arrived to burn the grasses crisp and turn the road verges to dust, allowing me to drive through a lush, subtropical fantasy land where everything but the road itself had some kind of plant growing from it. I crossed a narrow river with improbably green water and passed countless houses half obscured by spring blossom. The traffic was a stream of lorries, scooters, mopeds, pick-ups, ancient three-wheeled trucks (all with green cabs) and buses. Buses had a habit of cornering at speed, using most of the road and a lot of air horn, which apparently made that all right. I quickly learnt to listen as well as look as I drove, feeling small and squashable in Morva's tiny underpowered car. And yet after a while I began to relax into it, windows open, elbow on the sill, driving more slowly, breathing more deeply. The further south I went, the more the traffic thinned out.

I braked. If Morva's description was accurate, then this had to be it. The place where Kyla Biggs's car had been found abandoned was right in front of a long wall of cactus by the side of the road before the turn-off to a place called Chlomós. Morva had mentioned the cactus – it had formed the backdrop to the photo of the car, published in the local paper. I pulled off on to a narrow unmade road leading into the hills and walked across to the cacti. They were the prickly pear type, taller than myself and already bearing small flowers. There were no houses on this bit of road, just a blind stone hut that looked as though it was trying to shrink into the ground. Further along stood a rusted metal shrine. I walked over to it. It had a lopsided pointed roof and a glass front. Inside were the picture of a saint, a bottle of olive oil, an oil lamp, a box of matches and four dead flies.

What I had hoped to find at this place I couldn't have said. I hadn't expected the car to still be here, nor was I hoping to find an explanatory note pinned to a tree. Only, somehow, it seemed like the right place to start looking, since it was the only one I knew of that Kyla had been.

Or did I? Thinking about it, I realized I knew no such thing. Just because her hire car had been here didn't mean she had been in it at the time. I circled the wall of cactus, a couple of car lengths of it. There were cigarette butts and bits of paper rubbish at its base. Here and there, carvings had been made in the cactus, a pentangle, a swastika, a lightning bolt, some initials, the letters K and X inside a badly executed heart pierced by an arrow. This had been carved recently – I could tell by the lighter colour of the scabbing over the deep wounds in the plant's skin. Kyla and Mr X? Was I looking at Kyla Biggs's cactaceous declaration of her love for a mysterious stranger for whom she abandoned her former life, job and hire car? Possibly not. The cool black-and-white look in her photograph kept telling me that infatuation of the type that carves love hearts wasn't behind her disappearance.

The road had fallen quiet. I could smell cigarette smoke on the air but saw nobody. One more time for luck, I circled the cactus, and when I turned back towards my car, I found myself faced by a man who had to have sprung from the stone hut that very second. Either that or he had grown out of the ground. He stood motionless in the road, a couple of feet from the verge, a mattock over his left shoulder and a cigarette in the right corner of his mouth for balance. He was watching me with dark yet wide-awake eyes.

I said 'hello' and remarked on the warm weather with my bit of Greek, which he accepted as unremarkable. He made a dismissive gesture with a work-scarred hand: no, this wasn't hot, not hot at all. Then he startled me with a question that sounded just a little gruff to my unseasoned ear: 'What are you doing here?'

I shrugged. 'I'm on holiday.' Then, making a nonsense out of my statement, I pulled Kyla's photograph from my pocket and held it out for him to peruse and asked, with equal directness, 'Where is she?'

He lifted both eyebrows and nodded his head back in that tiny gesture that I was quickly learning had many meanings, from 'no' to 'impossible' to 'mind your own business'. The ash on his cigarette had grown long and curved downwards but survived the gesture. He added some rapid-fire Greek in which the only word I understood was *amáxi* – car – and walked off into the olive groves behind me.

I had paid no heed to the approaching engine noise until I saw the twinkle of blue rounding the corner. I ducked back behind the cactus and spied out between two close-growing lobes. The Toyota was being driven at speed, unfortunately on the opposite side of the road. Its right-hand steering wheel put the driver too far away to make out through the tinted glass, yet again I got the impression of white hair as the car flashed past, braked for the next corner and disappeared round it. It looked like the same British number plate, but I hadn't managed to memorize all of it. Next time I saw it, I'd take a photo. Even considering the fact that it was the main route to the south of the island, this was one sighting too many. Whoever was following me had not been put off my scent by my spending the night in Morva's hideaway, but it looked as if my car in the side road had not been spotted. If I was wrong about that, I would soon find out.

I took the turn to Chlomós. I'd been able to admire the village from miles away. It had been superglued to the top of the mountain at a time when the land between its base and the sea was still a mosquito-infested zone where malaria bred at night. The narrow road rose immediately up in a tightly twisting serpentine through the silver green of the olive groves. This was what car horns were made for, warning of your approach as you urged your underpowered engine to heave you through the next bend, but I didn't feel like advertising my whereabouts. Coming to an unsignposted turn-off, I hesitated for a moment. Should I slip down there and wait for something blue to turn up? I decided height might give me an advantage and carried on. I was halfway up when the mountain road opened into a lay-by, a tiny green hire car already parked there. I squeezed the Fiesta behind it and got out. Nearby stood a man in khaki shorts and a flak jacket with heavy binoculars supported on a monopod which he swung about like a Bren gun. It was the birdwatcher from Neo Makriá. For a moment I stood at the edge of the lay-by pretending to admire the view. It wasn't long before I *did* admire the view. Below us stretched the dense forest of olive trees, seemingly uninterrupted by other plantations, with here and there a collection of roofs or a spiral of rising smoke. Further away, I saw what looked like a lake or lagoon, quicksilver below a cloudless sky, and beyond that the hazy shimmer of the Mediterranean. I could imagine how in the days before proper roads this height made people feel safe, allowing ample warning of anyone approaching.

Not so in these days of tarmac roads, of course. The Toyota was back. Now and then I could see a flicker of blue below as my pursuer negotiated the switchback mountain, much faster than I could manage with Morva's clapped-out Fiesta.

The birder looked at me with the disinterest of the specialist – I was entirely the wrong species. I still gave him my finest smile. 'Amazing bins you've got there. Would you mind if I had a look through them?'

He shrugged. 'I've lost him now, anyway. I thought I saw an Egyptian vulture as I drove up and pulled in immediately, though I may have been mistaken. He moved off north, I thought. I only caught a glimpse while I was driving.'

'Ta.' I took the heavy binoculars from him – more Zeiss hardware – and pointed them down the mountain, trying to bring my blue quarry closer. What was I thinking? It was I who was the quarry.

'You won't see anything down there; north of the lake is where you should be looking. Over *there*,' he said, tapping me on the arm, exasperated.

'Oh, I don't know. It's more the performance of your binoculars I'd like to check out.'

'Yes, you said you had no interest in ornithology.'

'That's not what I said. I said I didn't come here for the birds. These bins are brilliant; mine are rubbish.' I meant it. The magnification was such that when I found the Toyota zooming up the hill I had to take my eyes away from the glasses to reassure myself that its arrival wasn't imminent.

'What kind of glasses have you got?' the twitcher asked, more friendly now that I had acknowledged his superiority in the bins department.

Below me, the Toyota had reached the unsignposted turn-off, slowed and come to a stop. I had a good view of it now below a rocky outcrop devoid of trees. The driver's door opened and my silver-haired pursuer got out.

She was dressed entirely in black: black trainers, jeans, vest top and gloves. She was about mid-thirties, her hair was bleached – her darker roots were showing – and a nose-ring or stud glittered by her left nostril. It was the gloves that worried me. 'Mm? Erm, I have no idea what make they are, to be honest. I bought them at a jumble sale.'

The woman stood with her hands on her hips, staring down the turn-off. Then she suddenly swung round. Had the sun reflected off the binoculars? She seemed to look straight at me for a couple of seconds, then swung herself back into the driver's seat.

'Well, small wonder,' the twitcher said. 'You always get what you pay for.'

I handed back the binoculars. 'Oh, I don't know. Sometimes you get more than you bargained for. Must dash.'

The Fiesta's wheels spun as I drove off past the twitcher, whose puzzled look clearly spelled 'never talk to strangers' across his face. I laboured at the wheel and tormented the little engine, but there really was no point: the Toyota had probably four times the horsepower. At every bend I could see it below me, getting closer. I should just stop, I told myself, and have it out with the woman. But perhaps not on an empty road on the mountainside. It wasn't the fact I was being followed that worried me; I myself had followed people many times and some of them were still alive. *It was the gloves.* Only seriously weird people drive with gloves on. Avoid them at all costs.

The Toyota was getting very close – I could catch glimpses of it in my mirrors now. A few houses began to appear, then at last I heaved the car into the village proper. *Which way, which way?* These streets were narrow, some not made for cars at all. What if I got stuck somewhere? The Toyota was now just a street corner behind. A small lorry, loaded to the gills with propane gas bottles, was in the process of pulling out of a yard and into the road. It would take up all the available space. I parped my horn as I squeezed past, then looked back. The lorry lumbered into the middle of the narrow street. An angry Toyota car horn blared behind me. I chose the quickest way out, back towards the north. I calculated that I had bought myself no more than three minutes' head start before the Toyota would again be eating up the distance between us. Where horsepower was lacking, bravado would have to do.

In a Ford Fiesta no one can hear you scream. I flung the car down the mountain, past some astonished sightseers who had pulled up at a beauty spot. I had no time for the views; the bends arrived at alarming speeds and the car cornered like a crateful of fish. Not once did I dare look in my mirrors. For all I knew, the Toyota could be nudging the rear bumper. I flung the thing about on the potholed road that seemed to go on for ever, then at last I made it to the coast and slipped the car among a healthy amount of traffic and felt a whole lot better for it. There was no sign of my pursuer. With any luck, I had given her the slip.

For a while I just bumbled along the coast road, with the sea glittering to my right and the land rising on my left. I knew I was going in the wrong direction, but just now I didn't really care. When I got to a place called Benitses, I stopped, slid the car between a couple of tourist jeeps and sat down at a cafe table within commando-roll distance of the driver's door. An Australian waitress served me iced coffee; a boy tried to sell me a pair of sunglasses, despite the fact that I had a pair on my nose; half-naked British tourists studied the menu boards promising all-day English breakfasts. All the clichés appeared to be intact and all seemed well with the world. I leant back in my plastic chair, stretched out my legs and tried to relax. The narrow strip of beach was dotted with bodies sizzling in the unusual spring heat, and the predominant smell in the air, even with the road between us, was of factor eight. Benitses was obviously built to cater for a large number of summer visitors, yet right now its cafes and restaurants looked impatiently unfrequented. The place had an eager, expectant air I wanted to lose myself in. I felt like skiving. For a while I tried to imagine myself at the beginning of a carefree few weeks of holiday, with nothing much to do apart from rattling ice cubes in my drinks and reading bilingual menus by the dazzling sea.

Until the Toyota crawled into view. I sat up so quickly I swallowed an ice cube. Even though Gloves looked straight at me through the tinted windows, I found it impossible to read her face. A local bus arrived behind her, its driver half obscured by religious medals, beads, effigies of saints and bunting. With no room to overtake, he laboured his horn, bullying Gloves into driving on. I dropped some euros on the table and lunged for the Fiesta. As quickly as traffic allowed, I drove in the opposite direction, ignoring the first opportunity to turn off the main road. I chose the second turn-off, a narrow tarmac road, and took to the hills. After half an hour's aimless drive, I was sure I had lost her. But for how long? If Gloves had picked me up so easily today despite my having changed cars, then she was either very lucky or she knew exactly where to find me.

EIGHT

'**N**ot just a pretty face, I see.' It was Helen who had sneaked up behind me under the orange trees in the neglected little grove near the church. I didn't look around, just kept sketching. I had it bad.

The sight of painters at work in the landscape, among the ridiculously picturesque decay of Ano Makriá, was timeless. On my return to the village I had found the house deserted by all but the chickens and the painters out at work among the ruins. They presented a sight that could have belonged to any time in the last three centuries: straw-hatted figures in paint-spattered clothes working at wooden easels under sunshades in the early evening light. The lure had been too strong; I'd simply had to join them. Morva generously kitted me out with all I needed from her considerable store and I soon found myself sitting on the remains of a broken barrel, sketching the overgrown tumble of stone where the wall surrounding the grove had fallen down. The sun had long disappeared behind the rim of the valley, but I was still drawing.

'I thought you said your work was abstract?' Helen went on. 'I think your talents are wasted on abstract work. That's such a sensitive drawing – you'll simply have to paint it.' She was standing very close behind me now, close enough for me to smell her flowery perfume.

I looked up. Her raised eyebrows were demanding an answer. 'That's what I'm afraid of. It's been tugging at me from the moment I got here. This stuff –' I waved my pencil at the offending landscape – 'just cries out to be painted.'

'Good. We'll seduce you away from the dark side yet, back into the world of light and form, Mr Honeysett.' She strode off in her long, loose flower-print dress. I watched her disappear into the nineteenth century or thereabouts, her progress a painting every few yards. Ridiculous. Surely one sketchbook of landscape drawings couldn't turn you into a figurative painter?

The sky would remain light for a long while yet, but when I heard the signal for supper – a metal rod struck against a rusty bit of iron on a rope – I packed up my sketch pad and pencils. After struggling so long with my work back in England, I had now become obsessed all over again with drawing and painting, even the very smell of art materials. But I never subscribed to starving for my art. Not even Van Gogh starved for his art; when he went hungry, it was only because he had spent his brother's allowance in the whorehouse.

By the time I turned into the courtyard the table was already laid, and Helen, Sophie and Morva were toasting my arrival with glasses of red. I fancied a beer myself so went inside to see if there was a cool bottle in the half-barrel of well water in the kitchen where essentials like beer and butter were kept cold. A strong smell of burning food greeted me as I came near the kitchen. I hastened my steps to catch a glimpse of Margarita at the stove, incinerating what looked like quarters of chicken in a gigantic black-iron pan. She jumped with surprise as I entered and whisked the pan off the heat. It was smoking and the chicken looked well cremated. Margarita let loose a flood of excited Greek, of which I understood not a single word, while she tumbled the smoking chicken pieces into a serving dish. She looked at me with gestures of despair not seen in ham acting since the arrival of the talkies. There was something strange about this girl and I thought it best to leave her to whatever she was up to. I grabbed a beer from the half-barrel under the table and turned to exit. Just then, from the corner of my eye, I caught a quick movement, but when I looked back all I saw was Margarita trying to stare a hole in the wall. Salt crystals crunched underfoot as I left the kitchen.

'I'd stick to the salad tonight,' I announced to the table as I prised the top off my bottle of Amstel. 'I'm getting a strange feeling about your Margarita,' I said quietly to Morva. 'Either she's not all there or she's just deliberately burnt supper.'

Almost immediately, Margarita rushed to the table, hair

flying, dumped the cremated chicken and a dish of potatoes on the table, then ran on out of the courtyard towards her moped, ululating in Greek all the while.

I looked at Morva who shrugged deeply. 'Don't all look at me; even I didn't understand half of that. Something about the evil eye and pixies. Or it could be sprites – not sure.'

Sophie prodded the smoking chicken with a knife. 'Mm, interesting. As a variation of Blackened Chicken, it's pretty hard-core.'

'Sorry about that, I don't know what's got into her. She's a good cook, I was told; she must have taken her eyes off it for a second. Or . . . or quite a few seconds, I guess.'

I sat down next to Helen. Sophie, as before, had settled a little apart, her sandal-clad feet on the chair beside her, as if to make sure it remained empty.

'Where's Rob, I wonder?' Morva asked. 'Poor Rob; chicken is his favourite.'

Helen brushed at the back of my tee-shirt. 'What's that on your back – salt? There's some in your hair as well.'

'There was loads on the kitchen floor just now.'

'Have you been rolling in it?' Helen said. 'Rob started a new painting today up behind the old olive press. Maybe he didn't hear the signal for supper.'

'Perhaps someone should go and find him,' Sophie said, not volunteering.

The whine of Margarita's moped drifted away, leaving nothing but the timeless sounds of scratching chickens.

'I'll have a look for him,' I offered. 'You start without me.'

I hadn't gone far beyond the courtyard walls when Morva came up beside me, carrying a hunk of bread. She tore it in half for me to share and we munched as we walked up the gentle slope. 'Do you know where the old olive press is?'

'Erm, good point. It's that way, isn't it?' I pointed to a group of buildings above us to our right.

She pushed my arm forty-five degrees to the left. 'Are you glad I came yet? Actually, I came to apologize for Margarita. Chucking salt behind someone is supposed to ward off the influence of the evil eye. She must have got it into her head that you're an evil presence or something.'

'Told you she gave me a funny look when you told her I was a private eye. Are you sure that's what you told her?'

'Pretty sure. My Greek's not brilliant but it's not that bad, either.'

'I wouldn't have thought her generation still believed in that kind of stuff, would you? Ghosts and the evil eye?'

'Think again. Out here in the sticks they're surrounded by it from the day they're born. The old women are full of the lore and the mutterings are everywhere. It's catching, too; you'll find yourself not walking under ladders before you know it. That's the old olive press over there. No sign of Rob.' She called for him. 'Rob, where are you?'

No answer. The building stood a short way apart from the rest, its wide double doors broken. I had a look inside. Nothing but a large circular stone in the centre of the ground floor remained; everything else had rotted away or been removed. A few wooden steps to the left led halfway up the wall into nowhere. I stepped on something crunchy and lifted my foot – a packet of Marlboro, looking new apart from where I squashed it. I straightened out the box and opened it. Only a few cigarettes were missing. The fragrance was still seductive; it wasn't long since I had given up coughing through a pack of Camels a day.

Morva joined me in the shadowy interior of the mill. 'I found Rob's easel and stuff, but he's not here. His painting isn't, either; he's probably taken it back to the house to show me. I don't know why we're running after him. He *is* quite old and I feel a bit protective of him, I expect. He'll be heart-broken about the burnt chicken, I can tell you that.'

'Found these.' I waved the open pack.

'No thanks, filthy habit. Kids coming here to smoke, I expect. That would explain our night-time visitors.'

'Bit of a way to come for a smoke. By the time you're home again you'd want another one, surely.'

'Oh, let's go; Rob's probably long back at the house. We'll go this way; show you a different part of the village. Hey, is that him between those houses? *Rob?*'

Someone was moving quickly in the shadowy gap between two ruins. I couldn't make out who it was, but the figure moved fast and disappeared into or behind one of the houses – it was impossible to tell which.

'I don't think that was Rob. Rob doesn't move like that; he's only got one gear.'

I agreed. 'It looked as if whoever it was wore camouflage gear.'

Morva put on a spurt towards the place where the figure had disappeared from view, then suddenly stopped. She put a hand on my arm to hold me back. 'Forget it, Chris; let's just go back to the house.'

'You sure? I mean, we could . . .'

'No, I'm sure. It's a free country – anyone's allowed to walk around here, after all. Come on.' She pulled me away by my shirt. 'Let's see if we can salvage some supper.'

When we got back to the house, Rob was there, as predicted. Morva had been right: he was quite upset and not just about burnt chicken. 'My painting has disappeared.' Rob sat at the table, slowly prodding a piece of charred chicken remains. His face said he was not having a good day.

'Disappeared how?' Morva demanded to know.

'Disappeared like – *poof* – gone,' Sophie said helpfully.

'I took a break, went for a stroll, so I could come back to it with fresh eyes, see if much more needed doing. When I got back, it was gone. Simply not there. First I thought perhaps a mysterious gust of wind had blown it off the easel, but there was no sign of it on the ground. I had a good look around, went in ever-increasing circles round the place, but it's utterly gone. I worked four days on that canvas!'

'Did you see anyone? Any strangers?' I asked. 'Before or after it vanished?'

'No one, before *or* after. Or during, for that matter. Though sometimes, of course, it does feel as if there're people around. Ghosts, I expect, in a place like this. But they tend not to steal paintings.'

'We did see someone move about,' Morva said, 'but we couldn't make out what they looked like. It's bound to be a prank of some sort – kids, probably. I mean who in their right mind would want to steal one of *your* . . . erm, *unfinished* paintings?'

'It was so very nearly finished,' Rob lamented. 'They could easily have mistaken it for a finished canvas, just sitting there . . .'

As a painter, I thought I could imagine how he must feel. 'Perhaps Morva is right and it was a prank; they might just have hidden it for a laugh. We'll go and have a look for it once we've had something to eat. Plenty of light left.'

But by the time we had dined on potatoes, bread and salad, dusk had crept into the village and the hunt for the missing artwork was postponed until the morning. Even Derringer shunned the blackened chicken mess. With a builder's shovel, I dug a shallow grave some fifty yards away from the house and, in the gloom of the approaching night, gave it an undignified burial.

That night, sleeping with the door ajar so Derringer could come and go as he pleased without waking me, I dreamt of a whispering army of men with fiery eyes infiltrating my night-camp in the mountains. The air smelled of electricity and rain as I hunted them in the dark, naked, armed only with a rock. Lightning struck with instantaneous thunder.

I woke with the noise of it still echoing in my mind, yet outside the moon rode low through wisps of white cloud and a west wind whispered in the olive groves. Derringer was out, hunting down the natives.

'It says "Back before you receive this, I'm sure. Love Kyla".' Morva turned the postcard over in her hand and examined the picture on the front again. 'She obviously expected to come back as planned.'

'Looks like it. And you haven't come across Niko's Taverna?' I tapped the picture postcard.

'Come across it? Every firstborn son on this island is called Spiros after the patron saint, and the rest of them are called Nikos or Dimitris. There could be fifty Niko's Tavernas.'

'But this one's right by the . . . ah yes, water, I take your point: we're on an island.'

'Yes, there must be thousands. Well, loads, anyway. Can't remember when I've last been on a beach,' she said, frowning into space, trying to remember.

'Really? I'd have thought that would be the big attraction, living in a place like this: the beach-bum existence.'

'Yeah, sure. You get over that very quickly. Walking on the beach in winter when the tourists are gone is fine, but you do that – what – once a month? No, I've never been a beach babe. It bores me and I can't think of many things that are improved by the addition of sand. One thing about this, though . . .' She turned the picture around and pushed it towards my breakfast plate. 'That looks like fishing boats in the background, so it's probably on the east side. I don't think there's mooring for fishing boats on the west coast. Too stormy. So that does narrow it down. I'm sure you'll find it eventually; depends how long you've got.'

'Not very. I don't have much money and I can't stay here sponging off you, so I'll have to get . . .'

'Rubbish, Chris,' she interrupted, grabbing my forearm. 'Listen, you're not sponging, I'm really glad you're here; in fact, if I had the money, I'd *pay* you to stay here. It's been so . . . well, it's been a bit . . . weird. Being here on my own, trying to get this painting school thing off the ground, spooky stuff at night, things going missing all the time . . .'

'You mean Rob's painting wasn't the first thing that went AWOL?' Rob and the others were already out among the ruins trying to find it.

'Things constantly disappear. Sometimes they just move about and turn up in the wrong place and sometimes they disappear for good. Rarely, but it does happen.'

'Like what?'

'All sorts. Petty things . . . a teapot walked and didn't come back. A wind-up radio was gone one day, back in its place the next. That sort of thing.'

'It's probably just kids, Morva, playing practical jokes on the foreigner.'

'I know, but . . . You know what's the creepiest thing?' She picked up my coffee cup and saucer, then set it down again half an inch from where it was before and with the handle facing a different way. By a fraction. 'Stuff like that. Someone obviously picks something up, has a look at it, then sets it down again. *Slightly* out of place, but just not enough out of place to be sure you're not imagining things. It spooks me, Chris. People creeping around at night and just a couple of women and an old man out here. I'm beginning to get worried about it all. I can't even get workmen to come out here and finish the accommodation. And I thought I could get connected to the grid and bring at least a bit of civilization to Ano Makriá . . . This candlelight thing is fine with good company when the wine is flowing, but when you're by yourself . . . Please don't worry about money. Go and find your missing Kylie . . .'

'Kyla.'

'Same difference. But hang around. Stay the summer. Hell, *stay*.' Morva tried to make the invitation sound light-hearted, yet I could hear the tension crackling behind it. She squeezed my arm, then quickly got up and helped Margarita to clear the table. The girl was back, being her strange surly self. For breakfast she had served up the finest fried eggs I had ever tasted.

Morva grabbed her sun hat and walked off. 'Good hunting, Honeysett. I'll go and see if Rob's painting has turned up yet and then perhaps I can get down to some actual teaching.'

I drove south in the Fiesta, mulling it over. Morva obviously needed help, but of course I couldn't just stay here. I had stuff to do like . . . painting . . .

Stay the summer.

The impossible blue of the Ionian Sea filled my vision as I turned a corner on the shoulder of a hill, then it continued to flash glimpses past me in the gaps between dense vegetation: sea, olive, myrtle, sea, myrtle, myrtle, olive, sea.

Hang around.

These potholes would drive me barmy for a start. Snatches of music drifted on the air – a violin, a mandolin, singing, strange, ancient, fading; kaleidoscopic smells – pine scent tingling on the breeze, tourist coach heat haze laced with diesel fumes, hot tyres, suntan lotion, freshly baked bread.

Hell, stay.

A small white-and-blue village, giant plane tree and village pump, a whitewashed taverna with a terrace shaded by a twisted vine; I parked the car.

But of course Kyla had eloped with some Adonis down here – who wouldn't want to? A new life, slower and simpler . . . Sunnier, for sure. I ordered fiercely fizzing orange – *portoka-láda* – on the sun-dappled terrace of the taverna and showed my picture of Kyla to the boy who served me. He scrutinized it, shook his head and called over his shoulder for his mother. She wiped her hands on her apron, frowned at me, frowned at the picture, lifted her chin and raised her eyebrows: *ochi*. Not in this village. I sighed contentedly: *good*. I wasn't sure I wanted to find the woman; it was bound to mean trouble, and right now I felt like a bit of peace and quiet, like sitting here in the shade, slurping luminous orange through a straw, watching that woman walk behind her donkey loaded with bundles of greens, just breathing. Each smell was distinctly etched into the air: the orange fizzing in my glass, the cigarette smoke of the old man across the road, the purple cascade of pink blossom at the corner of the terrace. Was I really being paid for this? It was simply too good to be true.

But if it wasn't true, then why did they really send me here? I paid for my drink and drove to Corfu Town with my eyes glued to the mirrors, suspecting every flash of blue. But I didn't spot the Toyota.

Morva probably hoped I would be cruising around the island all summer, searching for Niko's Taverna, but I was looking for a short cut. I parked the car, then went to the offices of the tourist police. These, according to my language guide, were the people to ask – friendly and helpful and they'd all speak English.

They did. A young man in a blinding white shirt and tight black trousers led me into a drab office with venetian blinds across the windows and a ceiling fan stirring the smoke that rose from the cigarettes of the three uniformed men working there. I was shown to a cluttered desk, behind which sat an irritable-looking officer with neon-bleached skin and black walrus moustache. He looked relieved when he learnt I had not come about any larceny committed against my person. Finding a taverna was a lot more pleasurable. One look at the picture and he said he didn't recognize it. He called over a colleague who gave the picture barely a glance, shrugged, fired

off a blast of Greek and went back to his desk. I stretched my
hand out for the postcard but the officer had started fanning
his face with it.

'Why do you want to find this taverna? Special taverna?
We have many, many *tavernes*. My cousin has taverna in
Sidari, you go Sidari yet? Veeery long beach. Veeery nice.'

'A friend recommended it but forgot to tell me where it
was. I just thought you might recognize it. It doesn't really
matter.' I stretched out my hand for the postcard again.

He shrugged, smiled, turned the card over and read Kyla's
inscription. His smile wavered and faded. He scrutinized me
with more attention now. 'Perhaps it does matter. You are
tourist, we are tourist police. We will try make your stay here
. . . for you remember long time. Perhaps my boss know, I
ask now. *You wait here.*' His last words were not an invitation.
As he left, he shot a sentence at his colleague who immediately
came over and perched himself on the corner of the desk at
which I was waiting. He was large enough to block the airflow
from the fan and I soon felt sweat rising on my forehead. My
guard just nodded and smiled at me like a Greek fisherman
might smile at a good-sized octopus before turning it inside
out and bashing it against a rock.

'*Káni leego zésti, eh?*' he asked in Greek. A bit hot, eh? I
understood but wanted to keep what little Greek I spoke to
myself. I looked at him blankly. He made no attempt at translation. Instead, he offered me a cigarette from a flat packet of
Karelia and, like the idiot I felt, I accepted. Months of struggle
against the weed instantly wasted, I inhaled the fragranced
smoke as though it had the power to make me invisible. I had
finished it by the time the walrus returned with my postcard.
He handed it to me casually, saying, 'Nobody know and we
know all *tavernes* in Kerkyra. We think this picture not Corfu.
Probably other island postcard. We think must be taverna on
Kefalónia.'

'Do you really? What's it like there?'

'Kefalónia veeery beautiful island this time of year. Perhaps
not so hot, also,' he added temptingly.

'Well, I think I'll go there, then.'

'Good. Where you stay now?'

'Benitses,' I said without hesitation. 'Good base for bird watching.'

As I left the office, I heard the two exchange a couple of sentences of which I only understood the last word: *vlákas*.

It means idiot. Under the circumstances, I had to agree. Why had I trusted the judgement of my language tape over that of Morva who had warned me against going to the police? *Tourist police*. Somehow it had sounded more like tourist information – helpful and harmless. I had given the game away, but I hoped they'd think, at least for a while, that I was shifting my search to the neighbouring island of Kefalónia.

I stopped abruptly in front of the window display of a patisserie as though captivated by the display and turned round towards the entrance door. I knew my paranoia levels had risen considerably in those twenty minutes I had sweated in the building, yet there was no mistake: I was being followed, by the young man with the blinding white shirt. If he was trying to do it secretly, then he was making a mess of it. He suddenly pretended to be studying the display of the shop he was passing, then looked embarrassed since it was selling ladies' swimwear. Inside the patisserie I bought a few tiny squares of baklava to make my move look plausible. Further on, in nearby Theotoki Square, I bought a packet of Karelia and a lighter, lit a fresh cigarette and gratefully filled my lungs with carcinogens. Then I walked into the nearest travel agent and asked about ferries to Kefalónia. I took a leaflet with me which I pretended to study as I walked back, with my new shadow in tow, past the tourist police building to the car. Then I got the hell out of town.

NINE

'I'm not sure it's supposed to be quite that green,' was my first observation.

'I know, it's very bright,' Morva conceded.

'What else did you use?'

'I don't remember, a bit of everything, quite a lot of some I liked the look of.'

'Have you tasted it yet?'

'Are you supposed to do that?' The wooden spoon with which she had been stirring the evil mess in the large cast iron pot faltered. 'It's Margarita's night off. I thought I'd cook them some sort of curry.'

'Made curry before?'

'No. I thought I'd just add spices until it tasted the way I liked it, but the point never seemed to arrive. The more I added, the worse it got.'

'Have you done much cooking?'

'Me? Hell, no. Boiled an egg, yes, but actual cooking . . . no. Dan was the cook. He was a bloody good cook . . . bloody, *bloody* good cook, bloody Dan the *bloody* bastard *cook*.' Morva stabbed the spoon into the pot as though she had spotted visions of Dan rising from the heaving surface of the gunk. 'Probably cooking some perfect bloody 'roo steaks for his perfect bloody girlfriend on his barbecue in sunny Oz this minute.'

'It's four in the morning there,' I said helpfully.

'On his bloody barbecue *with built-in bloody lights, then*! I don't suppose you can cook?'

'Thought you'd never ask. You go and teach your students; I'll fix this.'

'Can you fix it, you think?'

'No problem.'

'You're a marvel.' She planted a kiss on my neck that was just a bit longer than is traditional when kissing cooks and left the kitchen, humming a Greek tune to herself.

Now for the food. There is an easy way to fix any curry where the cook has been a little over-adventurous, heavy-handed or plain stupid with the spice-box. You pick up the pot, scrape the lot down the toilet and start again with a sensible recipe. I lugged the heavy casserole over to the outhouse and left a bunch of flies terminally surprised by dumping the sizzling content on top of them. It improved the smell in there immeasurably.

Next I checked the available ingredients in the kitchen, had a good laugh and walked back to the car. By now I had quite a good mental map of the worst potholes in the roads around the two Makriás and drove a lot faster than when I had first arrived, yet even so it was quite late in the afternoon for shopping when I rolled into the square and parked near the palm trees.

Dimitris, the owner of the *kafénion*, gave me a smile hovering somewhere between doubt and complicity. 'Greek coffee for you, Chris?'

I was glad Dimitris didn't pronounce my name *crease*. 'I don't think I have time for coffee, Dimitris; I need to shop for food and then feed, let's see, five people and a cat. Are there any shops still open?'

'In Greece, if we are awake, we are happy for business. And if they are asleeping, we wake them up. Come with me.' Instead of showing me to a shop, he led me through several crazy-paved alleys and we did business in backyards and at narrow front doors. Sap green olive oil decanted into a wine bottle and stoppered with a paper bung from one place, the first knobbly tomatoes of the season from another, tiny lettuces and a plastic tub of *tsatsiki* at the next house. One man produced a dish of broad beans in a spicy sauce, and Dimitris admonished me to return to him the metal bowl it came in. A two-litre bottle of wine I hadn't asked for also appeared. Small amounts of money were negotiated and handed over. A young man was dragged away from a card game to open the butcher's shop near the square. Nothing was on display here but I had no say in the matter anyway. Dimitris told Spiros the butcher what to get and a paper bundle was handed over and paid for. 'Tonight you make *souvlaki,*' I was ordered. A bundle of split bamboo skewers made an appearance and I was given detailed instructions as to how to cook my souvlaki.

Dimitris helped me carry my purchases back to the car. 'The police are looking for you. They come here one hour before,' he said casually.

'Did they?' I said, trying to sound unperturbed. 'I wonder why?'

'They do not say. They think you stay here. They will be back, I fear.'

'What did you tell them?'

'I say nothing much: you were here, now you no longer here. But they also talk to the Englishman who looks at birds. He says to them about you drive first camping car, now drive red car.'

'I see.'

'Yes. Perhaps is better you now get green car. I have a cousin in town who rents cars. All green.' He handed me a card from his shirt pocket.

I took it and drove off, promising to bring back all the containers once they were empty. At no point did Dimitris ask why the police might be looking for me and what I had to hide. I liked Dimitris.

Back at the ghost village – that's how I thought of it now – Morva had spread the good news that I was at the helm of the good ship *Kitchen*. Despite the cooking smells, I recognized Helen's perfume as she tried to sneak up on me again. 'He draws and paints and now he cooks, too. Why couldn't I have met you ten years earlier?' She leant against the table while I prepared what the tourist menus called Greek salad and the Greeks, I had learnt from Dimitris, *choriátiki,* village style. It means throwing into your bowl anything that's around – in our case, one spiny cucumber, some knobbly tomatoes, crumbly feta cheese and last year's olives.

'Because instinct told you to avoid self-obsessed young artists painting nonsense in Turkey?' I suggested.

'That's probably it.'

'And I didn't know how to cook then, so count your blessings.'

'I'm counting them now. I think you're probably the only one in this ghost town who can make an edible meal. I'm a disaster in the kitchen, like Morva, and I'm not sure Rob knows how to boil an egg.'

There was a pause. I filled it. 'And Sophie?'

'Sophie?' She fished a slice of tomato from the bowl, shook out the seeds and took a bite out of it. 'She'd serve up a dish of toads and lizards. And tuck in with gusto herself.'

'Not impressed with life?' That would explain the strange vacuum she created around herself.

'Her son drowned. Right here, off Corfu. Diving accident while the whole family was here on holiday. Eighteen years old. She was there, in the boat, waiting. But he never came back up. And they never found the body. The boy just disappeared. That was three years ago, but Sophie won't leave the island. As if there was a chance of her son rising again from the depths of the sea. Her husband gave up in the end and went home, back to England. He rented a flat for her near Corfu Town from where she can see the stretch of the sea where it happened. Morva says that taking up painting is helping and that she's much better than she was. If that's true, then I'm really glad I didn't meet her earlier; she can turn pretty dark sometimes, quite out of the blue. Two suicide attempts. I'm starving. Will supper be long?'

In the courtyard, the coals on the barbecue had quietened down to a perfect heat and I cooked the kebabs Greek-style: rubbed in olive oil, highly seasoned with pepper and oregano and doused with lemon juice.

The best that could be said about the local wine was that it was cheap and there was never a shortage of it. Derringer wasn't hungry for once, presumably because he had recently eaten someone small and Greek. Rob's painting had not been found. He had embarked on a new canvas, a view of the overgrown churchyard, and his mood had much improved by the time we popped the cork on the third bottle.

*   *   *

I woke at an uncertain hour but with a definite wine-induced headache in the darkness of my room. The door was ajar, allowing Derringer to move in and out, and I had the vague feeling that he had just slipped from the room. As I felt around for my bottle of Loutraki water in the near total darkness, I could hear the cat outside, making one of those small noises that mean he is not quite sure about something. I thought of lighting the oil lamp but changed my mind as my eyes were adjusting to the dark. I got up and stepped into the yard. The air smelled cool and clean. The moon was just setting behind the shoulders of the hill, leaving enough light in the sky to see by. Perhaps a stroll in the ozone-laden night air would clear my head enough to get to sleep again. I went back inside, dressed and, with provisions of water and Greek cigarettes, walked out amongst the ghosts between the ruins.

I quickly realized that unless I stuck to the paths I remembered I would be stumbling on every hidden root and stone. Aiming for the olive press, I walked uphill, feet crunching across dried leaves and small twigs snapping under my weight. The rhythmic sighs of the sea were a faint background to the rustlings in the undergrowth and the night calls of some bird I couldn't identify. Two or three crickets kept up a desultory chirp in the long, dry grass.

Somehow my memory of the village layout failed to connect with the realities of the night. Each dark, looming presence I took to be the press turned out to be a different ruin or else shrank back into its shadows to reveal itself as a mouldering outbuilding. Not that it mattered; I just thought the press would give me something to aim for. I sat down on the uneven rim of an old well and lit a cigarette. Temporarily night-blinded by the bright flame of the lighter, I sat and smoked, the fragrance of the Greek cigarette curiously sympathetic to that of wild oregano on the night air.

That's when I heard a small sound. Somewhere to the left, in the direction of Morva's house, something moved. Dog, I thought immediately, since it was probably what I feared most at that time: an encounter with a wild Greek dog who might consider me an intruder on his turf. Being a coward, I decided to arm myself with a stick and go back. I dropped the cigarette

butt down the well where it disappeared into the void without
the expected hiss. Bone dry like the surrounding countryside.
The only stick I managed to lay my hands on in the dark
wasn't big enough to frighten a puppy, but it felt better than
nothing in my hand.

There was the sound again, and it was definitely moving
about. I advanced slowly towards it. In the dark, something
was stalking the high grass. The sounds moved slowly from
left to right, then died down again between the ruins. Two
legs or four? I thought of calling out a challenge but changed
my mind. As Morva had said, anyone had the right to walk
here, but whoever this was did not behave like someone taking
the night air. Instinctively, I adopted a low loping gait,
following some genetic imprint from hunter-gatherer days. But
even in those days we were probably armed with more than
a short, slightly bendy stick. I heard a click further away, and
thought it was a mechanical, not natural noise. Whatever moved
out there did not use the paths but negotiated the high grass,
perhaps familiar with the lay of the land.

Just then I thought I saw a light in the corner of my eye,
above and behind me, near the spot where I had smoked a
cigarette. Trying to focus on it and determine its origins, I
stopped. It was a tiny light source, whatever it was, quite low
to the ground. It was also moving towards me. I turned around
to listen for the clicking but instead found another tiny light
had appeared further down. This one quivered, diffused by the
high grass. These were no electric lights; they moved and
danced in the soft sea breath that sighed through the ghostly
valley. They had to be flames. Another one sprang up further
down and only seconds later a fourth and fifth just where the
dark shape of Morva's farmhouse squatted. I made a beeline
for the closest light. What I saw made me stop dead.

Coming towards me through the dry grasses with madly
glittering eyes was a large tortoise. On its back it carried a
stumpy white candle and in its wake it was leaving a trail
of smouldering grasses, here and there fanned into flame by
the breeze. Trying to get away from its own fire-trail, the
big tortoise was moving at quite a pace. I snuffed out the
candle and started a stomping war dance on the smouldering

grass. As I looked back, I could see I had six other dance engagements further down. I'd never do it by myself. I had to call for help.

'Fire!' My voice fell dead between the ruins. Once I thought I had stomped out the first fire I galloped towards the closest glow of light and kept calling. 'Fire! Wake up, everyone!' Even though I was shouting at the top of my voice, I wasn't sure it would wake anyone at the other end of the village.

It didn't. The patch of burning grass was beyond dancing on. I doused the candle on the fleeing tortoise, emptied my half-litre of water on the grass and beat at the flames with my jacket. There were still five fire-tortoises marching about between the ruins, laying ever longer trails of smouldering grasses. Two of the fires were close to the house. 'Fire! Wake up, you deaf bastards! Fire!' At last I could hear calls and excited voices from the direction of the house and soon I saw movement, too. A silhouette looking much like Helen's was beating out flames close to the house. Morva shouted something from the direction of the cistern.

Just as I realized I was losing the fight with my spreading circle of fire, Sophie appeared next to me carrying a two-litre bottle of plonk in each fist. 'Seems a waste but it was the first thing I could grab on my way out.'

'I've got a blinding headache that says that wine can't be wasted. Start pouring the evil stuff.'

Sophie began a leisurely but well-aimed libation and between us we smothered the fire. It left us standing in the dark and smoke, the place smelling like a burnt-down wine bar.

'What the hell is going on?' asked Morva as she panted past us carrying two buckets of water, not waiting for a reply. I ran towards the patch of fire furthest from the house, an S-shape of flames licking up at the branches of a twisted olive tree. My now smouldering jacket made little impact. 'Someone help over here!' I called. Then I remembered Matilda. There was a tiny fire extinguisher hanging next to the cooker. I made it to the motorhome and back in record time, aimed the nozzle and slapped the red knob on the top. The extinguisher was pathetically small, but at point-blank range the hissing powder jet did an excellent job. When it fizzled to a stop after ten seconds, most of the fire was out and I flailed the rest with my seriously singed jacket.

Dawn was breaking at last. I could see no more flames anywhere, just thin curls of smoke rising from a few patches of ground here and there. I could see Morva coming from the cistern, carrying buckets of water but unhurried now, making sure of things.

By my feet sat a tortoise, withdrawn into its shell on a patch of blackened ground, the candle it had carried completely melted away. I picked it up. The shell was intact and didn't look burnt at all. There was no immediate way of telling whether the reptile had survived his ordeal by fire. I brought my mouth close to the front. 'All right, spit it out: who put you up to it?'

TEN

'**A**ttack of the Fire Turtles.' I set the reptile on the kitchen table. It was either dead or still happier inside than out.

'That's a tortoise,' Rob corrected me. 'Turtles live in the sea, terrapins in fresh water. On land, it's tortoise.'

'But with candles on their backs, it's fire turtles. Special branch of the land turtle, subspecies *candelabrum*. I still can't believe you slept through all this.'

'I'm a heavy sleeper – I could sleep through a bomb going off.'

'Let's hope it won't come to that,' Helen muttered.

'Still think it's kids?' I asked Morva.

Morva prodded the motionless shell on the table with an accusing finger. She bent her face towards it and asked the same question I had asked earlier. 'Who sent you, you fiend?'

'I think you're talking to its bum hole.'

'Yuck.'

We were slurping much needed Greek coffees – except for Sophie who had found another two-litre bottle of red and was making a start on draining it. 'It's the sort of thing kids would do, though, isn't it? Half-arsed, with no guarantee it would work. A sort of hey-let's-just-see-what-happens. A real arsonist would pour some petrol round the place and chuck a match on it.' She raised her glass in a toast to the thought. 'It's moronic kids from that weird village down the hill.'

This time I disagreed, yet kept it to myself. Sophie was right, of course: throwing petrol around would have guaranteed results for the arsonist, but it would also be detectable afterwards. Candles, on the other hand, will melt away unnoticed in the fire or else disappear on the backs of the surviving tortoises as they made their way back to where the firebug had found them. As I looked out over the landscape around us, my perception of it changed; idyllic became isolated, deserted turned to desolate, and the lack of phones and electricity was beginning to lose its eighteenth-century charm.

Only Rob and Helen felt like painting that morning. Sophie wandered off into the ruined village without her painting gear. Ever since Helen had mentioned the suicide attempts, Sophie's habit of suddenly stopping and staring at a tree or a dried-up well looked to me as though she was asking herself whether it would support a rope or be deep enough to throw herself away in it. I felt she needed looking after, but Morva disagreed. 'You can't be there day and night. If someone wants to kill themselves, they'll do it somehow. I actually think she's improving. At least she doesn't ride her motorbike drunk along the cliff tops any more.'

'Quite an improvement.'

'Especially for the sunbathers below.' I could already see the headlines: *Grieving Kamikaze Mum Ruined Our Hols*.

We wandered among the trees near the shuttered but roofless church. The adjacent churchyard, from where Rob was painting a view of the bell tower, was less overgrown than the surrounding land. 'Apparently, one or two of the old folks still make the pilgrimage up here, usually just before Lent, to visit graves of relatives. They clear up a bit, leave bunches of wild flowers.'

'Are those actual photographs?'

'Yeah. Go and have a look if you like. I'll wait here; they give me the creeps.'

Set into many of the low, simple headstones were fading black-and-white photographs of the deceased. They were looking out from behind glass in mostly round or oval metal frames. The earliest examples I could find dated back to the 1940s. Apart from some flocking and the inevitable fading, the pictures had held up well. Many were of old people, often in traditional garb, but a few, poignantly, were of children. The photographs brought a ghostly quality to the silent, sun-flooded place. I was almost glad I couldn't read the mournful inscriptions. There were a couple of unfinished graves. Both were marked with blank stones and their round picture frames stared blindly. They probably dated from the time when the village was at last abandoned.

I was glad to rejoin Morva outside the crumbling churchyard wall. 'So where is this private little beach you promised?' I still hadn't set foot on a beach and had seen the sea mostly through the windscreen of a car or in paranoid glimpses in the rear-view mirror.

'Don't expect too much, Chris. It's one hell of a climb unless you're a goat, and when you get there, it's a tiny cove with a pebbly beach. In winter it completely disappears under the waves. But I'll show you where you can get down without breaking your neck. It's just off the track to Neo Makriá.'

We walked on past the last blackened patch of grass near where the broken cobble path stopped and the drivable track started. We both stared at the fire damage, but neither of us spoke. Morva now seemed eager to have the children's pranks theory accepted for everything that happened in the village, yet she was clearly tense and uneasy. Thinking back now to the welcome she gave me, carrying a murderously sharp bill-hook, made me wonder whether perhaps she had moved here for reasons other than those she had given. But from time to time I tried to remind myself that not everything had ulterior motives or needed investigating.

We passed Matilda and the Fiesta which I had parked at the top of the track and walked downhill in the baking sun. Now and then we heard small startled sounds in the growth along the verges. 'Snakes and lizards,' Morva explained. 'Here it is.' The ground between two olive trees on the seaward side, eroded through hundreds of years of use, showed where the descent to the cove began, though from up here only a glimpse of the sea was to be had. Much of the path and the cove itself were hidden from view.

Boyish excitement bubbled up as I stood at the top of it. 'You sure you don't want to come?'

'No thanks. As I said, I hope you won't be disappointed. Have you got some water? It's a thirsty climb.' I patted my shoulder bag in answer and started the descent.

Climbing down is as tiring as climbing up. My muscles started protesting instantly as the uneven path, no more than two feet wide, first zigged and then zagged steeply down. 'Don't break your neck now,' Morva called from above.

'Are you still there?' I grabbed hold of a tuft of dry grass to steady myself and looked up. Morva was standing at the edge above, waving. I waved too and prepared to turn back to my path when a movement in the corner of my eye made me look up again. All I could see from my low vantage point was the rust-red roof, but it was clear that the Fiesta was on the move, coming fast down the hill on the narrow track. 'Look out!' was all I got out, but Morva too had seen or heard it. She turned and moved rapidly out of my sight. There was a thud and a low cry, then the whole car bounced into view through the verge above me, tilted and crashed into a stunted pine tree growing out of the very edge of the cliff. The back of the car bucked and slid towards me. I ducked away from the shower of stones kicked up by the impact, then looked up. The Fiesta had come to a precarious rest against the tree, right next to where the goat track began. I was sure that if I sneezed it would come tumbling towards me. There was no sign of a driver. 'Morva? Are you alive up there?'

Her voice was shaky. 'Yeah. Kind of. Get up here, will you?'

The goat track would lead me right under the gravity-defying car, so I decided to find an alternative route to the right, then straight up. Hand over fist, I pulled myself up on the sharp, tufty vegetation and baking hot rock, sending crumbling soil and stones seaward every time one of my feet slipped. Did I mention I'm no good with heights?

As I crawled over the edge on all fours, I could see straight away that Morva was in trouble. She was lying on her side, clutching her legs and looking pale. 'The bastard car ran me over. There was no one driving the damn thing. You must have forgotten to put the bloody handbrake on. I think I broke my ankles; the tiniest movement makes me want to scream. At you, mostly.'

'Shit, that's terrible. I can't tell you how sorry I am. We'll need to get an ambulance up here. I'll call one from the village.'

'I don't want a bloody ambulance. At least not until I know they're really broken. There's a doctor in Neo Makriá; he'll come out. You'll have to get me back to the house. But first give me some of your water. Ow!'

Morva sat up a little to accept the bottle and more apologies from me, with one or two qualifications. 'I'm truly sorry, Morv. Only I seem to remember not only putting the handbrake on but leaving the car in gear as well. I always drive ancient vehicles; it's second nature to leave it in gear.'

She gave me a hard stare for a few seconds, her lips pressed tightly together in pain and disapproval, then inhaled noisily. 'Damn, and I believe you, too. Bloody hell. I wanted it to be your fault.'

'I can imagine. Doubly sorry. Someone around here really doesn't like you, Morv.' We both looked at the Fiesta, hanging precariously against the tree, one rear wheel off the ground. 'I'll go and get the others; we'll carry you back to the house.'

I sprinted up the hill. Rob was painting in the churchyard, but it took me a moment longer to find Helen at her easel. There was no sign of Sophie. Morva, it turned out, couldn't stand up at all, the car having bashed her knees and run over her ankles. Together, the three of us managed to carry her back in a woollen blanket. It was a stupid way of doing it and caused her considerable pain. She swore all the way back to the house, mostly in Greek, some of which she refused to translate. When Sophie turned up, just as we deposited Morva on the sofa in the living room, it was clear she had polished off the two-litre bottle of wine. 'Oh, I'll fetch the doctor on my bike; take two mins that.'

All four of us protested immediately and loudly. 'All right, no need to shout, I was only trying to be helpful. Bike's quicker than your old van, that's for sure.'

'You've got a point. Can I borrow it?'

'Don't see why not.' She tossed me the keys. 'Don't crash it.'

There were enough scrapes and dents on the little red Honda to show that Sophie was used to crashing. All levers were bent and had the ends snapped off, and the tank was so dented I doubted it could hold much petrol, but the engine started straight away and I hassled the bike downhill. I managed not to drop it and zipped into Neo Makriá only to realize I had no idea who and where the doctor might be. Dimitris started his chiding straight away. 'Living in that place is trouble. Someone will get killed because there is no help near. You

are in luck; the doctor is just crossing the square.' He pumped
up his lungs and shouted, '*Yatré!*' A slightly built man in a
dark suit carrying a newspaper and a carton of cigarettes looked
across. Dimitris waved him over and talked rapidly at him in
Greek, pointing at me, the bike, the direction of Ano Makriá
and the heavens. The doctor, who was probably not even forty
yet but seemed to cultivate a middle-aged style, looked at me
through old-fashioned gold spectacles and sighed. He stretched
out a well-manicured hand for me to shake. 'I'm Spiros
Kalogeropoulos. Just call me "Doctor" if you find it a
mouthful.' Doc Kalogeropoulos spoke good English with only
a hint of a Greek accent behind a definite American twang.
'I'll come right away. I'll just get my bag.'

'I can take you on the bike,' I offered.

'No *thanks*. You know what they call bikers at the hospital?'

'Organ donors?'

'So you heard that joke. Anyway, I'll use my car, if you
don't mind. I know the way.' He walked off briskly.

I kick-started the Honda. Dimitris laid a hand on my arm.
'One moment.' He dashed inside the darkness of his cafe and
emerged a minute later with a small stoppered bottle filled with
an amber liquid. 'For the painting lady,' he said, 'for the pains.'

I pulled the cork and sniffed. 'Metaxa?'

He waggled his head and shrugged his shoulders lightly.
'Nearly. Maybe one star only. My uncle makes a barrel every
year.'

The doctor drove past in a white Citroën that had seen
better days and many bad roads. I followed him at a distance,
avoiding the dust cloud his wheels chucked back at me as
he negotiated the broken road at breakneck speed. He didn't
wait for me at the end of the track. When I parked up the
bike, he was halfway to the house, lugging his black leather
bag and a blue plastic carrier. It occurred to me that anybody
who had grown up around here had to know their way around
the deserted village with their eyes shut simply from playing
Cowboys and Indians, if that was what Greek children played.
I uncorked Dimitris's bottle of brandy and took a fortifying
swig that left me hissing several bad words until the burning
stopped; it was easily the strangest stuff I had ever tasted.

I heard Morva's scream even before I got across the court-yard. When I got inside, the doctor was bending over her legs. 'I am sorry but I have to see if they are broken. I think you may have been lucky with this one. Now the other one. Please.'

'Lucky, was I?' Beads of sweat were gathering on Morva's forehead.

I held out the bottle. 'Take some medicine first. Dimitris sends it.'

'The stuff his uncle makes?'

'The very stuff.'

She snatched it from my hand. 'Give it here. It's eighty per cent alcohol and twenty per cent weirdness.' She pulled the cork with her teeth like a gunslinger, spat it away and took a large gulp. '*Now*, Doc,' she croaked, 'while my throat hurts more than my foot . . .'

Five minutes later Morva's ankles were packed in the ice the doctor's foresight had provided and I was walking the man to his car. He let his eyes travel over the ruined village and shook his head sadly. 'You see the problem with living here: that sort of thing can be nasty, even life-threatening for someone by herself. If no one had been there to call me, she would still be lying over there. Accidents can happen any time. I don't know what Miss Morva paid for the place, but it could turn out to be too expensive. Anyway, she'll need looking after now.'

'For how long, do you think?'

'She won't be walking for ten days, and perhaps shouldn't for a couple of weeks.'

'A couple of weeks?'

'Yes, a sprain can be worse in that respect than a break. At least with a broken leg you can move about with it in plaster, but she won't be able to put any weight on either ankle for a long time. If you had iced the injury immediately . . . but, of course, there is no ice here, either.' He dropped his bag on the rear seat and got into his car. 'Can you not persuade her to move away from here? You must see it's not a healthy place to be. For a foreigner.'

'Yes, I'm beginning to see that. I get the feeling there are those who don't want Morva up here.'

The doctor shrugged. 'Cars don't suddenly run amok by

themselves. Not even around here. None of my business, though.' He closed the door and started the engine. I wondered if the doctor could tell me anything about the strange girl Morva had hired. I knocked on the window.

He let it slide down. 'Yes?'

'Morva has some help, for cooking and such – a girl from the village called Margarita.'

'What about her?'

'It's just that she seems a little strange, especially with me, ever since Morva told her that I'm a private detective.'

'You are? That's definitely something I'd have kept to myself. Too late now, everyone will know. It can only make matters worse.'

He was turning the car round now, but I kept up, walking alongside. 'What matters? What's going on here?'

'I'm not sure and I don't want to get involved. I only moved back here recently to support my mother who is frail and I am not getting . . . entangled. Understand me well, now. I am a doctor and treat patients. Sprained ankles are easily treated. I don't want to treat worse. Much worse.' He held my eyes for a moment. There was no menace in his look, only concern – helpless concern – and it made me more uneasy than open threats could ever have done. I watched him slowly roll downhill. At the site of the crashed Fiesta, he briefly stopped, stuck his head out of the window and looked back at me. He opened his mouth as if to call something, but changed his mind. He simply shook his head and drove on.

It was while I sat next to Morva, who was self-medicating from Dimitris's bottle at regular intervals, that it sank in. *Two weeks.*

Morva dismissed it. 'Two weeks? Rubbish. What does he know?'

'True. A mere doctor at that.'

'Exactly. But until I'm up and about again, it may mean . . .'

'Yeah, no problem. I'll look after you, don't worry.'

'Do some of the shopping? Drinks and so on, anything we'll need from town . . .'

'That won't be a problem, either. I'll be whizzing about the island every day anyway to find that Kyla character.'

'Any materials the students might need . . .'

'Sure.'

'And then there's the teaching, of course.'

'*Teaching*? What do you mean, *teaching*?'

Morva looked about her to check that none of her students were within earshot. 'Well, don't you see? They came here to be taught painting, out in the field at their easels. Not to watch me lie on the sofa. They can sit in the sun and paint for free anywhere. Painting holidays are about having a tutor by their side, pointing things out to them while they work, lots of encouragement. They'll want their money back if they get no tuition out there, and I'm sunk if that happens.'

'You want me to teach them?' Things were looking bleak.

'You've done it before, haven't you?'

'Yes, but . . .' There was a good reason why I had given it up: I'd hated it. That and having been fired.

'There you go. You'll be good at it. And it's only for a few days . . . *Please*?'

I didn't know why I was hesitating. I knew I was going to do it anyway, because even though I was sure I wasn't responsible for the accident, I still somehow managed to feel guilty. And Morva had a strange, casual persuasiveness I had always found hard to resist.

'Thanks, Chris, you're a star. Here –' she held out the half-empty bottle – 'have some. It'll dull the pain.'

Whatever medication Dimitris's bottle had provided me with had worn off by the time I stood impatiently at the kiosk in Ano Makriá, dialling the Mill House number for the third time. Something had to give and, as usual, it looked as if it was going to be me. At last I got a ringing tone, so faint it was difficult to have faith in it. Even the gurgling of my stomach was louder. I was about ready to hang up when Annis answered the phone.

'Have you finished that painting yet?'

'I have. Last night. Where exactly in Corfu are you? How am I going to find you?'

'You mean you're coming? You mean I don't have to beg you to come down here?'

'You were going to beg? How sweet; let's hear it.'

'Hurry. I have made no progress, Morva got run over by a driverless car and I am now a hungover painting tutor, grocery boy and private eye all rolled into one slightly sweaty package.'

'You make it sound so attractive, how can I possibly stay away?'

'I'm also being followed by a weird woman in a big blue Toyota *who drives with gloves on.*'

'Stay away from her. I'm on my way. I'm looking at flights on your coal-fired computer as we speak . . .' I could hear her hum to herself as she scrolled through web pages. 'There's one from Bristol, gets into Corfu airport on Saturday, at twenty past seven in the evening, your time. Hang on . . .'

I hung on while Annis booked her flight online. The same three men were sitting outside the *kafénion*; several figures shrouded themselves in smoke in the deep gloom inside the *ouzeria*; a man was weighing produce for a small group of women in floral-print dresses at the back of a pickup truck packed high with crates of vegetables and fruit; a lorry with a heavy load under a green tarpaulin squeezed into the square at one end and out the other. A group of young men at the corner were playing pig-in-the-middle with a small boy demanding his tiny red ball back. It was hot. I was hot.

'Yup, it's booked. Will you pick me up?'

'Sure.'

'Do you want me to bring anything?'

'Now you mention it. Jake's got a mate, Charlie – he's a builder. When I left, he was out of work. Ask him if he fancies a job in the sun. It won't pay much but the food will be . . . interesting and the company . . . diverting.'

I hung up and dialled again, this time a long UK number I had found in the envelope along with the money and the picture of Kyla Biggs.

Naively perhaps, I had hoped to talk to John Morton. What I got instead was a well-groomed, wide-awake corporate female voice.

'Is Mr Morton expecting your call?'

'He should be. By the way, I'm using a public phone in a village square.'

'One moment, please.' While I waited with expensive static in my ear, something blue in the corner of my eye made me turn. And there it was: the blue Toyota, creeping slowly into the village. I put as much of the kiosk between me and the new arrival as the cord on the receiver allowed. The car stopped by the palm tree, but no one got out. 'Mr Morton is not available at the moment. But he'll get in touch soon. Goodbye.'

'Hang on. How's he going to get in touch? My mobile doesn't . . .'

'Please don't worry about it. He'll find you, Mr Honeysett.' She hung up, leaving me with the much cheaper purring sound in my ear.

Mr Honeysett? Who had said anything about Honeysett?

If I was supposed to be impressed by how easily Morton could find me, then, no, I wasn't. Everyone seemed to find me far too easily just now. I stepped around and paid the taciturn man a fortune in euros for the phone calls and wondered how to deal with Gloves; I could hardly hide behind this kiosk all day. I feigned interest in some of the plastic toys dangling from the roof and peered around the corner. The car was gone. This unnerved me just as much as its arrival had done. I preferred my mysterious strangers to be where I could see them, or else stay away and be strange somewhere else. I got back on the bike and took the tarmac road out of the village.

ELEVEN

I've never been any good at multitasking, so the imminent arrival of the energetic Annis Jordan cheered me up immensely, and if she'd manage to bring Charlie the builder with her, it would cheer Morva even more.

So I relaxed. I couldn't help drifting back into holiday mood. There was nothing but grey metal stubs where the Honda's mirrors had once been, so perhaps I didn't check behind me quite as often as I should have done. I tootled on the Honda along the narrow tarmac roads through the tree-covered hills. The odours of verdant land baking in the sun were marbled with ribbons of other smells – of goats tethered by the roadside, of distant charcoal grills or gusts of ozone on the breeze. At junctions, often with even narrower dirt tracks, road signs were either missing or obscured with paint. One sign looked as if someone had used it for shotgun target practice. The bald patch on the tree trunk behind suggested there was room for improvement in his aim.

Tootling on, I pleasantly lost all sense of where I was going. All I had was a postcard of a taverna. Which the police seemed eager for me to believe was on a different island. From time to time I stopped at the roadside to show the postcard to people waiting at bus stops or walking donkeys, but always got a negative reply. I had no idea where this road was heading and didn't really care. Some of the vistas were too beautiful to whizz past so I slowed down even further. Which must have taken the Toyota driver by surprise, since the car suddenly appeared round the bend behind me, its three-litre engine surging noisily.

In the tinny old Fiesta I had felt a little vulnerable; now I felt positively naked. On this road there was nowhere to go. Here, if I had wanted to avoid being caught by the Toyota, I'd have been better off on foot, had it not been for one thing: I didn't think of it.

Instead, I opened the throttle and ran with a screaming little motor under a dented little tank with a dubious amount of petrol in it. Behind me, Gloves put her foot down. The road I was following rose and fell, following the contours of the tree-clad hill. The Toyota's engine had thirty times the capacity of the Honda's and stayed unshakeably a few yards behind me, even on this downhill stretch. After a dip, the road rose again and the contest became ludicrously uneven. The clapped-out Honda wasn't at all happy going uphill and very soon I would fall into the Toyota's clutches. I tilted up through a bend with idiotic speed and nearly came a cropper as my saviours came bleating the other way. Driven by a young boy, a flock of twenty or so goats were just then pouring on to the road. A narrow gap allowed me to whine through on the Honda and to watch over my shoulder as Gloves stood on her brakes to avoid massacring the lot.

I ran on. The road levelled out and then fell away sharply again. The goats wouldn't delay Gloves long and I'd be back to square one soon. To my right, a low, crumbling wall and a ruined stone hut. It wasn't much, but I'd take it. I wrestled the Honda to a snaking stop and wheeled it off the road. Behind the wall, I lay it flat on the ground and dropped down myself next to the ticking, hissing machine. Not a moment too soon. Gloves came flying down the hill seconds later and whizzed past. I stuck my nose over the wall to watch her take the next bend. She slowed, then stopped. A moment later she got out of the car.

A new engine noise, much quieter, instinctively made me duck lower. Wearing black helmet and dark sun visor, denim jacket, jeans and trainers, a broad-shouldered figure on a tall BMW trail bike slowed right down and stopped level with me on the opposite side of the road. The big engine purled, the twin exhausts gently putting. He sat motionless for a moment, observing Gloves as she stood by the verge and peered downhill with one hand shading her eyes.

I had hoped to turn the tables on Gloves and follow her for a change, but it looked as if someone else already had that job. Gloves looked back in our direction, but the rider was well hidden by dense oleanders between roadside rocks. She got back in the car and as soon as she had driven out of sight the tall rider followed.

'Well, what do you know?' I said to the lizard who was sunbathing a few inches away on the wall.

'I know your bike's been leaking petrol because you didn't close the petrol tap when you laid it on its side' is what the lizard might have said, had he shown any interest in the matter.

The Honda had taken exception to being made to lie down. I had to work the kick-starter for what seemed like for ever before the engine reluctantly fired. As I went after bike and car at full throttle, a new set of questions kept me busy: quite apart from *who was Gloves*, I now had *who was following Gloves* and *why?* Did Gloves know she was being followed? Did the tall biker know she was following me? And, if so, did *he* know *why* she was following me? And would he notice that now I was following *him?*

Well, trying to. Every time I went beyond forty miles an hour the engine started misbehaving. Fortunately, Gloves was taking it easy. I caught up with the back of the train further down the hill, the biker once more hiding behind trees on a bend, Gloves a hairpin further down, once more out of the car and looking down, probably wondering how she had managed to lose me. The bike rider, I noticed, held one hand up to his helmet and his head was moving in the way it does when humans talk, especially to people who aren't there. He was talking either on a phone or a radio. Sitting astride his big idling machine, I hoped he wouldn't hear me as I coasted close to him with my engine turned off. I was sending silent incantations to the back of his head: *don't look round, nothing behind you, keep talking, no need to turn around.* I rolled the last few yards with my breath held until I was no more than three bike lengths behind him. He was listening to a squawking voice from a tinny loudspeaker, then suddenly spoke in fast Greek of which I understood only very few words – *amáxi, yináika, mikaní* (car, woman, bike) and several Greek swear words I thought I remembered Morva using – but I heard distinctly the mention of Neo Makriá. I could see now that he was talking into a grey radio with a stubby little aerial.

Below us, Gloves climbed back into her car and drove off.

The biker terminated his call, stashed the radio in his jacket. We were on a sharp bend and I hoped I wouldn't show up in his right rear-view mirror, but I needn't have worried. As soon as the Toyota had disappeared from sight, he zoomed after it without a thought for what lay behind him. I was left pumping the kick-starter again, then launched myself after him. I wished I had at least the protection of gloves and helmet as I dodged the potholes down the hill. There was no sign of bike or car on the next stretch of road, so I opened the throttle and squeezed a trembling fifty out of the little bike, then had to throw the anchor out sharpish as the next bend rushing up turned out to be full of gravel. The engine sounded increasingly rough, but I thought this wasn't the moment to worry about it. The bottom of the hill approached when a gap in the vegetation afforded me a view of a straight road on the valley floor where I could see Toyota and bike disappearing fast towards the south-west. As I rolled up to the junction, the bike gave a tortured squawk, followed by a loud bang which blew the engine out.

After I'd worked the kick-starter a dozen times without effect, I unscrewed the filler cap and peered with foreboding into the tank. Shaking the bike from side to side did not produce the desired sloshing sound. I bent down to turn the tap to reserve. Ah, already on. I had come down the hill on nothing but fumes and was now entirely fumeless.

A minute ago I had wished for a helmet. Another minute and I was wishing for a hat. No sea breeze reached here to cool my troubled brow. Nor any other parts, troubled or other-wise. There wasn't a cloud in the sky and not a village or petrol station in sight. After pushing the squeaking bike for half a mile in the heat, I was already thoroughly tired of cars zipping past me with their horns blaring. I lit a cigarette to dangle in the corner of my mouth while I pushed my nag along, trying to remember the words to the *Lonesome Cowboy* song and wondering why I had hated teaching art. Surely it had to be easier than this malarkey. Now I'd have both to do and it hardly seemed fair.

Pushing the bike in the heat was sweaty work. Wasn't there a single kind soul on this island with some spare petrol in the boot who'd stop and sell me some?

A large silver Mercedes passed uncomfortably close, then stopped in front of me. Mind readers? The passenger door opened and a man in white shirt, black trousers and shiny black shoes climbed out and walked to the back of the car without seeming to notice me. The boot appeared to open magically without his assistance. I was about to wheel past this obstacle when he extracted a petrol can from the boot and laid a hairy hand on my handlebars.

'Oh, how kind of you. I drove around on reserve without noticing. Just a splash will get me to the next petrol station, I'm sure. You wouldn't know where to find one, would you?' Something about the man made me prattle on like that. Was it the expressionless face? Or the fact that he appeared to look straight past me through mirrored sunglasses? As he glugged petrol from his plastic can into my tank, I thought I could feel the cold he had brought with him from the air-conditioned interior of the car. He was about forty, I guessed, and he looked Mediterranean. I checked the number plate – it was Italian. The expensive car was covered in grey dust and looked as though it had been driven non-stop for a thousand miles.

I was thinking he would never open his mouth when at last he spoke in heavily accented English. 'Perhaps you are a careless man? Driving all over island alone, on little bike . . . Easy to have accident. Big truck on roads, Greek truck, *Italian* truck . . .'

'Yes, I noticed.'

'Easy to have little accident on little bike.' Mirrorshades deemed me sufficiently fuelled up and carefully replaced the filler cap on the tank. 'My advice – you listen good: no drive around villages any more. Go lie on beach and *enjoy life*.' He turned away, replaced the petrol can in the boot and climbed back into the car without a further word. The Merc quickly scrunched away on the gritty tarmac while the boot was still closing by itself.

I was left talking to an empty space. 'Thanks for the advice, Mirrors. Bye. Have a nice . . . whatever it is you're having.' Somehow I didn't think it was a holiday.

Enjoy life. Had I just been warned or been *warned off*? If it was just a friendly warning, then why the mention of *Italian* trucks? Was I getting paranoid?

I turned the valve on the tank to 'normal', took a deep breath and stood on the kick-starter. The little engine fired first time.

There was no point in bumbling around in the sun with the vague hope of running into Gloves and Co. when I had Kyla Biggs to find, students to keep happy and Morva to look after, though I wasn't entirely sure yet what that would entail. The sooner Annis got here, the better.

At the first petrol station I came across I topped up the tank, then followed the signs into town. If anything, Corfu Town had turned hotter and dustier since my first arrival. It was also busier with tourists. The bike had no lock, so I relied on the scratched and dented rat-bike look to keep it safe from any self-respecting bike thieves.

Morva had asked me to buy a few things Margarita couldn't find locally, such as something resembling Cheddar cheese for Rob who wasn't keen on the local varieties. For me, shopping was difficult only because whenever I find myself abroad I want to buy everything I see. Even the most mundane things become interesting in a foreign country, with their invariably better-looking packaging and strange writing. I make a point of never taking much with me, buying things like toiletries when I get there. It allows you to imagine you have started a new life as you try out the unfamiliar toothpaste and the curiously coloured shampoo. A new life in a fresh place. A place where nobody knows your inglorious past, your chequered history. Wiping the slate clean, starting afresh, starting over. A second chance, perhaps a new name, too. Was that what Kyla Biggs had done? Was that why I had been sent after her, to make sure she couldn't shed her past like a snakeskin that had grown too tight? Was she *that* valued an employee?

I stopped at a hole-in-the-wall souvlaki grill and bought two of the seductive little skewers of meat, fragrant with oregano and lemon juice and each presented with a small morsel of bread. Munching these at the street corner opposite a colourful greengrocer's display, trying to remember where I had left Sophie's battered bike, an unflattering thought occurred to me. If John Morton's secretary was right and he'd have no trouble getting in touch with me – or rather 'find me', as she put it – I couldn't see what trouble he could have finding Kyla Biggs. And if he had, why didn't he hire someone more competent than Chris Honeysett, the private eye painter? I had few illusions about the efficiency of Aqua Investigations, since all its operatives preferred drinking beer around the barbecue to doing an honest day's work, and unfortunately that included the boss. So why let an incompetent like me amble down here in a campervan with very little hope of finding her, rather than engage some large hotshot agency like Bentons of Bristol who'd have flown a couple of sharp ex-police officers down here to do some methodical searching?

I dropped the denuded skewers into a waste bin and walked back to the bike, carrying my shopping and a vague feeling of foreboding. It was quite possible, then, that I was not supposed to find Kyla Biggs, that I had merely been sent here so that Morton could say he had tried. But why? There was something missing in that train of thought and the whole thing was beginning to give me a headache. I decided to forget all about it until the sharp-eyed Annis Jordan turned up, when we could pull it apart over a few bottles of Henninger and a good meal, preferably not one cooked by a distracted Margarita.

I rode back to Ano Makriá, wishing there was more than one way to approach it. If anyone wanted to keep an eye on my coming and going, then it was all too easily done. Everyone in Neo Makriá would know who was or wasn't further round the mountain in the old ghost village, and if Greek villagers were anything like their Turkish counterparts, then foreigners and their queer ways were a favourite topic. As I rolled past the square in Neo Makriá, I noticed another thing that made this place so strange and decided to ask someone about it at the next opportunity.

I found Morva on the sofa in a worse mood than when I had left her, propped up against several pillows and moving only her eyes, which did not look kindly upon me. By now, the ice pack had long melted and the pain in her ankles was probably worse than ever. The little bottle of Dimitris's tonic was empty by her side. It turned out that the flip-side of its painkilling magic was that it gave you a correspondingly vicious hangover unless you kept drinking it.

'You look worse than when I left you.'

The brandy had scoured her voice to a croak. 'Thanks a bunch. My ankles feel like someone cut them off and loosely stitched them back on with barbed wire. And unless I hold my head very still, it will explode into tiny fragments.'

'That's bad news.'

'Yes. If I find the bastard who took the handbrake off my car, I'll lock him in the boot and push the thing over the cliff just as soon as I can walk again.' She gave me a dark look through narrow eyes, as though her suspicion that I was somehow responsible had made a return in my absence.

'OK, good plan. In the meantime, can I do anything for you?'

'Yes, find a brick or something and render me unconscious with it. Then have a look at my students' work and teach them to paint properly.'

Rob had chosen his spot well. His painting camp by the churchyard was conveniently shaded by a large olive tree, while his subject, the little bell tower, remained in sun for most of the day. He had worked steadily – Rob did everything steadily – on his new painting. His method was to draw in pencil on the canvas, then fill it all in with paint, starting in the centre of the painting and working outwards, not stopping until he hit the four corners. I had never seen anything so strange in my life. There was little point in challenging this eccentric method since it (sort of) worked for him. In fact, I'd have paid money for a time-lapse film of him painting an entire canvas. Instead, I tried to discuss some of the muddy mixtures of paint he produced which I thought weren't doing the subject justice, but, just as Morva had feared, Rob seemed much more concerned with the security of the place.

'It all appeared so idyllic at first, but since my last painting was stolen I don't trust this place any more. I know it's probably nonsense, but I feel as though someone is watching, just waiting for me to leave the painting on the easel so they can pinch it. Needless to say, I no longer let it out of my sight now.'

I tried to reassure him, though after the past events I sounded unconvincing even to myself. 'Let's hope it was a one-off occurrence.'

'A one-off? You never know *what* will happen next around here.' He looked pointedly over his spectacles towards a large patch of burnt grass nearby. 'And then there's Morva's accident. Who ever heard of someone being run over by their own car? That has to be foul play. I think the police should be called and I told Morva so, but she won't hear of it; says they are more trouble than they are worth. Well, I strongly disagree. *Something* is not right here and *someone* has to do something about it.'

I agreed. And as I walked among the ruins on the lookout for the other two students, I realized that by *someone* he probably meant me. Typical. This only happens to very few professions, and private detective is one of them. A binman on holiday won't feel obliged to shift any rubbish he might encounter on his travels, and no one expects an anaesthetist to put everyone around the pool to sleep. But, then, I wasn't really on holiday. Just wished I was.

Sophie did more than just hint at it. 'You're a private eye, aren't you? *Well, then.*' She lifted a half-empty litre bottle of local red and toasted me with it before taking a long draught. 'Damn, the stuff's getting more'n a bit warm. Want some?' She held it out to me.

'No thanks.'

'Don't blame you. I realized here that drinking red wine at room temperature is a very British delusion. It doesn't really apply if your room's baking at ninety degrees. Of course, no bloody fridge here. But to get back to where we were. Where were we? Oh, yes. If Morva doesn't want the police round here, then it'll *have* to be you. Go sluicing. I mean, sleuthing. Surely more important than your missing person thing.'

'Possibly. But it's the missing person thing someone hired me for, so I can't just let it go.'

'Oh, piffle, just tell 'em there's no sign of her – end of story. What's "missing" mean, after all? She either fell down a well or she's around here somewhere. Everybody's some-where. Has to be. *Ergo* not missing. Just in an unexpected place, and it's not *their* fault no one expected it, is it?' She took another sip of wine and pulled a face in disgust. '*Missing* is neither here nor there. In fact, only if you *are* neither here nor there. See? My son, now, he is *missing*, they say. Out there.' Sophie pointed past my ear to the north-east. ''S'rubbish, of course. He's either dead or he is out there. Only I don't feel it. If he was dead, I should feel it and I'm not feeling his death.'

'I heard of the diving accident. You think he's still alive?'

Balancing the bottle loosely across the palm of her right hand, she looked past me as though choosing a place to throw it, then her hand slipped around the neck of the bottle and her gaze shifted back to my face. 'Think it? No, I don't think he's still alive. But I feel he is, and while I feel he's around I'll stay on the island, because if I left, then it would be like abandoning him here. Him, his spirit, my love for him, whatever. I can't see why people find that so hard to understand.'

I offered her a cigarette from my pack of Karelia. She accepted wordlessly and I lit both our cigarettes. 'I think I do understand.'

Sophie blew cigarette smoke skywards. 'Do you, fuck. Until you've had a child of yours disappear in front of your eyes, you'll understand fuck-all.'

'You're probably right. But I'm trying to. Perhaps I'll have some of that wine, after all.'

She put the bottle out of my reach. 'There's not enough to go around. There's never enough to go around. Of most things, I find. And why would you want to understand in the first place? It won't change anything. Not for me. Go find your own missing person.'

'I really came up here to talk about your work.'

'My *work*. Well, I wouldn't quite call it that.' She pushed herself off the overgrown mound of rubble where we'd been sitting and took the few steps to where a small watercolour pad was resting on a low wall. 'It's a mess. I wet the paper but in this heat it dries straight away. I either get big pools of paint that run everywhere or all these hard, darker edges when the paint dries.'

'In this weather, wet only small areas at a time. Mix stronger colours and use less water. Then soften the edges with a damp brush, not a wet one. A wet brush will push the pigment to the sides, which is what gives you the hard edges you don't want.'

'Anything else?'

'Yeah, try to hate it a bit less. As you said, it's not your work.'

'Smart-arse.'

I went to look for Helen. The houses were widely scattered, and trees and shrubby growth restricted the view. I could have called her name as I walked, but I did have things to think about, so just wandered aimlessly in the cricket-sawn heat. Someone was trying to scare Morva off this patch, and whoever that was had to have a fairly strong motive if they thought running her over or setting fire to an entire mountainside was warranted.

The abandoned village was cracking and creaking. Every rock, crumbling wall or fallen stone was radiating heat, and the cloudless sky was pumping more of it down on me. Sunlight bounced so harshly off every surface that I thought I should be able to hear it. What I did hear was very little. The crickets, so incessant only a moment ago, had slowed their rasping in this unseasonal heat to the occasional, half-hearted chirrup. There was no wind. Not a breath stirred, and I seemed to keep drawing the same deep-fried air in and out of my lungs. For me, feelings of spookiness had always been linked to the dark, to fogs and gothically driven rain and the dripping dankness of ill-lit places, but I felt that Greek ghosts would choose to walk now, in this wavering, over-lit, ticking silence of a Corfu heatwave.

After fifteen minutes of walking aimlessly among the groves and houses, I was ready to give up looking for Helen when I caught her fragrance, though the air was so still it might have been hanging here immobile since yesterday. I turned into what had once been the courtyard of a horseshoe of single-storey buildings and there, under an ancient, sickly looking vine, stood Helen's portable easel and her little rucksack. A set of watercolours and a tub of water stood balanced on an old plastic oil barrel. No sign of Helen. The horseshoe of buildings stood low and with shuttered windows, though their doors were open to the darkness inside. On the easel stood a watercolour pad with an elaborate pencil sketch of the yard, the vegetation within and the trees beyond it.

'What do you think?'

I turned around towards Helen's voice. What I thought was that she had a remarkable figure for a woman her age. She was wearing leather sandals, a straw hat and perfume as she stepped out of the dark doorway of the centre house. She walked up and stood beside me while I turned what attention I had left to the pad on the easel. 'It's . . . erm . . . yes, erm . . . not at all bad.'

Helen stood very close. 'Am I embarrassing you?'

'You're certainly doing your best.'

'And you're being terribly English about it, pretending not to notice that I'm naked.'

'Good Lord, so you are.'

'It's so bloody hot today, I thought I'd kill two birds with one stone: cool down and get a seamless tan. Though I'm sure I don't know what for.' She stepped past me to where her clothes lay folded across a bare arm of the vine and, after tossing me her straw hat, pulled her loose floral dress over her head. 'There, you're quite safe now.' She took up her place beside me at the easel again. 'More or less. Well?'

'I think you're overdoing the drawing a little. It's OK for a pencil sketch, but as a preliminary for a watercolour it's too much, too detailed. Keep it light and to a minimum.'

'Good advice, I'm sure, but I'm more interested in who is trying to frighten us away from this place. That runaway car was no accident. And the fire certainly wasn't. And I'm beginning to think the snake in my bed may not have found its own way there, either.'

'I've no idea. It's bound to be people from the village.'

'But why? What's up here? It's just ruins, and Morva does own her house. It's not as if she's a squatter – she has every right to be here.'

'True. It could all just be one xenophobic villager having decided to try to drive her out, perhaps fearing an invasion of foreigners in her wake.'

'That would be us, then. A handful of painting students hardly constitutes an invasion. And it would benefit the village – people spend money there. Or would if the place was friendlier. There certainly aren't any other foreigners around here, and apart from one birdwatcher I've not seen a single tourist in that village.'

'No, neither have I. Every other village is fighting for every last tourist euro, but in Ano Makriá they couldn't care less.'

'Perhaps they've seen how tourism can destroy traditional village life and decided against it. After all, that's what we're doing here, isn't it? Escaping from the tourism on the rest of the island. Whatever, they're a queer bunch down there. I'm starving. Isn't it time for one of Margarita's surprise suppers?' Helen stuffed her paintbox, watercolour pad and underwear into her little rucksack. 'Be a dear and carry my easel for me . . .'

TWELVE

S tick my nose in and see where it isn't wanted. That's always been my operating system when all the obvious avenues lead nowhere. Sooner or later it will get someone rattled and the sound of their rattle might tell us something. That it's time to run, for instance.

Loitering, preferably near a source of good food or at least coffee, is not the speediest or most efficient way to collect information, but it's certainly the least odious part of detective work and it's very me.

Dimitris's cafe, shaded by vines and overlooking most of the village square in Neo Makriá, was where I thought I'd start. The three old boys were there, or three others looking remarkably like them. With their backs against the peeling pink plaster of the wall, they took hours over tiny cups of coffee and practised synchronized smoking while watching the world. I turned the tables on them by installing myself in a shady spot where I in turn could keep an eye on them as well as all that went on in the square.

It was slow work. It would have helped if I had felt pleasantly relaxed and drowsy from the heat, but Dimitris's cups of Greek coffee, diminutive or not, kept my mind hyper-alert and ready to pounce on the smallest event. Had there been one.

Mid-morning. The old boys commented in mumbled Greek on anyone passing or crossing the square, like a sleepy team of secret service veterans on autopilot. For a while nothing at all happened. This was followed by a long period of very little happening quite slowly. People moved things from A to B. A young girl in a bright yellow dress yanked an unenthusiastic goat on a rope past the cafe. Women carried circular roasting trays of meat and vegetables to the baker's oven at the end of the square, from where they would collect them done to a turn later in the day. The barefoot village idiot made the rounds, begging for coins, and was skilfully avoided by the young and loudly chided by the old. He avoided the small groups of young men who were sitting astride shiny scooters, smoking and chatting, and those drinking in the shadowy *ouzeria* opposite the grill. Earlier, I had ambled across to the kiosk and chosen a dozen postcards from those on offer. All were slightly faded from the sun and none showed views of Ano Makriá. Writing these in super-slow motion with a leaky biro had given me a legitimate excuse for hanging around, but eventually I ran out of inane things to scribble. Another single customer arrived, a man in his fifties with narrow, fashionable glasses. He ordered coffee and lit a cigarette. His arrival meant that Dimitris, who spent long stretches of time standing in his own doorway scratching at mosquito bites, had sold his seventh Greek coffee in two hours, leaving him plenty of time to worry about his finances, I imagined.

I had shown several people, including Dimitris, the black-and-white photo of Kyla Biggs with no result. Now, scraping together my few words of Greek, I accosted the newcomer with it. He studied me for a moment with a deep frown before taking the print and scrutinizing it. 'You looking for this woman?'

'Oh good, you speak English.'

'A little.' He returned his attention to the picture, sliding his glasses towards the tip of his nose. 'Why you look for this woman?'

'She's a friend. We got separated. I thought she might have come through here.'

'Separated. Mm. I think maybe I see before here but I am not sure. Is OK I show my wife? She is better with remembering. One minute only. You sit.'

While he walked off, I allowed myself a tiny amount of hope. It was the first time anyone had even thought he'd seen the woman. I stuck the stamps I had bought at the kiosk on the postcards and looked around for a postbox but couldn't see one. I finished my coffee and sipped some water. I smoked another Karelia. I drummed my fingers on the table. I smoked another cigarette. Then I went inside to find Dimitris who was rearranging saucers on a shelf. 'That man with the glasses . . .'

'Yes?' He looked past me through the door.

'He walked off with the picture of Kyla that I showed you earlier.'

'Yes? Why you give him?'

'He said he'd go and show his wife, but that was fifteen minutes ago. Where does he live?'

'I don't know where he live. Not this village.'

'Damn. Who was he?'

'I don't know, Chris. I never seen him before.'

I followed him outside where he looked up and down the street, then barked a question at the old boys who merely raised their chins and eyebrows a fraction.

'No one know,' Dimitris translated and cleared the man's coffee cup and water glass away. 'You talk with lot of people you don't know – maybe will bring trouble. If girl was here, I would know. I said "no", so is end of story, OK? No more asking people. *They don't like.*' His eyes refused to meet mine. 'Is good advice, Chris.' He swiped the postcards from my hand. 'I give these to postman when he comes tomorrow.' He marched off inside where he flung the postcards on to a small pile of other mail to be collected.

For a moment I considered asking him to give them back – I'd been pretty rude about his village on some of them and thought he might be offended if he read them, but since my handwriting has always been inscrutable, even to myself, I didn't bother.

Instead, I went for a walk in the general direction Fashion Specs had taken with Kyla's picture, turning into the first paved alley by the corner which gently sloped away. It was narrow and shaded, undulating between houses shuttered against the heat. I ignored even narrower alleys leading off, not having a good memory for turnings. I found small shady courtyards, dogs that slunk away as I approached, for which I was grateful, and eventually came to the last house and the end of the crazy paving, of which I was equally glad. Here and there I had heard the odd voice behind closed shutters and barred courtyards, but I had seen no one. So there was nobody to ask for permission as I squeezed along a runnel between the last houses into the groves of olive trees beyond.

I had seen many olive plantations around the Med, but the trees in Corfu seemed much larger and older than most. Here was terrace after terrace of ancient-looking trees, some so old their boughs had been propped up with stout pieces of timber to stop them from snapping under their own weight. I passed several specimens that were hollow at the base yet thriving further up, and some of these had been partially filled with concrete to prevent them from collapsing. I walked gratefully in their shade until I was no longer sure of which direction the village lay, so dense and large was the plantation. When I found a rutted dirt road, I followed the hard-baked mud of the tyre tracks, telling myself that they had to lead somewhere eventually.

Naturally, I had hoped the track might join a road or lead back towards the village, but it landed me against a broad aluminium gate set between concrete posts. Eight-foot-high chain-link fencing stretched away through the groves to either side. Above the gate, a large sign told me where I was: Thalassa Organic Olive Oil Co-operative. I pushed the gate – it was locked. There was no bell or intercom, so it didn't look as if they were hoping to attract passing trade. On the other side of the gate, the track continued and curved away into a hollow from where I could just make out the roofs of a few buildings. The faint smell of food cooked over charcoal made me turn away with a rumbling stomach. Nothing but coffee in there; time for lunch soon, surely. I retraced my steps along the rutted track, but I hadn't gone far when I heard engine noise behind me. From inside the co-operative two cars approached the gate. It was being opened now by a spiky-haired man in jeans and tee shirt and a single-barrel shotgun slung over his shoulder. The first car was a black BMW convertible with the top down, with three occupants I hadn't seen before. I recognized the second car with mixed feelings: it was the dusty Italian Mercedes that had stopped so that a man in mirror shades could give me petrol and advice. Something about sticking to lying on the beach. Everyone on this island seemed to volunteer advice I had no intention of taking.

As the leading car drove up to me, the driver, a pale young man in a short-sleeved white shirt, stretched out a hairy arm as though wanting to scoop me up, talking rapid-fire Greek at me. He made impatient get-away-from-here gestures towards the village, and when he didn't get an answer, he suddenly stopped and switched languages. '*Yermanos?* English?'

'English,' I confirmed.

'This no for tourist. Is private. Go away. *That* way.' He gestured impatiently again. 'Holiday *that* way.'

I apologized. 'I went for a walk and got myself lost. Which is the quickest way to the road?'

He threw up his hands. 'No road, is no road, is private! Back to village *that* way.' He pointed behind me, away from the drivable track.

'OK, thank you. Sorry if I trespassed.'

'OK, go, quick now.'

Through all of this his passengers had sat without seemingly taking any notice of me. The man in the back was a dark-haired, bored-looking man in his forties. The front-seat passenger, somewhere in his sixties and grumpy with it, had remained motionless apart from tiny movements of his arm as he checked his wristwatch several times. I walked away quickly as I had been told, feeling distinctly unwanted, and soon the cars moved off. The deeply tinted windows of the Italian Mercedes had prevented me from seeing whoever was driving or being driven in it. The man at the gate stared after me for a while, then turned away and soon disappeared from view.

When the cars had vanished too, I checked all around. I could see nobody, so I stopped. Just in case I was still being watched, I pretended to have a stone in my shoe. Leaning against the trunk of a tree, I took my time taking off my shoe, shaking it, peering inside it. I could still see the gate and the fence that ran away into the distance on either side. It was something about the way that man had checked his watch and his driver had insisted I go quickly that made me want to hang around. Funny that. It was very quiet now, apart from hissing cicadas and the distant crowing of a cockerel. I tied my shoe-laces, walked on a few paces, then stopped again. There was a faint drone in the air now. It was difficult to make out where it was coming from, but it was getting louder. For the benefit of hypothetical onlookers, I struggled with my plastic lighter to get a cigarette going. Now I could clearly make out the whine and rhythmic beat of a helicopter engine and blades, and soon I glimpsed the crop-duster at work above the treetops beyond the fence, gliding first left, then further away on a reciprocating course. I lit my cigarette and puffed back to the village.

Dimitris's cafe was closed. It was siesta time and all sensible folk were dozing indoors or lying around on hammocks in shady courtyards, sipping cool drinks. The ubiquitous tourist business was eroding such practices in many places, but here, away from the demands of foreigners, the village had fallen ghostly silent. Who was I to argue with thousands of years of local custom? A short bike ride up and round the hill and twenty minutes later I was lying on the bed in my room at Morva's place. Staring wide-eyed at the ceiling. Too many Greek coffees.

Yet I did doze off eventually and woke late in the afternoon, ravenously hungry. Today I would dodge Margarita's fare (which could be excellent one day and inedible the next) and instead hunt for Niko's elusive taverna with the help of Kyla's postcard. I'd try to remember not to let this scrap of a clue out of my hand, having still not quite got over the embarrassment of having lost Kyla's picture to what I had now come to think of as *the opposition*. Well, Morva had warned me. Dimitris had warned me. So had an Italian with a petrol can. Yet somehow I always suspected that it wasn't curiosity that did for the cat, but someone with a blunt instrument and something to hide.

Ablutions at Morva's place were a decidedly retro affair, consisting of what was basically a tin bath by the side of the house and a few enamelled ewers of water. Morva had always made sure there were at least three of cool water drawn from the well, with Margarita supplying a pitcher of scalding hot water on demand. Now that Morva was laid low, it was every detective for himself. Her current students had been sweettalked into putting up with it, but I doubted that would work on everybody.

Dispensing with Margarita's offices, I drew water from the

well and gratefully poured the cold stuff over myself, which left me extremely awake and gaspingly refreshed. Since Morva's 'accident', Sophie had elected to stay at the house all the time, sleeping it off each night in Morva's room. She shrugged when I asked to borrow the bike again. 'Be my guest.'

Sometimes, astride a motorbike is the only place to be. When the heat becomes oppressive and the air is still and stagnant, there is noting better than a blast down country roads on a motorcycle. Here, even the uncertain horsepower (ten? fifteen?) of Sophie's rattling Honda brought instant relief and a fragile smile to a hungry and frustrated private eye on his way south. I had no idea where I was going, having deliberately left the map behind. Somehow, today I didn't care. Had I thought about it, I would probably have said that I no longer believed I could find out anything at all about Kyla Biggs's disappearance. Perhaps Sophie was right: everyone had to be somewhere, and so she was either dead or alive somewhere, just not wherever I was. Corfu was not a huge island, but trying to find someone here was still like looking for a penny on a football pitch. A penny that had turned green with verdigris at that. It would be pure chance if I found a trace of her and chances aren't marked on a map.

Where the hell was I? I'd already forgotten the name of the village I was driving through – another two-donkey affair, low houses dribbled along a narrow tarmac road that looked as if it was still a novelty to the kids on bicycles and the scooting chickens. One cafe-cum-cornershop, no Niko's Taverna and no stretch of water. There was water and the masts of boats in the picture postcard, so perhaps I ought to head for the coast. Well, nowhere was far from the coast – that was the whole point of being an island – so I simply carried on. My stomach growled louder than the engine as I rode through two more villages with otherwise perfectly good tavernas, restaurants and cafes that didn't fit the bill. I carried on south until I was sure I'd keel off the bike if I didn't get my teeth into something edible very soon.

Lefkimmi appeared to be a small town with quite a sizeable population if the number of churches – all yellow, white and pink – was anything to go by. There was little evidence of tourism here. As I tootled slowly downhill through its streets, I saw several women – mostly over sixty, granted – in traditional costume that included a headdress apparently devised from checked tablecloths.

Unexpectedly, I arrived at a bridge over what looked like a canal, which was not only home to a long row of fishing boats but also lined with trees and tavernas. Journey's end for my stomach and willpower. I left the bike under a tree and walked into the first little taverna to my left that had tables by the edge of the water, pointed at the first thing on the menu that looked good and was soon settled with a large bottle of beer in dappled sunlight at a table by the canal. Thankfully, only a few minutes later I was twirling thick spaghetti and chasing bits of octopus with my fork through a thick, fuliginous sauce. Had this been a holiday, then I'd have considered myself truly arrived at last. The clientele at this and the other two tavernas I could glimpse was a mix of tourists and locals and the menu had shown a refreshing absence of moussaka or chicken and chips.

I never think well on an empty stomach and a certain amount of drink always seems to help lubricate the cogs of my mind. Having vacuumed up my last strands of spaghetti and replenished my glass with beer, I took out Kyla's postcard. Stretch of water, masts of boats, trees, taverna. I was there. Niko's Taverna was one of these restaurants – had to be. All I had to do was match the postcard to the view.

After crossing the canal via the narrow bridge, I turned left along the row of low houses. Niko's Taverna was only the fourth one along. Despite the noisy Greek bouzouki – which sounded uncannily like the music played in all the other establishments – the place was nearly empty. Or perhaps because of it. I matched the spot from which the image on the postcard had been taken and felt as if at last I had come to the end of a long journey that had started in Mrs Walden's icy flat in a distant season.

Only two tables were taken under the strings of coloured lights festooning the awning and unfortunately none of the diners was Kyla Biggs. The man behind the bar beamed at me. 'Welcome, you are alone?' He craned his neck to see behind me.

'Yes, it's just me,' I confirmed. 'So this is Niko's Taverna. And you are Niko?'

'I am he.' He opened his arms in an expansive gesture of surrender.

Did he remember a woman called Kyla?

'Kylie? Kylie Minogue!' He beamed as though he'd found the winning answer to a quiz question.

'No, no, *Kyla* – different name.' I wished I'd still had her picture as I struggled to describe to him a woman I knew only in black and white.

Niko was apologetic. 'Every year so many tourist, so many names. Is quiet now, but in two, three weeks, very busy.' He swept a hand towards the many snapshots of happy- and drunk-looking punters that covered half the wall behind the bar.

'She sent this postcard.' I held it up for him to inspect.

He beamed again. 'Yes, our postcard.' He pointed out a stack of them on top of the bar. 'You get free with meals. Is what is called *gimmick*. And works, no? You got postcard, you come here.'

'She only sent it a few weeks ago. There can't have been that many tourists around then.'

Niko put on a conspiratorial air and leant across the bar. 'Is too many faces every week,' he said in a tragic voice. 'We like tourists, but every day is same job, different people. Sometimes people come many years, then you remember, but if come for one or two weeks only, then you smile, you say how nice, how wonderful, and when they go away, you forget same day. Because is already more people. To you is holiday, important event, OK. But to us is just people come and go, come and go, always.' His fingers drummed a tattoo on a laminated menu. 'You want to eat now?'

I have been rightly called a glutton, but another meal so soon was beyond even me. Besides, I have a rule about eating in places with laminated menus. You guessed. I climbed on to a bar stool. 'No, not tonight. I'll just have a drink, please.'

Niko set an ice-cold bottle of beer in front of me. 'Enjoy

your drink. Sorry, I must go kitchen now.' He ducked away through a narrow door, leaving me to contemplate my various ineptitudes as a private eye over a glass of Henninger. My only clue as to where Kyla Biggs went on her holiday hadn't got me very far. They didn't remember her – or else Niko was a good actor. And he did have a point, after all; I didn't for one minute imagine that I myself would remember foreign names and faces over a hectic twenty-eight-week season of moussaka and chips. Sipping my drink, I sat gloomily unfocused, not knowing what my next move should be. Sometimes, I tried to tell myself, the answer was right there in front of your nose, if only you could see it. '*Focus!*' I admonished myself. I drank more beer and sat up straight. My eyes focused on the dense patchwork of tourist snaps blu-tacked to the wall behind the bar. It was an excellent showcase of how even the worst photographer somehow managed to capture at least some of the atmosphere; happy, pink, possibly drunk examples of tourist-hood smiled from every picture, now fading in the strong Greek light almost as quickly as they did from Greek memory.

And there she was, right in front of my nose, looking back at me from a square Polaroid: Kyla, sitting outside this very taverna, smiling, tanned from the sun, red-eyed from the flash and flushed from drink, raising a glass towards the photographer. To her right sat Niko, smiling at her. Next to him, badly lit and half cut-off at the edge but easily recognizable, sat the chap I had seen only this lunchtime, sitting in the leading car emerging from the Thalassa Organic Olive Oil Co-op, checking his watch. And to Kyla's left, with bleached hair and sparkling nose stud, holding a bottle of beer by the neck, unsmiling and watching the others, sat Gloves.

THIRTEEN

I slid off the barstool and peered into the doorway Niko had disappeared through – a cluttered gangway leading to the kitchen. There was no sign of him or any staff. Good. I had just changed my mind about Niko's acting skills. Or perhaps the state of his memory. I walked behind the bar, snatched the picture off the wall and rearranged its neighbours a bit. There, no one was going to notice that. My first impulse had been to point the photo out to Niko to refresh his memory; only then I remembered how the police seemed quite keen for me not to find this place. Or perhaps any place Kyla had visited. I heard a noise from the doorway. The Polaroid disappeared into my pocket and I swiftly resumed my place at the right side of the bar. Not a moment too soon. Niko reappeared. Too smiley now somehow, and tidying things that didn't need tidying, while keeping a nervous eye on the open entrance door. I felt a little tingle at the back of my head that made me think I shouldn't be sitting here with my back to that door. Peeling euros on to the table, I thanked Niko, who suddenly came to life.

'You go so soon? Is early. Have another drink.' He pushed the money back towards me as though refusing all payment.

'No thanks, I ought to be going.'

With lightning speed, he set two glasses up on the bar and splashed a generous amount of ouzo into both from a large bottle. He pushed one across and set a carafe of water next to it. 'You must take one drink with me. Is ouzo – you mix with water if you like. On the house, of course. Is traditional, for welcome people. I forgot before, very sorry.'

If one large shot of this ubiquitous aniseed horror was going to be enough delay, then I really had to get a move on. 'Very kind, but I'm allergic,' I said on the way to the door. '*Iássu*, Niko.'

He followed me outside and put a heavy arm around my

shoulder. 'You have allergy with ouzo? Come drink whisky. One whisky. Is on the house.'

'Scotch whisky?'

'Greek whisky.'

'Tomorrow,' I promised. 'I'll have a drink tomorrow.' But most likely not in this place. And definitely not Greek whisky.

I had reached the edge of the taverna area by the canal and he had to let go of me now. Guests from the two tables began to notice this excessive display of hospitality and two more couples, talking in loud, happy voices, were just arriving, greeting Niko like a long-lost friend.

I shrugged past them and hurried. It was getting darker now and the retro street lamps along the canal were glimmering against the remnants of the sunset. I had nearly reached the bridge when a police car came flying across from the opposite side. Hastily joining a family reading a billboard menu outside a cafe, I watched as the car stopped abruptly by the little supermarket at the corner. Two men jumped out, one in uniform, the other in a dark suit. They walked fast towards Niko's Taverna.

Not as fast as I legged it across the bridge to the bike. I had little doubt that the police had arrived in response to me having quizzed Niko and I had no intention of hanging around to find out what they thought about it. The wretched little bike responded to my working the kick-starter with a tired snuffling sound. Four, five, six times – I was just going to flood the tiny engine if I carried on. I pushed the bike along the road, faster, fell into a trot, then jumped on the thing, slid it into second gear and dropped the clutch. It coughed, the engine fired and I opened the throttle wide, listening to its agonized whine, urging it to gain speed as it crawled uphill through the town. There was no point trying to hare down the side streets in an attempt to hide; the police were bound to know every short cut and would simply scoop me up round the next corner. I joined the thin traffic through the centre, checking behind every few seconds, my paranoia at a fresh peak, then left the town north-bound. Soon I was just a tiny light on a rural unlit road, being frequently overtaken by faster vehicles, though none of them turned out to be the dreaded police car. Perhaps I had got it all wrong and the arriving police had nothing to do with me. Or perhaps they had decided to believe my promise to come and have a drink there tomorrow and would be waiting for me. Or perhaps they were confident of getting me later. We'd see about that. For the first time since arriving here I had taken the advice given to me; Morva had said, 'If you see police, scram', and I was scramming north as fast as the little Honda would go.

The roads around Neo and Ano Makriá felt familiar now, which is how I managed to find my way home in the dark with only the feeble glimmer from the bike's headlamp and the stars for company on the narrow unlit roads. A few potholes and a couple of prowling dogs took me by surprise, but I skilfully panicked the bike around those without riding it into a ditch. I was relieved when I reached the prosperous lights of Neo Makriá. Dimitris's cafe, though, stood dark and deserted as I passed it. The treacherous dirt road up to Ano Makriá seemed to go on for ever tonight and Morva's crumpled Fiesta by the tree was a sharp reminder of just how close to the edge it ran.

Once I had parked the bike by the van I waited for a while, allowing my eyes to adjust to the sudden darkness and my ears to the absence of engine noise before taking the path towards the house. The display of stars in the Greek sky was spectacular tonight, the starlight strong enough to make out the shapes of the church and churchyard to my right and the rest of the ruined village squatting in the hollow darkness to my left.

Only in a setting like this one could the oil lamps and candles that were lighting Morva's sitting room appear so bright. The three students were keeping the invalid company, cheering her – and themselves – with the help of quite a few bottles of wine. I fended off the repeated invitations to join them. In the kitchen I pulled the cork on a private litre bottle of red Corfu plonk and let myself out of the back door into the ghostly starlit village. Not too far from the house I found a comfortable place between the roots of a giant olive tree where I intended to drink every drop of this stuff. Tomorrow Annis would touch down and I would talk sense to her about this whole Corfu lark, but tonight I would indulge in the solitary romantic pleasures of starlit inebriation.

After a third of a bottle, my taste buds were sufficiently numb and I no longer shuddered after each gulp. Lying back against the tree trunk, I looked up at the patch of sky above the silhouetted church and fell into schoolboy musings about whether up there on a distant planet some other idiot was drowning his brain cells and thinking the same. In which case, it was hardly worth us going there; it was bound to be painfully similar at the other end of the galaxy.

Even quiet footfall travelled far in the stillness of the night. A dark shape appeared near the house, then stopped. There was no way of telling who it was. No noise came from the house and the figure stood motionless now. I kept equally still, hoping to pass for a gnarled root shape under my tree. Then the shadow moved off towards the groves near the church and I lost sight of it. All was quiet again. Should I care? I had never felt less inclined to investigate anything than in that warm, hidden, starlit moment, slightly soured by cheap red wine and serenaded by just one insomniac cricket, still sending its simple message to the stars.

I took a long draught from the heavy bottle. When I set it down again between my knees, the shadow was back, much closer and in front of me, standing motionless.

Perhaps aliens used this last quiet corner of Corfu to beam down on to our planet. Yes, that was it. Bound to be the most likely explanation. I lifted my wine bottle in salute. 'Hail, alien shadow. Welcome to our planet; population: five. We are a peaceful race and taste horrible.'

The figure moved straight towards me. I smelled her perfume long before the amorphous shadow sharpened into a recognizable shape.

'How did you find me?' I asked. 'Thought I'd be invisible under here.'

Helen let herself slide down the trunk next to me. Close. 'You were, more or less. But I could smell the wine.'

'You must have a sensitive nose.'

'Let me ruin it by drinking some more of that paint stripper.'

I transferred custody of the bottle to her, remembering what Sophie had said in a similar situation: 'There's never enough to go around. Of most things.' Sophie had a point there – a sad little point – yet there was, just possibly, enough sour wine on the isle of Corfu.

She took a swig from the bottle. 'Why the lonely vigil?'

'I just fancied a quiet drink under the stars.'

'Sorry if I'm ruining it for you.'

'Don't be. I think it already yielded all the metaphysics it was going to.' I lit a cigarette. The flame from the lighter briefly illuminated Helen's face, her eyes bright from the evening's drinking. 'I wonder what it was like up here when people were still living in the village. Life must have been quite simple.'

'Nonsense, Chris; village life is never simple.'

'Basic, then,' I amended.

She ignored it. 'City life is simple. You don't know anyone and nobody knows or cares about you. The freedom of the ant heap. But in a small community you have to think carefully about what you say and do. Everyone knows your business, too; watches every step.'

'You make it sound less than idyllic. You're speaking from experience?'

'Mm? Yes, I . . .' She sighed impatiently. 'I lived in quite a small community; didn't care for it at all.'

'And what about here? You couldn't live like Morva, then?'

'No. And neither can Morva. But she's stubborn.'

She felt for my cigarette and took it from between my fingers, then took a puff.

'I didn't think you smoked.'

'I don't. I just wanted an excuse to touch you.' She felt for my hand again, found it and held it in that suddenly awkward six-inch canyon between our bodies. My body remembered hers, naked, among the sun-baked ruins. For a while we just sat quietly. She handed the cigarette back, which I finished all too soon, but she kept my hand, caressing it with her thumb; a tiny, delicate gesture, yet electrifying, magnified by the wine, by the night. She stretched out her other arm towards me.

I cut across the gesture, reaching for the bottle, and re-arranged my body, freed my hand. 'I do have a girlfriend . . .'

'I know.'

'She's arriving here tomorrow.'

'I know. Morva mentioned it.' There was a pause in which I took a swig, then lit another cigarette. Helen took the lighter from me and held a flickering flame between our faces. 'That's tomorrow. How about tonight? Why waste the night? Go to bed with me. Make love to me under the stars.'

'Look, it's . . .'

'If you say "Look, it's not that I don't fancy you, but", then I may just do something . . . unexpected.'

'Like what?'

'How should I know? That's the thing with unexpected things, I find; you never know what to expect.'

'I don't want a one-night stand, but I don't want to complicate my love life, either.'

'This lighter is getting bloody hot.'

'Then let it go; I can't see the stars.'

The flame went out and I heard the lighter drop in the sudden darkness. 'I'll not try to compete with your stars.' She stood up with a little groan, brushed her skirts with her hands and walked off, sure-footed. 'I can see like a cat in the dark,' she called over her shoulder. 'It's just during the day that I don't see so clearly.'

Matilda wouldn't start. Annis's plane was touching down in two hours and the damn van sulked in the heat. Since the Fiesta still sat crumpled against a tree, the van was my only hope of bringing Annis up here without paying a fortune in taxi fare, always presuming I could persuade a taxi driver to make the journey up here. With the amount of luggage Annis normally lugged about, I knew the little bike certainly wouldn't do.

Being under-endowed with mechanical genius, I kept on worrying the starter and senselessly drained the battery. I shrugged at Dr Kalogeropoulos who just then arrived in his own battered car to check on Morva.

'Engine trouble?' he enquired.

'It may just be a flat battery.' The starter motor stopped turning over altogether. 'Quite flat now, I expect. You wouldn't have jump leads by any chance?'

'No, I'm afraid not. Someone in the village, perhaps. Or a battery charger?'

I checked my watch. 'No time for that, I'm afraid. I'm supposed to pick someone up from the airport soon.'

'I'll drive you,' he offered instantly. 'It's no problem.'

'Are you sure?'

'I said, it's no problem.'

'No patients to see?'

'Not until tonight. But now I must go and see how Miss Morva is getting on.'

Today Morva was getting about again for the first time, albeit only on the ground floor of the house, on the crutches the doctor had provided, taking as much weight off her ankles as possible and moving extremely slowly.

'The less you move about, the sooner you'll recover,' the doctor warned.

'The less I move about, the sooner I'll go mad,' Morva countered. 'And you'll never get a shrink to hike all the way up here.'

The doc shrugged. 'I have a psychiatrist colleague who would be interested in your case, I am sure.'

'Ha. Now get out, both of you; Margarita is about to run me a bath.' She nodded at the zinc tub waiting by the stove.

'Run?'

'Well, pour, anyway. Out, both of you.'

A photograph of Dr K behind the wheel of his car would have shown a cautious-looking man grasping the steering wheel at the recommended ten and two o'clock positions while squinting through his gold-rimmed glasses through the windscreen. Yet the sun-drenched landscape beyond the car windows would have been a blur; Dr K drove as though the pothole had never been invented and he cornered at ambitious speeds.

I braced myself against the door and worked an imaginary break pedal, usually seconds before the good doctor felt any need to. He noticed it. 'Relax. Trust me, I'm a doctor.'

'They teach rally driving at medical school?'

'They do in Finland, I think. Good rally drivers, the Finns. Lousy doctors, I heard. Everything quiet at the old village now? No more strange things happening?'

'Not for a few hours.'

'Good, good. And what about your own . . . mission? The missing woman. You have not found her.' This was not a question; he was stating a fact. 'But you must find her before you can leave, yes?'

'I can't stay for ever. If I can't find her soon, then I'll have to pack it in and go home.'

'But you believe this woman, Kyla, she is still here. Not . . . gone somewhere else.'

'No. She could be dead, of course.'

'Oh no, she is not dead. I mean, let us *hope* not,' he quickly corrected himself. 'So . . . how much longer do you think you will look for her?'

'Oh, I don't know. Another week or so.'

'Well, that is good. But you have somebody coming to help you?' He frowned, first at me, then at a pickup truck backing from a side track on to the narrow road we were barrelling along. Our car hurtled towards an inevitable collision until, at the last moment, Kalogeropoulos swerved madly and we flew past the truck in less time than it took to scream his name.

It wasn't just his driving that got to me; this interrogation was beginning to make me uneasy, too. 'Just a friend who needs a break from the British weather,' I told him. I decided to forestall further questions by posing a few of my own. 'Neo Makriá seems a strange little village.'

'Does it?'

'It looks fairly prosperous, though.'

'People are surviving.'

'A lot of people seem to own cars,' I mused. 'And a lot of satellite dishes. And all that stone paving everywhere must have cost a bit.'

'Probably. I wasn't here when that was done.'

'Very well done, though. Not like some villages.' Most I had seen appeared to make do with tarmac or ancient paving, much repaired with concrete. 'It doesn't seem to get many tourists, though. None at all, in fact, as far as I can make out.' Apart from one stray birdwatcher, of course.

Dr K sighed. 'No, not many tourists make it to Neo Makriá. Or if they do, they'll soon leave. Nothing to do there, you see.'

'Most people on the island seem to make money from the tourist business, yet in Neo Makriá there are big groups of working-age men just hanging about at street corners or in the *ouzeria*. And they're all quite well dressed. Doing nothing except play with their worry beads. Shouldn't they be working in bars and hotels at this time of year?'

Kalogeropoulos shuffled closer to the steering wheel and squinted into the thickening traffic; we were getting close to the airport. 'Sorry, I have to concentrate now. Lots of *cars*,' he said as though *cars* were the last thing he'd expected to find on the roads. I couldn't tell whether he was simply avoiding my question or really did need to concentrate, though perhaps he had a point; the way he was driving when he *was* concentrating made distracting him seem like a bad idea. He got us to the airport with minutes to spare, which he decided to spend in the car with the seat reclined and his eyes closed.

I stood in arrivals watching the gate. I hadn't really forgotten how beautiful Annis was, but the sight of her in shorts and tee shirt pushing her luggage trolley still electrified me. We did the airport scene of reunion properly, with greedy kisses and tangled limbs, oblivious to our surroundings. 'We'll have to catch up on things real soon . . .' I started, but Annis disentangled herself.

'You've met Charlie, haven't you?'

I'd forgotten about Charlie the builder. So she'd managed to persuade him to come.

'You came – how brilliant.'

'Didn't have nothing else on, so I scraped together enough for a one-way ticket. Bloody hot here, though, isn't it?'

'Wait till we get outside,' I promised. What I had forgotten was how curiously good-looking *he* was. Six foot tall, without any sign of a builder's beer gut, and darkly bloody handsome. I suppose the only time I'd seen him he was covered in dust and muck and standing halfway up a ladder at Jake's. He scrubbed up extremely well.

Charlie travelled light, which was just as well or we'd never have got all the bags into the back of the doctor's car. Since she's fearless, I let Annis sit in the passenger seat, while I folded myself into the back next to Charlie. Then I regretted it. The doctor was obviously instantly and utterly smitten by his passenger and seemed barely able to keep his eyes on the road. Annis turned round in her seat so as to be better able to talk to me, unconcerned about the good doctor's jerky driving. 'You haven't found her, then?'

'Not a sign.'

'Not a single lead?'

'Not a one,' I lied. I semaphored Annis to change the subject and she did so seamlessly. 'Have you at least been to any good restaurants?'

I shook my head with genuine sadness. 'I've been trying to save my money. I might not have enough to get home as it is.'

'Snap,' said Charlie. 'Perhaps we should go into business together. I'll do the building stuff; you can do the painting bit. Just say the word.'

'I will.' I already knew exactly what that word would be.

'Well, I'll take us all to a brilliant restaurant I went to last time I was here,' Annis promised, 'if it's still there. And if I'll remember how to find it. You see, you're not the only one to have had a cheque in the post. Glasshouse Gallery paid up, so you can all stop worrying.'

'Blimey. Now that's a notion I haven't entertained for a while. Stop worrying about money. I'm not sure it can be done.'

'I can't get used to it, either,' she agreed. 'But I still think you should call your supermarket chap Morton and ask him for more money.'

I wasn't imagining it: the good doctor's hands tensed on the steering wheel and his back stiffened at the mention of Morton. I semaphored Annis some more and she pulled an apologetic face and started rattling on about her last painting, how freezing the studio had been, how hard it had been to get the Glasshouse Gallery to cough up for the three huge paintings of hers they'd sold, but her eyes frequently drifted away from mine. Not towards the handsome builder next to me, as I had first thought, but out through the rear window.

I didn't bother turning around. 'Blue?' I asked.

'Blue,' Annis confirmed.

FOURTEEN

I had kept the possibility of importing Charlie the builder to myself, not wanting to raise Morva's hopes. She greeted his unexpected arrival like the second coming, casting away her crutches and commanding Margarita to produce a loaves-and-fishes miracle in his honour. But first I took him on a tour of the promised land.

'Only the first of these rooms is finished; Annis and I will sleep in there. Until you get another one fixed up, it's the motorhome for you, I'm afraid.'

'No sweat.'

'Well, actually, *yes sweat*. It gets pretty hot in there.'

'I just spent the winter in a damp bungalow with night-storage heaters; it'll be a while before you'll hear me complain about the heat.'

'That's OK, then. Morva will want to see these rooms done because without them she can't really continue running her painting school. But before you get stuck in there, I'd be grateful if you'd put your mind to constructing a communal shower, which would greatly enhance the hygienic arrangement round here. At the moment it consists of a zinc tub and buckets of water.'

'Sure. Where does your water supply come in?' he asked, looking around for pipe work.

'Ah. Well, it doesn't – that's the problem. Let me show you . . .' I walked him up the hill. He didn't seem in the least put-out when I showed him the cistern that supplied all our non-drinking needs.

'Yeah, right, bit of a distance. But I'll think of something. What kind of a budget have we got?'

'No idea. None to speak of, probably.'

'No leccy, no water. No gas, I expect?'

'Nope. Not unless lugged up the hill in bottles.'

'Wind power?'

'Look around you.'

'Solar?'

'Maybe next year.'

'Bit of a challenge, I don't mind telling you, but then I do like a challenge.'

'There's loads of material, though, from when the last lot of builders walked out; use up what's there and then scream for more.'

'Good system. How come she had problems finding anyone to finish the rooms? I don't see the problem.'

Good. I was hoping he'd get them finished before he did see. The last two lots had either been paid off or warned off by whoever didn't want Morva to succeed up here. 'No idea, Charlie. Too hot? Too much hassle? Better offers?'

He looked about him from our uphill vantage point, surveying the decaying houses. 'What a spot. Looks just like a film set. Are they fixing up the other houses?'

'Nope, just Morva's place.'

'Shame; they should.'

'No one wants to live here. You'll soon see why, once you get your eye in.'

But I'd lost his attention; he was getting his eye in elsewhere. 'Who's that?' he asked in a suddenly soft tone.

Following his gaze, I saw Sophie staggering through the tall grass in front of a ruin some fifty yards away, wearing a gloomy-coloured top and jeans, swinging a wine bottle on one finger and apparently talking to herself. I presumed what Charlie saw was a more romantic version of the same: a wild-haired female with gothic ruins and a churchyard in a wild corner of a foreign country – that kind of thing. He probably imagined she was reciting poetry.

'That's Sophie. Needs cheering up.'

'Really? If she needs help with that bottle of wine, I'm her man.'

'Go introduce yourself, then.'

'I think I will, ta.' He strode off after her through the tall grass in the softening evening light. I could see he was going to fit right in up here.

When I got back to the house, I could hear raised female

voices from the kitchen. Already? They belonged to Morva and Margarita, arguing in torrents of Greek.

Annis, sipping coffee at the courtyard table with her feet up on her pile of luggage, shrugged her shoulders. 'A wage dispute, I think. The Greek girl wants more money for the extra work our arrival brings.'

'Fair enough,' I said and meant it. Shopping and cooking for that many people was quite a job. Especially if you were as erratic as Margarita. I'd asked Morva why she had hired someone so unenthusiastic about cooking and was told she was the only one she could find. So I thought I already knew the outcome of the argument.

'I'm willing to help out, of course,' Annis offered. 'Though I'm surprised they haven't put you in charge of the kitchen; that's what normally happens wherever you turn up.'

'I can't be expected to do everything around here. Morva already has me giving lessons to her three charges. I'm supposed to find the Kyla girl *and* someone round here is trying to spook Morva and her students out of this place.'

'How?'

I gave an account of the strange happenings. 'Some of it could be coincidence or accidents or children's pranks, but the thing with the tortoises certainly wasn't and it really was freaky. Not to mention dangerous.'

'And the out-of-control car that could have killed Morva. Any possibility it could have been meant for you?'

'You really know how to cheer a man up. I never thought about that. I just assumed . . . But no, I doubt it. I was already off the track and climbing down towards the beach. Unless the car took longer to gather momentum than whoever pushed it downhill thought it would.'

'There's that. And did whoever let the car roll downhill *know* you were going to leave the track?'

'Ah. That's a point.' I ran through the events in my mind. 'No, I still think it's aimed at Morva. Someone wants her to leave this place. People from the village. There's something odd about the place and the people there.'

'But, then, why did they sell her the property in the first place?' she asked, not unreasonably.

'Ah, but they didn't. I don't think they'd ever have sold her a house up here, however ruined. She bought it off a Greek-American from New York who had inherited it but had no use for it.'

'Mm. But it somehow doesn't suit the locals. Could it be just simple xenophobia? It's a Greek word, after all.'

'Is it? You've been at the books again. But endangering the lives of everyone up here by setting fire to the place? Getting Morva run over? It's all a bit extreme.'

'That's why racists are called extremists.'

'There is that thing about Neo Makriá not catering for tourists; only I don't see how a whole village can be totally anti-foreigners when the rest of the island depends on them for a living.'

She mulled this over for a bit. 'If someone contemplates murder – if we ignore the common or garden psychopath for a moment – then the stakes are usually high. There's something going on around here that we can't see. Perhaps quite literally. You obviously don't trust the doctor, I noticed.'

'Oh, I don't know. I don't trust anyone at the moment. He's very evasive when I ask him about what goes on here. But he's very helpful otherwise.'

'Being helpful means he gets to be around to see what goes on. Though I'm not sure he can see very well through those specs of his.'

'He saw you well enough. He doesn't half fancy you.'

'You think everyone fancies me. Face it, Chris, it's just you.'

'There's Tim.'

'There is,' she admitted and changed the subject: 'Blimey, can those two argue.' The voices from inside the house still rose and fell in Greek argument. 'Come on.' Annis drained her coffee. 'Show me to our bed.'

'Oh sure, sorry. You must be tired from the journey.'

'Eh? Who said anything about tired, hon?'

Sweaty, hot and close, breathless and sweaty. Did I mention sweaty? While Annis and I were busy getting reacquainted in the cloistered austerity of my room, thick billows of oppressive, dirty umber had crept over the rim of the hill like smoke from a burning tyre. The evening had grown prematurely dark. Lamps were lit and the table was being laid for our evening meal as Annis and I slipped off for a wash by the cistern.

'I swear I'd forgotten what clouds look like,' I told her.

'Well, I haven't. In fact, I seem to recognize that one over there. Looks suspiciously like the sky I left behind. Except in England they put oxygen in the air. I came here for the sunshine,' she grumbled.

'Tough luck.' I poured a pitcher of cold water over her head and ignored her sputtering protests. 'The problem with living in the picturesque past is that weather forecasting is pretty rudimentary. I'd say them's rain clouds up there and I wish they'd get on with things. Ready for another pitcher?'

'I *suppose*,' said the soapy girl. I poured. She blared. 'Waaah! The sooner Charlie gets to work on a shower, the better. You never mentioned it was quite so basic here.'

'I forgot.'

'What about the shower in the van?'

'A dribble. And by the time you've fought your way out of the cubicle you're bathed in sweat again.'

'Pour away, then . . .'

When we got back to the house, we were the last to sit down to the meal Margarita had prepared, apparently still under protest and with dark Greek mutterings even Morva had trouble decoding. But apparently Helen had helped in the kitchen, with the result that not a single item of food had been incinerated. Everyone praised the dishes and Morva translated every compliment until Margarita was visibly struggling to keep her scowl from slipping. But she said she was far too busy to join us and swept back into the house, a happier grump.

Morva, had her ankles not prevented her, would have hopped around Charlie like a fussy hen; instead, she got everyone else to do it ('See if Charlie wants another . . . has Charlie got enough . . . pass that to Charlie . . .'). He accepted it all graciously, though right now would probably have eaten a dish of spiders without noticing. He only had eyes for Sophie, who in turn was hardly eating at all. She had occupied a chair at the end of the long table, leaving her usual gap between herself and the rest of us; only Charlie had moved his place setting from across the table and had filled the gap and was chatting away at her relentlessly. Good.

Helen was quizzing Annis, who hated discussing her work, about her paintings, while pretending that I was invisible. Rob was sitting quietly, never speaking unless spoken to and even then starting every sentence with 'Hm? Oh, erm . . .' as though startled from deepest thought. He might as well have been invisible, a quality I had noticed about him before. One tended to forget he was around at all. Left to his own devices, he would fold in on himself and shrink a little, but once you had his attention he was quite capable of holding down a conversation, like a voice-activated automaton.

Margarita left for the village earlier than usual, saying she wanted to avoid getting caught in the downpour we were expecting. Those who had had enough of the heat were positively willing it to rain, but Morva wasn't one of them. 'Be careful what you wish for. Corfu rain isn't like normal rain,' she complained. 'It's more like a monsoon. A *watered-down* version of a monsoon. But it's good for the water table, so I shouldn't complain.'

The weather still hadn't broken when we all went to our beds and bunks, lighting our way with an assortment of candles, oil lamps and wind-up torches. But when it did break a few hours later, we all knew about it. If there had been distant rumbles to give warning, then I had certainly slept through them, since the first thing I knew about it was when a thunderclap detonated right above the house. It practically lifted me out of bed. I opened the door to the courtyard and Derringer flew in, wet, muddy and complaining that he'd never liked thunderstorms anyway. Thunder and lightning followed each other closely, the lightning giving a short-lived ghostly substance to the ruined village beyond the courtyard walls, then the thunder rolling around the stony hills like a shipload of empty oil drums. The rain hit the ground with such force that it bounced upwards again before feeding the muddy tide that was already sloshing towards the door. Then the scene went almost white and the thunderclap that crashed above seemed to crush all the oxygen from the air around me. Someone screamed and the hairs on my forearms mysteriously straightened.

'Blimey, I felt that,' said Annis.

'It struck somewhere close, on the hill behind the house.'

'Close the door quickly and come into bed.'

I did. 'OK, now what?'

She drew the bed sheet over our heads, with a damp Derringer between us. 'The best defence against lightning strikes,' she assured me, 'is hiding under the blankets until it's all over. *Everyone* knows that.'

'I didn't. But I'm so glad you're here to tell me these things.'

'It was the smell of Greek coffee that woke me up,' Annis said, 'so I thought it might work on you.' She held out the tiny cup she had wafted under my nose to bring me round.

'Ta. What's it like out there?'

'Muddy.'

It was. The sun had returned, though, running in and out of clouds and quickly steaming away the moisture and drying the mud, leaving just a few puddles behind by mid-morning. A blustery wind from the west promised changeable weather. Morva, still unable to walk around on the uneven ground, had devised a teaching schedule that sent her three students out into the field to draw, then report back to her at intervals for advice and critique.

There was no sign of the much feted builder anywhere, so I went looking for him in Matilda. He was sitting in the open door of the van, wearing just shorts, boots and some Celtic tattoos on his arms. Head supported with both hands, elbows on knees; the cigarette in the centre of his pout made me think of a rectal thermometer. On fire.

'Looks from here like you discovered the full potential of the local wine.'

'What *do* they put in it?' he groaned without taking the cigarette from between his lips.

'Enough preservative to keep you just as you are now for ever.'

He gave me a look that eloquently spelled out what he thought of his current status. 'Didn't get much sleep, either – what with that racket going on,' he complained.

'It sure woke me up. There was a lightning strike up in the olive groves somewhere, quite close by.'

'Rain hammering on the roof. *Through* the roof,' he continued.

'Sorry about that. I hope you didn't get too wet.'

'Not as wet as some.'

'Like who?'

His cigarette had burnt down to the filter. He spat it elegantly at a nearby puddle. It missed. 'A couple of figures came slithering past the van just when it was at its wildest out there. I only saw them because of the lightning.'

'What did they look like?'

'Wet. Like they were in a hurry. Jackets or something over their heads against the rain.'

'Can you remember anything else about them? Sex? Age? Number of legs?'

'Nah. Only saw them for a split second lit by lightning, going that way.' He pointed down the track. 'Why, is anything wrong?'

'Just wondering who was mad enough to splish about in the storm last night.' The last thing I wanted was to worry him. I hoped he'd recover from his introduction to the local wine soon and set to work before he could get spooked. Though Charlie didn't look as if he spooked all that easily. So I left him to it. I wasn't going to suggest anything sensible like not smoking, avoiding coffee and taking lots of fluid to aid his recovery. Every man knows best how to get the most from his hangover.

When I went looking for Sophie's little Honda, it wasn't there. 'She's gone to her place for a dip into civilization, I expect,' was Morva's prediction. This left me with no usable transport. I had another look at the rusting Fiesta by the edge of the road. It was quite bent and needed unbending in a garage. I just kept on walking. The torrential rain of the night had re-sculpted the already rough track in some places, but had kindly washed a lot of gravelly soil into the ruts, doing quite a convincing repair job.

The same three characters at Dimitris's cafe. One of them called Dimitris's name as I approached the place. To my ears, it sounded more like a warning this time than an attempt at soliciting service for a stranger. My paranoia levels had risen and my weirdness radar was sweeping the area. Did those guys outside the *ouzeria* elbow each other in the ribs and nod their chins in my direction? Did those boys loading half a pig into the back of the van pause in the midst of what they were doing? Did they load half a pig into a van every time I was here? And did Dimitris's smile fail to reach his eyes as he greeted me today? '*Iássu, fíle*, what can I do for you? Coffee?'

'Yes, why not? What I also meant to ask is: what time's the next bus into town?'

His head to one side, his palms raised to heaven. 'No bus, my friend. No bus comes to Neo Makriá. Not for many years. I'll get your coffee.'

I sank on to a chair, feeling deflated. I had been so sure that there'd be a bus that I hadn't even bothered to ask Morva about it. *All* Greek villages were served by buses – that's how most of the population got around. I wondered how I knew this . . . Ah yes, my language tapes had told me so. It was definitely true, then. Thirty years ago.

My coffee arrived. 'So how do I get into town from here?' I asked.

Dimitris gave the briefest of shrugs. 'Perhaps you can call taxi. Very expensive. Taxi don't like coming out here – too far. Bad roads.' And that was that. He wiped a couple of tables and went back inside.

I considered my options. It didn't take long. It was time to get some transport, wrap up the Kyla thing and perhaps squeeze in a couple of days on the beach. Then it would be high time to get the van back on the road – the road home. Now that I knew what it involved I didn't look forward to it. For a while I slurped my coffee and watched the world go by. Today the world consisted of a three-wheeled truck delivering bottled gas, an old man riding a tiny white horse, a spade and some empty feta tins tied behind the saddle, and finally a depressed-looking dog being dragged along by a kid on a small bicycle. Then, at a house on the road leading into the square, I could just make out Dr Kalogeropoulos getting out of his car. Since he carried a shopping bag and at a narrow house unlocked a door through which he then stepped, I surmised that he had just entered his own abode. I wasn't a detective for nothing.

Perhaps the good doctor was going into town soon – or at least near a village served by buses – and would give me a lift.

It took me a while to locate the bell button, at child height and painted over with the same blue as the door frame. Pressing it produced a fierce ringing inside, yet it took a long while before the door was snatched open by the doctor.

'Ah, it's you.' His eyes wide. 'What has happened?'

'Nothing.'

'Nothing?' He appeared to find this hard to believe. 'I thought perhaps . . . So . . . good . . . well. How can I help, then?' A Greek female voice called from somewhere inside. 'You'd best come in,' said the doctor. Then he called in melodious Greek to the voice inside the house. I heard the mention of my own name. He turned back to me, apologetic. 'My mother. She is an invalid. The reason why I came back to live here, for the time being anyway.' The voice called again. 'Oh dear. She wants to meet you. I hope you don't mind.'

'Not at all. Why should I mind?' Rash words.

'She now lives entirely in the kitchen, I'm afraid. This way.' He led me to the back of the house and through a short corridor into a large kitchen. It was a simple and old-fashioned room, similar to the one at Morva's place, only this had at least some mod-cons, like a fridge; the big TV set on top of it looked as if it might soon succeed in squashing it. The door to the backyard stood open. A cat slinking by stopped, gave me a tail-swishing look and slunk on. Next to the door stood a daybed and in the corner a large solid-fuel burner. Beside it, in a wheelchair, sat a woman who might be seventy or ninety years old from her looks, but the strength of her voice and the alertness of her eyes seemed to belie both estimates. She was dressed in traditional black and wore a bun of grey hair that had to contain a length of several feet. The doc made the introductions and I heard the Greek for private detective that Morva had taught me. The old lady propelled her chair to a sideboard on which stood an eight-inch replica of the *Manneken pis*, the statue of the urinating boy from Brussels, lovingly rendered in brown plastic and mounted on a square pedestal. A shot glass was set within easy piddling distance, after which the old lady pressed a button at the back of the pedestal and with a whirring sound the boy peed an arc of (mercifully colourless) liquid into the glass which she then held out to me.

Behind her, the doctor shrugged apologetically. 'I do regret having brought her back that thing. In this house it pees ouzo. You'll have to drink it, I'm afraid – traditional Greek welcome into a house.'

I accepted and knocked back the yucky stuff. The old lady was off towards the fridge next. Her son smiled resignedly. 'It looks like you're getting the full works. In a minute you'll have to swallow something incredibly sweet on a spoon and wash it down with some water,' he warned me.

'More Greek welcome?'

'It wouldn't feel right to my mother without it. She would offer it to a burglar before screaming for help, I'm sure. Ah, candied rose petals. You're lucky – there are worse spoon-sweets.' The lady now held out to me a little tray, containing a charged spoon resting on a saucer and a glass of water while the doctor gave me instructions. 'Swallow the sweet, drink some water and drop the spoon into the glass.'

The rose petal conserve was a taste revelation, concentrating the fragrance of a garden rose on to a spoon. Why did we bother with quince jam?

At last Mother Kalogeropoulos relieved me of the glass, having performed the whole ceremony with an expression one might wear while clearing up dog mess. 'She doesn't speak English,' said the doc in a tone that suggested this was not altogether a bad thing. Mother and son instantly appeared to start a short sharp argument, after which he said, 'She wants me to translate.' Which he did, very fluently. 'Welcome to my house.'

I thanked her in Greek. She laughed mirthlessly, presumably about my pronunciation.

'You are a detective?'

'I am.'

'But not with the police?'

'No. A private detective.'

'Looking for Kyla Biggs?'

'Indeed.' Well I never. It appeared the only person who remembered her, even her full name, was the doc's mum.

'I don't think the police will like you coming here.'

'Anyone can ask a few questions, surely.'

The old lady shot several arm-waving sentences at me without the doctor translating a word, which sparked off another ding-dong argument between them, during which she thumped the armrests of her wheelchair for emphasis. I heard Morva's name several times in the fusillade the lady directed first at me, then her son.

'I think what my mother is *trying* to say is that it is not good to stir up things around here, and perhaps I agree. The police will not be too happy having their investigation called into question, I expect. And the people around here don't like foreigners, erm, let us say *looking around* everywhere. *Trespassing* was the word I was looking for. Apparently, you've been walking in the olive groves.'

'I went for a walk. Got lost.'

The old lady had got a second wind and started haranguing her son again. 'I think it's best we go next door and discuss whatever it was you really came for,' he suggested.

I bid the lady goodbye, which didn't interrupt her flow as she wheeled her chair towards the TV set. A minute later, when the doc had led me to a sitting room in the front of the house, the noise of a Greek soap opera came booming through the wall. We remained standing in the room which was crowded with furniture. Several prints of Orthodox icons adorned the walls and a red and gold plastic lantern flickered electrically in front of a picture of the Virgin Mary on a shelf in one corner.

'I do apologize for my mother; she does not like foreigners much. Which really means anyone not born in the village. She never forgave me for going abroad, either. She wanted me to go and study in Thessaloniki or Athens and then practise here.'

'But you are practising here now.'

'I see a few patients, yes. But I came back to look after her, really, and she thinks I'm waiting for her to die so I can leave. I am sorry; you did not come for my family history. How can I help?'

After all that, I'd practically forgotten what I'd come for. 'Oh yeah, I was wondering if you were going anywhere near Corfu Town or even just a bus stop today. And, if so, could you give me a lift?'

'You have business in town?'

I had no idea how much to trust the good doctor, so I fed him what he might like to hear. 'I have some things to organize for my trip home.'

'Is your lady friend coming into town also?'

I realized I was missing a trick here. 'Not today.'

His disappointment was clear: 'I will drive you to a bus stop.'

Nothing but the high density of cigarette ends on the ground gave any reassurance that the rural crossroads in the hills where the doctor had deposited me was indeed a bus stop. Standing there gave me ample opportunity to wonder whether his assertion that 'there'll be a bus along soon' was the British type of 'soon' or the Mediterranean one. According to him, the only timetables worth knowing were the ones in the bus station in town, telling you when the buses left. Beyond that, the bus would get there when it got there. In the time before everyone carried watches and mobile phones, people here estimated time by the number of cigarettes you could smoke in the interval. This was a three-cigarette wait. I flagged down the bus, told the conductor '*Stim bóli*' – to town – as instructed and took a seat in the back. This wasn't so bad. This thing really moved. The driver was working hard, cranking the wheel, heaving the big hissing vehicle through the tight bends, helped by scores of religious medals, miniature icons, garlands, beads and football scarves that festooned the windscreen and by an enthusiastic application of an air horn which he sounded like a steam engine driver by pulling on a looped cord. I soon learned the form on Greek buses: *stási parakaló* told the driver you wanted to get off, *mia sakoola* told the conductor you were about to puke from motion sickness and required a little plastic sack to throw up in. The acidic smell soon set off the neighbouring travellers and by the time we turned into the bus station there were six or seven people all holding little bags of their own vomit and the bus smelled accordingly. As I escaped into the fresh air, I resolved that this introduction to Greek public transport was all the education I required. I'd have to hire some kind of vehicle, no matter how broke I was.

Commerce in Corfu Town was relentless. Predictably, many of the more picturesque and colonnaded streets were devoted to tourist tat, though even here there was a sprinkling of useful shops such as greengrocers and cheesemongers. I happily drifted around for half an hour, stopped for a coffee in a little place that mysteriously offered 'pressed eggs' and 'curdled milk' on its menu, while the bakery next door had a hand-written sign in English promising 'Fresh Dread Every Day'. No thank you. I had my own supply.

Just when I thought I'd best ask someone, I stumbled on the very thing I was looking for: an internet cafe. Outside, the weather was close as more cloud crept in from the west; inside, the stuffy air was being stirred by a buzzing fan that jerkily shook its head at the task like a faulty robot. Internet cafes like these had practically disappeared from Britain, but here they clung on with battered clacky keyboards and an assortment of monitors that looked as if they'd come out of various skips. I ordered a beer and started.

Tim is an IT consultant at Bath Uni when he's not doing jobs for me, so he is usually found within eight inches of a computer. First I mailed him my woes and worries. I had lost the only picture I'd been given of Kyla. Could he find the group photograph he had unearthed, scan it and mail me a copy? Then I lied a bit about the weather and how much time I was spending lazing around on the beach, to pay him back for not lending me his car, and hit the send button at the precise time that thunder cracked overhead. By the time I'd paid and got to the door, it was raining hard, sending tourists running for cover. Within a couple of minutes, the only people still walking in the street were locals carrying umbrellas.

I remembered the card Dimitris had given me in case I ever needed to hire a car. It had moulded itself to the curve of my bum in my back pocket. Under the picture of a small green car, I recognized the name of the street; it was near the police station. I stayed out of the rain by skitting from

colonnade to colonnade until I ran out of shelter. Then I
stepped into the pouring rain and accosted a well-dressed
middle-aged umbrellaed local with my card and asked the
way. He said something like 'Oh, it's not far, please share
the shelter of my brolly so I might walk you there'; only
naturally it was in Greek and I couldn't swear to the precise
wording, and he did sigh a lot but was simply too polite to
chase me from under his umbrella. It was only a five-minute
walk and he usefully filled the time by muttering to himself
in Greek. In front of the rental place, I thanked him profusely
for getting me there nearly dry. Actually, my right shoulder
was soaked and so was his left since his brolly wasn't really
big enough for two. Without a word, he trotted back the way
we had come. Bless.

It was a tiny office. A tourist couple were just completing
some business at the desk and the man behind it was talking
to them in English while simultaneously holding down a Greek
conversation on his mobile. When I saw passports being
returned to a handbag, I realized that I didn't have a scrap of
ID on me. Tricky. The couple completed their business and
stood by the door, and the man, after a few final words on the
mobile, turned his energetic attention to me.

'Yes, can I help you, please?' he said brightly.

'Erm, yes, I need to rent a car. A very cheap car, if possible.'

'You have come to the right place – cheapest cars in town.
Welcome, please take seat.'

I took a seat, while outside the couple's rental car was being
delivered – a shiny green Citroën Something or Other.

'How long is your stay here, Mr . . .?'

'Honeysett. One week,' I told him confidently.

He pointed out the types of car they rented out in a laminated
holder, all lime-green Citroëns, then added that the only one
they had left was the Citroën *Something*. Fine.

'I will need to see licence and your pass-a-port, please.'

'Ah. I'm afraid I haven't either of those on me.' His face
fell. Outside, the rain was intensifying. Perhaps I could rent
an umbrella without a passport. 'Ah, here.' I found the card
Dimitris had given me. 'Dimitris, your cousin, I believe, gave
me your card. He'll vouch for me, I'm sure.'

Reluctantly, he took the card off me and angled it against the light from his desk lamp, then nodded. 'Is from my cousin. You see? Two little scratches under the picture of the car. Is his mark so I know is him.' He tapped the side of his nose. I presumed this had to do with family and commission and not being quite grown-up yet. 'Still, no pass-a-port . . . You will excuse me, please.' He speed-dialled on his mobile and soon bellowed into it. He talked and talked, listened and listened, perhaps reminiscing about their school days or warming up an old family feud – it was hard to tell. His smile, when he hung up, was unconvincing, but apparently the Dimitris connection had swung it for me. He made another bellowing phone call, took a wodge of money off me and told me to wait for the car to be delivered. What eventually arrived outside wasn't the expected Citroën Something, more the Citroën Something Else. It wasn't lime green, either – more the colour of a tomato you know will taste disappointing even before you bite into it – and it was squarely a last-century model. Which had arrived here through a mud-choked time tunnel. I opened my mouth to point this out, but the man pulled his shoulders up to his ears, laid his head on one side and said quietly: 'No pass-a-port . . .' It was raining as heavily as ever and the thought of a fuggy bus full of *sakoola*-clutching Greeks quickly won me around.

This was more or less the French equivalent of the rusty Fiesta, with the addition of a screeching fan belt, so I soon felt at home again as I splashed the thing out of town and into the hills. It was still raining when I got to Neo Makriá and beeped my horn outside Dimitris's cafe. He stayed in the shelter of his door. We exchanged thumbs-up signs. Then he went inside, presumably to roll on the floor laughing.

FIFTEEN

'You live in England; you ought to be used to changeable weather,' Morva said.

'Yes, but this is extreme,' I insisted. 'Yesterday you couldn't see five yards for the rain.'

'Listen, once the weather makes up its mind and summer starts, you might not see a cloud for months. After a few weeks you forget about the sky – it's blue and that's it. You forget about clothes, too; you wear as little as you think you can get away with, no matter what time of the day.'

'It's the strength of the sun that's so amazing,' said Annis who smelled strongly of coconuts this morning, her freckled skin glistening with factor fifty. 'There were three inches of water in this yard last night; now look at it.' She stomped one foot down on the dry, hard-baked ground in the courtyard where we were standing with our tiny china cups of Greek coffee. 'The mud has set like concrete.'

Morva nodded sagely. 'Which is just as well or the whole island would have slithered into the sea a long time ago. Listen: isn't that a wonderful sound?'

I angled my head in the direction towards which she had tilted hers. 'What sound? I can't hear it with Charlie's sawing and humming going on.' Charlie hummed continuously while working. Nothing you'd recognize.

'That *is* the wonderful sound. At last this enterprise is moving again. There's hope.' She called across the yard to where a half-naked Charlie was working on what was to be the communal shower. 'Do you want some more coffee, Charlie?'

'I'm fine, honest!' he called back without looking up. So far the construction consisted of a latticed floor and four uprights and no water supply, but last night, after shaking the last drops of red wine from a bottle, he'd announced he now knew how to solve the ablution crisis.

'Leave him be. You know what they say about watched kettles. Same goes for builders. Where are your students?'

'Out there, painting away. Rob's still by the churchyard, Helen is doing a study of a crumbling wall of one of the houses, and Sophie hasn't reappeared yet. I'll go and chat to them in a minute. Best go and gear up for it.' To walk anywhere outside the house and yard, Morva donned tightly laced boots over bandaged ankles and carried a rustic walking stick.

Annis held her pale freckled arm against mine where I had acquired the hint of a tan. 'I'll never catch up standing here. What's this private beach like someone mentioned last night? I think it's time I stuck myself in the sun for a bit.'

'Bad for you.'

'Factor squillionzilliontrillion. And it matches the price.'

'I've no idea what it's like. I've never made it down there. The one time I tried, someone rolled a car down the hill at Morva. No one thinks it's really worth the climb. The climb back up, that is.'

'Excellent, let's check it out, then.'

Kitted out for the beach – towel, drinks, sun lotion, book – we set out. 'Where's the path?' Annis asked.

'Right below that.' I pointed at Morva's crumpled Fiesta, still leaning against the tree on the edge of the track.

Annis gave it a speculative shove with one sandalled foot, then peered down the steep drop towards the glittering sea. 'I know it's been here a while, but perhaps we should try to pull it away before we go down there. Now we've got a working car. Is there a tow rope anywhere?'

There was one in Matilda. I backed the Citroën down the track, attached the rope to both cars, slowly took up the slack.

'OK, go!' Annis called from a safe distance.

It was at that moment, when I increased the pressure on the accelerator, that I realized what would happen. The Fiesta would come away from the tree that was holding it up, slip sideways and so put its full weight on the rope while hanging off the cliff face. Then it would pull me backwards over the edge into free fall towards the sea. Anyone with half a brain would have stopped there; *I* put my foot down. The tow rope strained, the engine strained, its wheels spun on the gravelly track, but the Citroën didn't move an inch. Fortunately, neither did the Fiesta. 'That's not going anywhere until we get a tractor up here,' I announced, somewhat relieved.

Tow rope put away and Citroën once more parked near Matilda, I gave the Fiesta a reassuring pat on the way down the track. The switchback footpath down the cliff widened and narrowed, sometimes disappeared altogether where a series of rocky outcrops forced us to scramble down backwards, holding on to tufts of grass and the occasional myrtle bush. Yet a few minutes was all it took before we dropped on to the beach below.

The minute bay consisted of a narrow sickle of coarse sand that turned first to shingle, then rock at the edges. Laid side by side, sardine-style, one might have fitted two dozen determined sunbathers on it. Just offshore, a series of large rocks calmed the waves before they reached the sand. The cove gave the impression of a very sheltered place, yet the tide marks well above head-height showed that the waves broke over the entire beach in rough winter weather.

'I think it's perfect,' Annis announced. 'Who needs leccy and plumbing when you've got a private beach?' She looked up. You couldn't see the crashed car from here. 'Told you we wouldn't need our cozzies.'

The sun may have been unusually hot for the time of year, but the water kept to a breathtakingly seasonal temperature. I was in and out in three minutes, enough to remind myself that the sea takes a long time to warm up in spring. I stood shivering on the sand, towelling myself, but Annis went on mermaiding it between the rocks and casting aspersions on my manhood (as opposed to mousehood).

'It's lovely. You don't feel the cold after a while!'

'That's because you've gone numb!'

'Come back in here, you wimp!'

'In a little while!' I promised. '*Like August.*'

Another five minutes and she was back on the beach, getting herself towelled down by the wimp while her teeth chattered. 'It's g–g–g–g–great out there, c–c–c–can't wait to do it again. In a w–w–wetsuit, perhaps.'

We huddled together and soon warmed up in the sunshine.

Another ten minutes and we were baking as the heat radiated from the rocks. I applied a fresh layer of factor fifty all over Annis's fair skin. Thoroughly. But however careful you are, you always end up with sandy bits, which means you have to get back into the sea, then towel yourself dry, reapply lotion, get sandy bits . . . the endless, insane cycle of life on the beach.

Eventually, Annis settled down with a swollen bathtub copy of *Harlot's Ghost*, while I failed to get enthusiastic about *The Naked and the Dead*, which I decided was a bad choice for the beach. After a while I gave up on it, put on my jeans and shoes and took a 'walk' to the edges of the cove. The left side was pretty disappointing, offering me a collection of worn plastic bottles, bits of tarry wood, the leg of a toy doll and cigarette ends. I scrambled over the rocks at the end to try to peer around the corner but nearly ended up in the drink and gave up on it.

The other side proved more interesting. The first thing I found was a small dead starfish. Next to it, the sharp corner of an angular plastic object showed above the sand. I pulled and wriggled it until the wet sand gave it up.

'Ha, look what I found!' I called to Annis.

She didn't. 'What?'

'A Monkees CD. Still sealed in cellophane. Aren't I the lucky one!'

'Beachcombing has its ups and downs. Keep looking till you find something to play it on. On second thoughts – don't bother.'

'You can't beachcomb to order, you know,' I complained. As I stood there, I heard a tiny noise above. Looking up, I saw a couple of marble-sized stones come bouncing down the cliff. I ducked instinctively, but they fell nowhere near me. Erosion . . . I went to explore the other end of the cove. It didn't take long and yielded no more treasure.

Another dribble of small stones landed near us on the sand. Annis picked one up. 'I suppose half of the stone down here falls from up there. The trick is not to be down here when it happens. Did you bring anything to eat with you?'

'Not a thing.'

'Bum. Neither did I.' We'd obviously reached a stomach-growling consensus since we were both putting on our clothes and packing our gear.

'What time is it?' Annis said, checking her watch. 'Bit too late for going into town for lunch. We'll go find something to eat at Morva's, but tonight I'll take you for dinner in my favourite Corfu restaurant. If it's still there.'

Gravity is still a mysterious, largely unexplained force. The one thing we do know about it is that it usually makes going up harder than going down. Climbing downhill, we hadn't paid much attention to how heavy rain followed by hot sunshine had produced cracks in the footpath and loosened stones. Now it was sending dribbles of stone and dried mud down towards the beach. As we got closer to the top, the presence of the crashed Fiesta began to loom above us. It looked somehow more precarious from down here than it had from up there. Now, out of breath and not liking heights at the best of times, scrambling around below the rusting hulk, I imagined I could hear gravity making it creak. When at last we had pushed and pulled each other up and over the top of the cliff, I stood panting with my hands on my knees. 'Well, I'm glad we got that out of our system.'

Annis glugged water down her throat, then agreed. 'Yes, I don't think we need to do that again.'

At Morva's place, the beautiful sounds had stopped for siesta. We had missed lunch and there was no one to be seen. Charlie's tools lay about the nearly finished shower cubicle; the table in the courtyard had not yet been cleared. Derringer sat by the well, watching the chickens; a fat black hen pecked at crumbs under the table with one eye on the cat. It was quiet, the chirping of the crickets so ubiquitous and incessant as to be practically inaudible until you thought about it – then it turned into the insane sound of Mediterranean summer.

'Welcome to the *Marie Celeste*.' I picked up half a slice of bread left on the table and gave it a speculative nibble. It had already gone stale in the heat; I rubbed it into crumbs for the hen under the table.

'It sure can get quiet here when it wants to. Let's find

something to eat and then I wouldn't mind a bit of siesta myself.'

'I suppose everyone's asleep. We'll tiptoe into the kitchen. I'll scramble some of those fabulous eggs these hens lay every day. There's usually plenty of those.'

We walked quietly through the sitting room and the adjoining little studio. The kitchen door was closed. I had never seen it closed before. I hesitated with my hand on the latch, feeling suddenly uneasy.

'What?' Annis asked. 'Please don't say "It's too quiet".'

'All right, I won't,' I said, hand on the latch.

'They're all asleep.'

'I'm sure they are. It *is* siesta time.'

'Exactly. Can you smell something odd?'

By now we were whispering. 'Not me. Silence doesn't have a smell.'

'Then why not open the door?'

I sprung the latch and slowly pushed open the door. The kitchen was empty. Despite the heat, both of the small windows were closed. I stepped inside. 'Close the door so we can stop whispering.'

She did. 'I'll make some coffee; sure Morva won't mind.' Annis stepped towards the cooker.

I looked round for something to eat. Under the table next to the half-barrel lay a hen, on its side, one eye staring up at me, unseeing. It looked very dead. I bent down towards it and got a noseful of it. I whirled round and closed my hand over Annis's as she was about to strike a match.

'Don't! You'll blow us sky high.'

'How so?'

I pointed to our feet. 'Gas. Bottled gas. The room's full of it, but it's heavier than air, settles on the ground. We're shin-deep in it. It doesn't mix with air, see? But light a match and whoosh, bye-bye Jordan and Honeysett.'

I reached across and turned the valve on the gas bottle. The rubber hose connecting it to the cooker had dropped off; the jubilee clip that normally held it in place was slack.

'I can get the odd whiff of it now – how creepy. Now what?'

'Hold the flambé. Open doors and windows and it'll

disappear in a while.' After a few minutes of draught and both of us waving tea towels around, the gas had dispersed. The gas bottle was completely empty.

'Was this an accident?' Annis wanted to know. 'Or was it deliberate sabotage? Meant to blow up the house.'

'Don't know. It wouldn't have blown the house up; at least, I don't think so. It would definitely have frazzled us to a cinder, though, had you lit that match. Or had Charlie walked in here with a fag dangling from his lips. And blown the windows out. But, then, I'm no expert on gas explosions.'

'What is your area of expertise? Remind me, hon.'

'*Weirdness*. And this place is weird. It's a weird house in an odd place full of odd people and weird stuff happens all the time.'

'That's your expert analysis, is it?'

'Yes. A bunch of mild eccentrics playing at being painters in a place where they're not wanted. I was going to say something like "idle foreigners being watched enviously by the hard-working locals", but no one down in that village ever seems to do any work at all. There's something weird about that, too. They don't look particularly frugal to me, so they'll have to have an alternative income.' I connected the spare bottle, making sure the jubilee clip was securely fastened this time, and lit the gas under a heavy frying pan. 'Is that bread over there still edible? Then cut us some slices.' I cracked a few eggs into a bowl, whisked them lightly with some seasoning, crumbled in some feta cheese and slid the lot into an oiled pan over medium heat. A shower of the ubiquitous wild oregano from a bunch hanging up near the stove speckled the egg mixture darkly. In the absence of a grill, I heated up a pan lid over the other gas ring and covered the pan with it until the frittata had set. We ate outside, watched by Derringer with a speculative eye. He was slowly growing fat from being spoilt by everyone and sleeping twenty hours a day in luxurious warmth. 'Don't get used to this,' I warned him. 'It's back to Blighty soon.'

We took our own siesta in our room and both fell asleep to the endless rasping rhythm of the cicadas in the groves behind the house. We woke late to the rasping rhythm of

Charlie's saw and for a while luxuriated in listening to him work in the yard, then drifted off again. When we finally woke up, it was to the sound of excited voices outside. We scrambled into our clothes and tumbled through the door just as Helen exclaimed loudly, 'Oh my god, it's *warm!*'

Everyone was in the yard, surrounding the shower cubicle. All except Helen who was standing inside it in a black one-piece bathing suit, laughing, under what looked convincingly like a working shower.

Charlie's pride as he demonstrated and explained was evident but well earned. The set-up was extremely low-tech. I approved. Morva was ecstatic. The cubicle itself consisted of nothing more than a phonebox-sized wooden construction with a slatted floor and sloping roof. The shower head looked suspiciously like the rose from an old zinc watering can connected to a bit of pipe with a simple on/off valve. It was fed from a green garden hose. The water came from a four-gallon tin thirty yards away uphill, which in turn was fed from the cistern behind the ruin further along. The water travelled via several lengths of hosepipe, on to which dozens of empty wine bottles, their bottoms knocked out, had been threaded. Exposed to the sun they absorbed and focused sunlight on to the pipe, heating the water inside to an astonishing temperature. Unfortunately, there hadn't been quite enough bottles for the entire length, resulting in an invigorating hot/cool/hot/cool effect, ending in a bracingly cold finale if your ablutions lasted for more than two minutes. On a sunny day it would take less than an hour to heat up.

'And I've had one or two ideas for when it gets cold in winter. It would simply mean extending your stovepipe . . .' Morva followed Charlie inside in rapturous admiration.

The rest of the afternoon was taken up with everyone taking turns at ninety seconds of bliss: showering, waiting, showering. Sophie returned late afternoon, looking as if she had indeed visited the twenty-first century, with its power showers, washing machines, electric irons and, I noticed, hairdressers. She admired the shower and hung around as Charlie began work on the room next to ours.

*   *   *

'I can't believe you rented this death trap – it's terrible.'

'It's a bit ancient.'

'It was crap when it was new.'

'The steering's a bit vague, but I'm getting used to it.' I demonstrated by skilfully wallowing all over the road when a pothole came up. I hit it with a back wheel on the rebound.

'I hope you realize that the number plates don't match.'

'Match what?'

'Each other. I noticed it earlier.'

'It's the next best thing to having James-Bond-style revolving number plates. Should keep the police guessing, anyway.'

'Start the police wondering, more like.'

We were driving towards Corfu Town, wearing our best clobber, trying not to look as if we had travelled all the way from the eighteenth century. 'Is it posh, then? Your restaurant?' I asked. I worried, since even my best efforts at dressing up had produced only rumpled results.

'No, not posh. Posh is boring. Just civilized. The view is brilliant, too.'

'It's not in town, then?'

'Lord, no. Just north of it.' She unfolded the map, ran a finger over it, flicked her nail at it. 'Turn left at the next junction.'

I turned left at the next junction and drove.

And drove.

'It's further away than I remembered it,' she admitted as she measured out distances on the map.

I pulled into a petrol station at the edge of a large village. They still had service at the pumps, a reminder of a more civilized age and something I hadn't experienced for years. '*Yemáto, parakaló* – fill her up, please,' I told the man suavely (cassette two). Annis was impressed. (Less impressed when it turned out I didn't have the money to pay for the *yemáto*.) While the man was still feeding the tank, Gloves shot by in her blue Toyota. Our tiny Citroën was partially hidden behind a sagging old van that had pulled in beside us, so she probably didn't see us. 'Looks like changing vehicles hasn't made much difference,' I observed.

Annis consulted the map. 'Next time we see her we'll grab

her, but right now I'm not in the mood. Tonight I want to eat under the stars. We'll go by a different route. Turn back the way we came, then left at the first opportunity.'

It appeared to work since we didn't see the Toyota again and Annis's map reading eventually dropped us via a tortured little track into exactly the right place, the road above Barbati beach. Villas, restaurants and cafes punctured the densely verdant slope between the road and the long curve of the bay. We left the car by the side of the road and walked back a few hundred yards to Annis's chosen restaurant, the Lord Byron. It occupied several terraces above the road and commanded five-star touristic views across the bay. It was fairly busy for the time of year. We managed to grab a table on the lowest terrace and sighed in unison as we drank in the view.

'Worth the drive?' Annis asked.

'Even if they only have bacon butties left.'

It was picture-postcard stuff. Beyond the bay, lights began to twinkle as darkness fell and the first stars appeared in the east. The Lord Byron's menu managed to match the view without being distractingly brilliant; it was simple Corfiot fare. It arrived in its own good time, allowing me to sample the beer and Annis, my designated driver for the evening, to slurp a few colourful fruit-juice cocktails. Just as Annis was assessing the doneness of her lamb and I was about to break into the enormous cube of *pastitsio* on my plate, I was distracted by the arrival of a new guest. Skipping lightly up the stairs, without his Zeiss binoculars, was the man I had met on the ferry from Brindisi. As he walked past our table, I raised a hand in greeting, but his eyes travelled over me without betraying recognition and by the time I'd remembered his name he had skipped further up the stairs.

'Kladders. Got it!'

'Kladders got what?' asked a mystified Annis.

'The chap who just walked by. I met him on the boat from Brindisi. He'd clocked that Gloves was following me before I did. He seemed to know the island extremely well, too. I think I'll go and pick his brain.' I put down my fork.

'After you have finished your food in a leisurely and

companionable manner. Unless you want to walk home,' she said sweetly.

'Naturally,' I agreed and picked up my fork.

Annis reminisced at length about the last time she'd been on the island.

'You make it sound as though it was all a long, long time ago.'

She paused, fork poised in mid-air, ready to skewer her next thought. 'Do I? It was, in a way. That was before college. Before painting, before Tim. And you, of course,' she added quickly in answer to something I did with my eyebrows. 'A different era. Years don't come into it, really; it's a bit like having a baby. Nine months, give or take, and you live in a totally different world and you'd better like it because there's no way back.'

'You've given it some thought, then.'

'My mother never lets me forget what a sacrifice having me has been, how I'm single-handedly responsible for her having missed out, career, opportunities, best years of her life, etcetera, etcetera.'

'Is that why you decided not to have children?'

She stabbed a few times at the remnants of lamb on her plate. 'Is that what I decided, then?'

Hadn't she? 'Well, I thought . . . you always said . . .'

'Ha! Your face! Priceless. Yeah, hon, don't fret. I'm far too selfish, and you don't exactly make ideal dad-material. And Tim . . . Tim would give a baby five minutes, then lose interest and look for the off switch.'

'Talking of Tim, I must see if he's mailed me another picture of Kyla. Actually, while I'm there, I might call him and ask him to check on one or two other things that would be useful to know. I'll do it first thing tomorrow. It's the weekend; he'll be at home.'

'Actually, he won't be. He's still at Mill House. Looking after the place while we're both away.'

Still. 'Was he at Mill House all the time, then?' This didn't come out as casually as planned; a sudden, illogical stab of jealousy seemed to have punctured my voice.

'Mm? Yeah. Does it matter?'

I hesitated. I shouldn't have hesitated.

'I really don't see why it should,' she said. 'Mill House or Northampton Street – what's the difference? It's not as if we're sleeping together in *our* bed.'

'No, sure, I mean . . .'

'And it made perfect sense because that way I could get a lot more work done than if I had bombed across to his place every day. I'd still be working on the painting now if I had, I'm sure.'

'True. It's no problem; it's just different from what I had imagined.'

'Your mouth is saying one thing and your eyes are saying something else. You're not jealous? Please say you're not jealous. And after how many years? It's you I live with. And if I preferred Tim's company, why am I here? I didn't *have* to come out here where I'm being shadowed by weird Toyota drivers, gassed in the kitchen and given evil killer looks by that Helen woman all day.'

'Are you?'

'I am. Did you make a rash promise of marriage or something? She constantly asks me a million questions and all the time I feel like she's pointing a gun at me under the table.'

'I hadn't noticed.'

'Of course not, Mr Detective. Anyway, I'm here with you, not there with him, so be a happy Honeypot or I'll fly home.'

'I'm happy,' I promised.

'You'd better be,' she said. She shut her mouth around the straw and noisily vacuumed the dregs of fruit juice from the bottom of her glass. 'Why don't you go and talk to the ferry man you saw and order us some more drinks while you're in there.'

'Good idea. Same again?'

'Hell, no, get me a beer. I can drive perfectly after a couple of bottles of this Amstel stuff. I remember it well . . .'

After delivering my drinks order at the bar, I looked around for Kladders. It took me a while to spot him at the head of a crowded table right at the back of the restaurant. Two waiters were busy depositing a multitude of dishes in front of the diners, which is why I was halfway to his table before I noticed who

he was eating with. All of his companions looked alarmingly
familiar. I made a hasty ninety-degree turn away which attracted
Kladders's attention. He gave the tiniest sideways jerk with the
head while he semaphored 'Scram!' with his eyebrows. No
need: I was making myself scarce at the double, hoping the rest
of the company had been too busy looking at the food to take
any notice of my odd manoeuvre.

'Cheers, hon.' Annis clinked her glass against my fresh
bottle of beer. 'Did you catch up with your man?'

'Nearly.'

'What's that mean?'

I took a long draught of beer from the bottle while I realized
I had no idea what it all meant. 'I didn't speak to him. He
had company. A lot of company. He pulled a face at me that
said "Not now, you fool", but I didn't really need the hint.
Right next to him was the police officer who had pretended
he'd never seen Niko's Taverna when I showed him the
postcard.'

'Perhaps he hadn't?'

'I doubt it. He was sitting opposite the bloke who runs it.
And *he* is the one who pretended not to recognize Kyla, even
though he had her photo on his picture wall.'

'Ah. Recognize anyone else?'

'Most of them. One of them, I'm sure of it, is the Italian
bloke I told you about – the one with the big dusty Mercedes.
He gave me petrol for the bike, but I thought even then he
was also threatening me. Now I'm certain of it. Opposite him
sat the bloke who runs the kiosk in the village and . . .'

'Margarita's dad.'

'What? Is he? How do you know that?'

'Morva mentioned it.'

'In what context?'

'Apropos of nothing. It's the kind of stuff women talk about,
who begat whom, relationships, connections. You know . . .'

'Yeah. Ta. Anyway. Next to Margarita's dad . . .'

'Thanassis.'

'What?'

'His name. Her dad's name is Thanassis.'

'Anyway, next to *Thanassis* sat a couple of chaps I saw at

the olive oil co-operative. One was an older guy in the passenger seat who kept looking at his watch while his driver told me to get lost.'

'And now they're all having a meal with the bloke from the ferry.'

'Yes. It's kind of spooky because that's most of the people I've met here so far and now I don't trust any of them for some reason.'

'Then what about your ferry man?'

'Kladders . . . I don't know. He pointed Gloves out to me.'

'But afterwards your notebook with Morva's old address in it had disappeared.'

'True, but then he gave me pretty good directions to her place. And just now he seemed to be on my side when he signalled me. I really don't want to meet that policeman at his table again; I feel happier with him thinking I've left the island.'

'Perhaps we shouldn't hang around, then.'

'On the contrary, we definitely should, but somewhere they can't see us.' I called the waiter over, asked for the bill (cassette one, part two) and pointed at my watch to show we were in a hurry.

While we waited, Annis finished her half-litre of Amstel, then relieved me of my bottle and drained that one, too. 'It's only fair if I'm missing the sweet course,' she declared. There was no arguing with that. This hadn't quite turned out to be the romantic starlit dining experience it was billed as.

Back on street level, I hesitated for a moment. The road was quite busy now with people strolling about and a row of cars parked on one side. 'I don't remember – could we see the entrance to the restaurant from our car?'

'Don't know. Let's try it.'

We were walking towards the Citroën when I saw them. 'Stop, turn round.'

'Wassamatter?' she asked as she turned on a sixpence.

'Back there, right in front of ours, are the cars of the guys from Kladders's table – the Merc and the BMW – and there's two guys leaning against the bonnets chatting. One of them is the BMW driver who told me to get away from the Thalassa

Oil Co-op. He might well recognize me and I have the distinct feeling I don't want him to. We'll look for somewhere else.'

Not far beyond the entrance to the Lord Byron, we found a bar with a few seats by the roadside from where we could keep an eye on things. I was too busy to take much notice of the fact that both of us were drinking beer now and my designated driver was on her third half-litre in less than an hour. We hadn't been there long when the two drivers came up the road towards us, walking quickly. They weren't chatting now and had a look of determination about them.

'That's the chauffeurs coming right at us; could mean trouble.'

'Now what?'

'We'll act stupid.'

'How hard can it be?'

The two determined-looking men never slowed down. They marched straight past us through the open door to the bar and demanded two large brandies which they instantly chucked down their throats. A minute later, and without having wasted a glance on the tourist couple at the table outside, they were walking quickly back towards their cars, talking animatedly now and lighting cigarettes, underling boredom temporarily relieved.

Just when the sentence 'We could be sitting here all night' began to form on my lips, Kladders's party tumbled into the road. We heard them before we saw them. A heated argument was under way and all of them were talking at once. I obviously had no hope of deciphering any of it, but I distinctly heard more than one language being abused. It appeared that in the heat of the argument everyone had resorted to shouting in their respective mother tongues, except Kladders who appeared to be trying to pour oil on troubled waters in both Greek and Italian, interspersed with English exhortations such as 'Calm *down*, everybody'. When the policeman and the Italian started pushing and shoving, Kladders threw up his hands in a gesture of mock despair and walked away from the brawl towards where we were sitting. Behind him, both the BMW and the Mercedes had pulled up to the entrance of the restaurant.

'There he is.' I got up from my chair and walked towards Kladders.

While looking in a different direction, Kladders said urgently, 'Go away.'

'I want to talk to you.'

'Not now, Mr Honeysett; ignore me and walk past.'

'OK, but I want to ask you some questions.'

'Another time.'

'Where can I find you?'

'You can't; I'll find you.'

Typical. Everyone was always confident they could find me on this island; so why did I have such trouble finding Kyla? We had passed each other by now and I stooped and picked an imaginary coin out of the grit by the side of the road, then turned round while studying it in the palm of my hand. I had come quite close to the brawl, which was now breaking up, and I was being overtaken by the police officer with the neon skin and walrus moustache. He crossed the road in an angry strut and got into a large and shiny red Nissan parked in the drive of a villa. He performed a hectic U-turn, which brought him close enough to our table outside the bar to make me think he might drive through it. He was frowning straight at me as he scrunched past, then accelerated away towards town. A couple of minutes later, first the BMW and then the Mercedes roared past in the same direction. Kladders had disappeared.

'Did you see where he went?'

'He got into a green Citroën – one of those hire cars.'

'Great, there must be a thousand of them.'

'Only one with this number plate,' she said, pointing at the table top. She had written it out in Amstel beer. She shrugged. 'It's all I had. Better get a pen before it runs.'

SIXTEEN

'Sorry, I gave my last Alka-Seltzer to Charlie the other day,' Helen said cheerfully. Then she clattered around with her portable easel for a bit before noisily setting off into the glaring sunshine for her painting session. I was convinced everyone was making a lot more noise than necessary this morning and I was sure the sorry apparition in the shape of Annis Jordan hunched beside me at the long table would have agreed had it been capable of coherent speech.

By the time we had got back to Ano Makriá from the Lord Byron the previous night, we had convinced ourselves that we had utterly and tragically sobered up. And for no reason at all, except that there was no beer in the cooler, we had started on a two-litre bottle of the local red. Each.

The planned trip into town to check emails and get in touch with Tim was postponed for obvious reasons: one pothole and my head was going to break open like a Chocolate Orange.

One by one, the ghost-village inmates had expressed their sympathy or amusement and gone their own way to paint, and eventually Morva had gingerly hobbled after them on two sticks to check on their progress. Charlie, who was now working on the room next to ours, had promised to find something quiet to do, clearing the place of rubbish and levelling the hard earth floor, but by noon he had run out of quiet pursuits. Without warning, he fired up the petrol engine of the ancient cement mixer in the yard to make concrete for the floor.

'Morva's beautiful sound,' groaned Annis.

'Let's get away from here.'

'Where?'

'Anywhere. Just away from that noise.'

'Into the bright stuff out there? I don't know what's worse.'

We slunk away into the grove behind the house.

'We're a pathetic pair,' I concluded.

Annis looked back over her shoulder. 'Margarita seems to think so. Did you see the look she gave us from the doorway?'

'She always looks at me like that. Let's keep under the olive trees – not so bright here. I think I know how vampires feel now.'

We clambered up several crumbling terraces into the overgrown olive grove until the noise of the cement mixer had receded like a toothache numbed by codeine, then slowly picked our way around the slopes on the edge of the village. The place was still lush from the recent rains, but already the fierce heat was trying to bake it into submission. The borders between sun and shade were hard-edged; the light shimmered painfully on the stones, reflecting blindingly on the bits of whitewash remaining on the back of the deserted church. Beyond the churchyard with its untended graves and waist-high grasses, I could see Rob dabbing methodically at his little canvas. Here the olive terraces came to an end and the shoulder of the hill sloped back towards the village. We clambered downwards on a stony goat track that took us in the direction of the holly oaks where the motorhome was parked. Every time my foot slipped on a loose stone, the juddering movement translated into a circle-dance of headache around my skull.

'Was it my idea to go for a walk?' I enquired as I negotiated the goat track like a tightrope walker.

'Certainly was. I feel much better, don't you?'

'I do hate young people,' I confessed.

Below us, somewhere among the holly oaks and myrtle bushes, a woman shrieked. Twice, loud and long.

'That doesn't sound too happy. Let's check it out.' Annis flew down the slope in the direction of the cry.

'Bloody hell, that's all I need now.' I ran after her as fast as my head allowed. I caught up with her by the van. Sophie was standing beside it, swearing continuously and repetitively; her hands fluttered.

'What happened?' I asked.

'A snake encounter,' Annis said.

'You could bloody say that. Snakes! That's all I bloody need! All I wanted was to have a look; I'd never been in a motorhome. I sat down on the edge of the bed and nearly sat down on the damn snake. I jumped up but it's so bloody small in there I ran smack into a cupboard before I made it out of the bloody door!'

'Did you see where it went?'

'What? Are you mad? I didn't hang around. I just got out and slammed the door shut behind me.'

'Still in there, then.' I pressed my nose against the window but it was too bright outside to allow me to see much. 'Well, we can't leave it in there to scare Charlie.'

'You're good with snakes,' Sophie said. 'Go and get it out somehow.'

'Yes, you should be used to it by now,' Annis agreed. 'Do some snake charming. We'll watch. You can pass the hat round afterwards.'

Great. Now I was the local pest control expert. *Wriggly things.* I wasn't keen on it, but it looked as if I'd landed the job, with another all-female audience to record any lapses in heroism.

Under the trees I found a likely-looking stick with a spur at the end with which I might do battle if it came to it. 'All right, you keep your eyes peeled in case it comes out.' I opened the van door with a feeling of doom and took my time going in. I quickly looked around. Nothing by my feet, on the bed or the table, as far as I could see. Of course, if Derringer could hide in here, then a long thin thing shouldn't have much of a problem. 'Where art thou, wee slitherous beastie?' I cooed. I trod very softly, hoping to find the reptile asleep again. Some movement in my peripheral vision. There it was, trying to get away into the furthest corner behind the driver's seat. Perhaps I could chase it out? The heat inside the van was cooking my hangover and my head throbbed as I bent down to give the thing the once-over. This one looked a bit different from the other: it had lozenge markings down the back. It wasn't all that big, certainly small enough to disappear into the woodwork if I didn't act quickly. On the worktop lay a well-singed oven glove. Better than nothing, I reasoned, and slipped it on my right hand. I didn't want to give the snake a chance to think about things so I struck snake-like first, pinning it closely with the stick behind the head into the corner where it writhed and wriggled, its fanged mouth gaping wide. On the tip of its nose it appeared to have some sort of warty growth. It looked well narked. Now for the tricky bit. Pressing down hard with my left on the stick, I gave the business end of the snake a wide birth and came at it from behind, grabbing it firmly behind the neck. It felt much meatier than expected and writhed and twisted frantically as I lifted it up and held it at arm's length. There were people who kept these animals as pets? I wouldn't have wanted to pet this one. I had the distinct feeling it hadn't taken to me.

'Got it, coming out now,' I called with the voice of a twelve-year-old.

Outside, Rob had joined the audience from his nearby painting camp. 'What have you got this time?' he asked.

'Don't know. Smaller one this time.' I held it out for inspection. 'You think it's poisonous?'

He waggled his head. 'No, not poisonous, strictly speaking.'

I relaxed a little. 'Strictly speaking? What about less strictly.'

'Well, I mean it would probably be safe to eat, so it's not poisonous as such. It's highly *venomous*, of course. Yes, quite deadly in fact, were it to bite you. Careful how you let it go now; it looks a little on the lively side.'

Strictly speaking, I had a sudden impulse to chuck the thing at him. With the snake fighting to escape my grip, fangs bared and ready to sink them into the nearest bit of Honeysett, I felt like a man who had accidentally pulled the pin from a grenade and then promptly dropped it down a drain. 'Any suggestions?'

'Yes, get rid of it. It looks horrible,' was Sophie's contribution.

'Make sure you chuck it a good distance away from you,' said Annis. 'It does look ugly. What's that at the end of its nose?'

Rob knew. 'That's one of its characteristics. It's a nose-horned viper,' he said, coming closer and peering at it with interest. I was sorely tempted to turn it into a Rob-nosed viper.

'How come you know about these things?' I seemed to remember him identifying the last snake I caught, too.

'There's a section in my guide to Corfu. It had pictures. Mind how you go, now.'

I minded. Never taking my eye off the stroppy serpent, I walked twenty yards towards the scorched patch of ground where the tortoise-fire had burnt. Then I picked my moment and flung the reptile away from me like a hand grenade. I didn't even wait to see it land, just legged it out of there in case it had thoughts of revenge.

Rob had already gone back to his painting. Annis gave ironic applause, but Sophie looked genuinely relieved. 'That was horrible,' she said with feeling.

'Tell me about it. You had a lucky escape sitting down next to it. I think you probably saved Charlie quite a nasty experience. If he'd have let himself fall on the bed after an afternoon's work . . . I never asked Rob whether there's an antidote available for nose-horned viper venom.'

Sophie shuddered, hugging herself. 'I don't know about you, but I need a drink after that.'

'No thanks, I'm still hungover from last night.' Was I? 'Actually my headache's completely gone.'

'That's the adrenalin.' Sophie smiled weakly. 'Erm, could you . . . could you please not tell Charlie that I went into the van uninvited? I know it's your van, but it's all his stuff in there. I feel a bit embarrassed about it now, I just wanted to take a look, you know . . .'

'Are you sure? I'd hate to take all the credit.'

'Please?'

'Oh, all right, I'll say I spotted the snake through the window.'

'Thanks,' she said, relieved, and turned away.

Then I got a sudden attack of the Columbos. 'Oh, just one other thing . . . Was the van door open or closed when you got there? We'd better leave it the way you found it.'

'Closed.'

'You sure?'

'Positive,' she called over her shoulder.

I went back to the van, had another quick look around the interior, then slammed the door shut. 'I may not be ready for a drink but I think I could take a little nourishment now. Let's see what's left in the kitchen.'

The rumbling cement mixer in the courtyard was no longer

threatening to fragment my skull, its sound having shrunk along with my hangover. I paused at the door to the room where Charlie was smoothing an area of cement with a wooden trowel. 'I passed the motorhome just now and saw something moving inside. When I checked it out, it turned out to be a snake.'

'Oh, shit.'

'I got rid of it for you. But be extra careful, just in case it had a mate. Quite poisonous – sorry, *venomous* – according to Rob, and he seems to know about these things.'

'Thanks. mate. That could have been nasty. I really hate snakes.'

'I'm beginning to feel that way myself.'

'Serves me right for leaving the door wide open. But it gets too hot in there otherwise.'

'You left it open, did you?'

'Yeah, stupid, I guess. I'll go and close it.'

'Don't bother; I shut it for you. But have a look through your stuff anyway, in case there's another one. You don't want to find you're sharing your pyjamas with a sleepy reptile.'

He gave a theatrical shudder. 'I only said to Morva last night how I really hate snakes and stuff like that. The quicker I get these rooms finished, the better. It'll be baking in the van tonight with the doors shut.'

In the kitchen Annis was throwing together a salad. 'I'm certainly going to check the bed before getting in tonight, but I guess this sort of thing doesn't happen too often.'

'I'm not sure it happens at all.'

She paused in mid-tomato-slice. 'Meaning?'

'I just asked Charlie and he said he had left the van door open. Because it gets too hot otherwise. But Sophie said that when she got there the door was closed.'

'Is there still feta under that upturned dish? So you think someone put the snake inside and then shut the door to make sure it stayed there.'

I lifted the china bowl and revealed a half-brick of feta cheese on a plate. Between the seven of us we got through mountains of the stuff. 'That's exactly what I'm thinking. I don't believe it's all that easy for a small snake to heave itself into a van anyway, though this one was quite muscular and it could conceivably have come down from the tree next to it. But it's quite another thing for a snake to get into a van and then close the door behind itself.'

'I take your point. But then, of course, one of the students may have passed the van, thought the door had been left open by mistake – oh, what am I saying? They're far too self-absorbed.' Annis finished the build of the salad with a scatter of black olives from a big stoneware brine jar.

We took our plates into the courtyard where a light breeze was stirring now. The grinding cement mixer drowned out the rasping cicadas. We had hardly started on our brunch when Margarita puffed by with bags of shopping, giving us a sour look and talking to herself in Greek. 'I think she disapproves of our helping ourselves.'

'You may be right,' Annis said, closely examining an olive on the end of her fork before closing her lips around it. 'Mm. It seems bloody obvious that someone around here is sabotaging the place.'

'But who?'

'Well, if this was an Agatha Christie movie with famous ageing actors and lots of adverts, then the murderer would naturally be the one you'd least suspect. It's easy.'

'OK, let's go with that. So in our case that would be who – Morva?'

'In Agathaland, yes. Either that or her evil twin sister. They were separated at birth. The evil twin grew up in poverty and, driven mad by jealousy of Morva's good fortune, has been living in the village for years, disguised as a man, plotting her twin's downfall.'

'Yeah, I buy that.'

'Meanwhile in the real world?'

'Occam's razor.'

'Whose?'

'Old Bill Occam – his razor. Franciscan philosopher.'

'Dead?'

'These five hundred years.'

'Then how's his rusty razor going to help us?'

'The principle of Occam's razor basically says that if there are several explanations, then the simplest one's usually right.'

'So in our case that means it's . . .'

'*Margarita*,' we both whispered in unison.

'But, then again, why?' Annis asked, looking over her shoulder to make sure we hadn't magically summoned her to the table. 'What's she got to gain? Surely she'll lose her job if this painting school thing of Morva's fails.'

'True. But.'

'But?'

'But, then, perhaps the job isn't the important thing. Hardly anyone in the village seems to work.'

'Her dad does. Runs the kiosk.'

'Call that work?' My mind flashed up the image of a spider in the centre of a web that covered the entire village.

'You know what I think?'

'As ever, no,' I admitted.

'I think you should concentrate on finding Kyla, or tell Mr Morton-Supermarket you can't find her and then we'll get the hell out of here before this really does turn into an Agatha Christie mystery.'

'It isn't one yet, then?'

'Of course not, silly – no dead body.'

'Not for want of opportunity.'

'Exactly. And I think I want to get out of here before someone taps me on the shoulder and says "You're it".'

'OK, let's turn the wick up a bit. I'll go into town and have a chat with Tim and see if he's sent me another mugshot of Kyla.' I pinched the last olive off her plate and got up. 'You coming, or what?'

Compared to the rest of the island, Corfu Town seemed busy. I found a parking space near the old bus station and left the car so only one of the unmatched number plates showed. From here it wasn't far to the internet cafe.

'OK, meet you back at the car in an hour,' Annis said.

'Why, where are you going?'

'Shopping.'

'We can go together afterwards.'

'*Clothes* shopping.'

'You're on your own there.' She wouldn't need me for that; her bum would never look big in anything for a start.

At the superheated internet cafe I skimmed my emails. How did so much junk get through this so-called spam filter? Among the rest were some possible referrals from a large Bristol detective agency – naturally, all stuff they themselves wouldn't touch with the proverbial. I sent a heartfelt 'No thanks, me and my bargepole are in sunny Greece' and then opened Tim's email. He had scanned the group picture with Kyla in it, the one from the food article. 'Best I could do' was Tim's verbose message. Was it possible to print this out, I asked the bloke running the cafe. The kid came over, grunted in the affirmative and saved the image to a memory stick, then disappeared. I had just started on a reply to Tim's baroque email when the kid reappeared with the picture printed out on matt photo paper. Kyla was one of six people standing outside the entrance to a posh-looking office building, all smiling as if they'd been told to. The photo was appropriately grainy and in black and white. For some reason, it looked like a picture of people long dead. I fanned myself with the print. Too hot in here. I abandoned the email and went to call Tim instead. The post office was air-conditioned and had the added bonus, presumably, of not broadcasting my conversation all over the island. At Mill House, Tim answered almost straight away.

'I never realized how bloody cold your place gets,' he complained. 'You're nearly out of logs again, by the way.'

I hadn't realized I had logs to be out of. Annis must have had some delivered. 'I had no idea Corfu could get this hot in spring,' I countered maliciously.

'I might have to come down there, then.'

'Seriously? I thought you were busy working.'

'I was. But the project fell through – cutbacks. I scraped a few days' holiday together. If a cheap flight comes up, I'll join you.'

'Don't leave it too long, I'm trying to wind things up here, one way or another, and get out.'

'Hide nor hair?'

'Couldn't have said it better myself. And it's a strange place, Corfu. All I keep turning up is people who aren't keen on me going around asking questions, and then the next moment I'm disarmed by acts of unexpected kindness.'

'Talking of "disarmed", you didn't take the Webley, did you?'

'I'm not mad, you know. You get caught taking a gun across an international border and you've had it. Just smuggling the damn cat across Europe was nerve-wracking enough. Actually, I don't think I'd feel any safer carrying a thirty-eight. A lot of weird things have been happening, though most of it hasn't been aimed at me, I'm glad to say. Spooky things. Stuff you can't shoot.'

'Oh, I mailed you a picture, by the way.'

'I know, I got it. Could you do me another favour?' I gave Tim a list of names. 'See what you can find out about them. I'll call again soon. Oh, here's a thought . . . if I call and seem to talk rubbish, then that's because I'm calling from a kiosk in the nearby village where they can hear every word I say. Just give me your news and I'll pretend we're chatting about the cat.'

'Why don't we? How *is* Derringer?' Like everyone else who'd met Derringer, Tim had become fond of the beast.

'Murdering the locals and getting fat. Greek rodents seem to agree with him. And I suspect there are seven people feeding him kebabs, chicken and feta cheese under the table.'

Annis and I had agreed to meet outside the church of Agios Spiridon, the much-travelled (and mummified) patron saint of Corfu, for no other reason than that its red-capped tower was hard to miss. I had some time left and allowed myself to drift about the narrow streets and alleys. Not all the shops sold useless tourist tat. If you wanted your shoes repaired, your dress mended or the tin lining of your coffee pot replaced, then you could still find the tiny workshops that served the permanent inhabitants of Corfu in the narrower and less glamorous alleyways of the town. Taking mainly left turns, I managed to come nearly full circle, keeping a lookout for a suitable cafe. Eventually, the alley I walked up widened and there, between a stationer's and a draper's shop, I found what I had been hoping for: a patisserie with little tables outside in the shade of the colonnaded building. Unfortunately, the only free seat to be had was opposite a balding, overweight, cake-eating police officer called Superintendent Michael Needham.

SEVENTEEN

I had a terrible urge to tiptoe past in cartoon style, or else run like hell, but I forced myself to keep to my normal pace so he wouldn't look up from his chocolate cake. I hummed 'Walk on by' to myself, all the time expecting to hear my name called in that stentorian voice of his. When at last I made it to the street corner, I leant against a wall and pinched myself just in case I was sleepwalking.

Superintendent Michael Needham, Avon and Somerset Constabulary's finest, had long been keeping a critical eye on the activities of Aqua Investigations. While 'meddling private investigators' in general never made it on to the superintendent's Christmas card list, I had somehow managed to achieve special disapproval ratings. Our paths had crossed frequently in Bath and environs, but the sight of him thousands of miles south of his patch was enough to send my paranoia count through the roof. What were the chances of Needham being on the same Greek island – how many did the tape say there were? – at the same time as me? Exactly. I tried not to hold my breath as I peered around the corner for a good look. I had a three-quarters back view of him now, so unless he really did have eyes at the back of his head as was rumoured, I should be quite safe. His hair, what was left of it after fifty-odd years, had a suspicious amount of colour left in it. Surely he hadn't taken to dyeing it? A waiter appeared, cleared an empty plate off Needham's table, then went back into the cafe. A few seconds later he reappeared with another piece of brown cake and put it in front of the superintendent who went to work on it straight away. Not the behaviour of a man who was waiting for someone to join him, unless, of course, he was just trying to sink as much cake as possible before that someone arrived. I checked my watch: it was time to meet Annis and tell her the good news.

'You're imagining things,' is how she greeted it.

'Large as life. Slightly larger soon. He's hoovering up cake at a frightening rate.'

'Certainly sounds like him.'

'He was slurping Greek coffee like a connoisseur, too.'

'That's very him.' Superintendent Needham was a coffee lover whose life had long been blighted by cop-shop coffee-machine muck. It wasn't beyond him to turn up at your house, drink your Blue Mountain first, then arrest you afterwards.

'But what's he doing here?'

'He could be on holiday, you know. Police must get some eventually.'

I closed my eyes for a second. 'White shirt and tie, suit jacket over the back of his chair.'

'Briefcase?'

I closed my eyes again. 'The scuffed brown one, under his chair.'

'Bum. He's here on business. But why should it have anything to do with us?'

'Because we're here on business.'

'Speak for yourself.'

I ignored that. 'Now, if we were here simply for sun, sea and sand in our sandwich, I wouldn't worry much, but we're not and so I do.' Not that Needham was strictly the enemy; he was just not convinced that we were entirely on the straight and narrow he so admirably squeezed along himself, no matter how much cake was on offer.

'How long ago did you spot him at the patisserie?'

'Not five minutes ago.'

'He'll still be there as long as there's a biscuit left in the place. Let's have a look at him.'

Walking towards Needham was entirely counter-instinctive. Only reluctantly did I lead us back to the street corner from which I had observed the superintendent. He hadn't moved an inch. He had probably put on an inch, of course, since – unbelievably – he was now staring at some other piece of pastry on his plate.

'That's his third, at least. This one looks a bit like your hair.'

'It's *kataïfi*,' Annis enlightened me. 'A bit like baklava, just . . . weirder.'

'He seems to have his doubts himself.'

'Did you do anything particularly dodgy recently? Anything that might be especially irritating to the super's hide?'

'Nothing I can think of. I sneezed near Manvers Street Police Station once.'

'Not an arrestable offence, I'd have thought, though I haven't checked recently. We could just go and have a chat with him – that would quickly clear things up. Oh hello, he's got company. Look, he's consorting with bikers now. Surely a good sign.'

A tall man in his thirties was shaking hands with Needham, who had risen politely from his chair. The younger man put a black helmet on the ground under the table. He wore jeans and trainers and was just taking off his denim jacket. Underneath, he wore a black tee shirt and under that gym-trained muscles. Clipped to his belt he had a radio with a stubby aerial. He unhooked it and laid it on the table.

'I think I recognize that bloke. He's the biker on the big BMW who was following Gloves. I seem to recognize his jacket and helmet and he's the right height. If I'm right, then he's Greek, or at the least he speaks fluent Greek.'

'Looks pretty native to me, in a tall, tanned, classical Greek sort of way. So why is Needham hanging out with him? You think he's a police officer?'

'I expect so.'

'One way to find out . . .'

'What, scream "Help! Police!" in Greek and see if he comes to your aid?'

Annis pulled me away from the corner and shoved two of her three shopping bags at me. 'No, I'll go and have cake and coffee; the table next to them's free now.'

'You can't; he'll recognize you.'

'Oh yeah?' She put her hair up in a twist at the back of her head and pulled a straw hat from her bag. 'Bought it for the beach. Men are notoriously unobservant. Change your hair or put a hat on and they swear you're a different girl. Watch.'

Before I could lodge further protest, Annis marched off and, as cool as you like, made for the free table. The biker checked her over, but Needham was talking through his cake and never even looked up. A waiter shot out of the door to take her order. So far so good, but I was still nervous. 'Please don't take out a make-up mirror to check over your shoulders,' I silently implored.

Soon Annis too was served with Greek coffee and strangely hairy pastry. Typical: everyone except me was eating cake. Out of sight around the corner, I sat on a doorstep and had time to smoke a couple of cigarettes while I contemplated the injustices of the world. I nearly choked on my fumes when Needham walked right past my nose, fortunately without giving me so much as a glance; I was just another tourist tired of shopping.

Annis appeared moments later. 'Did he see you?'

'I don't think so.'

'You were right: the bloke's a policeman, an inspector from Athens.'

'Did you find out what Needham's doing here?'

'Not really, but neither of them mentioned you, me, Aqua Investigations Inc. or Kyla Biggs.'

'So what did they talk about?'

'Cake.'

'Yeah, right.'

'They did, I swear. The bike cop insisted the stuff he was eating wasn't as good as the cake they make in Athens.'

'There's our answer: Needham flew to Corfu on urgent pastry matters.'

'They talked about other stuff too, but I'm not sure what, really. Someone disappeared, but it's a *he* they are looking for and he's Greek – that's about as much as I could make out. It's some investigation that's been going for a while. But they were saying things like "keeping a low profile" and "getting everything in place" and "making sure no one slips through the net", so they're up to something. But it certainly didn't sound as if they were after you or me.'

'An international counterfeit-cake smuggling gang, then. Well I never. I wonder how Needham got himself involved.'

'No idea, but we now know his favourite cake shop if you feel like asking him.'

'No ta, perhaps some other time.' I'd had enough of town

and definitely enough of Needham. A little goes a long way. 'Let's go back to the village, but first I'm going to get a huge slice of cake to take away from the patisserie.'

'Bad luck, hon. They were putting the "Sorry, we're closed" sign up as I left.'

On the drive back I irritably parped my horn in every corner and enthusiastically dodged potholes on the narrow roads. Cake deprivation always affects me strongly.

'Greece has the highest number of road deaths in Europe,' Annis said casually. 'Try not to make the statistics worse.'

'What's getting worse is the steering on this chariot. Please observe.' I turned the wheel several inches to either side without any effect on the direction of travel. 'I feel like I'm an actor in a forties movie with a back-projection screen behind.'

I checked the mirror. The back projection was lovely. I slowed down and tried to enjoy. It wasn't easy: there seemed to be too much to think about. When I first took the job in fogbound Blighty, I had imagined I'd be spending most of my time strolling on long sandy beaches or sitting in restaurants while keeping one lazy eye out for Kyla Biggs. I hadn't done all that much strolling. I'd also imagined I'd find the locals helpful and Kyla Biggs quickly, and neither could be said to be true. Dimitris, the cafe owner in Neo Makriá, had been helpful, of course, but seemed to become less friendly the longer I hung around. And the longer I thought about him, the more I wondered how on earth he could possibly make a living from selling a dozen cups of coffee a day. Like so many others in the village, he had to have some other income. Farming, perhaps, though no one ever appeared to do any. And though it was true that the landscape was lovely to me, it was also a place full of misplaced snakes and fire-spreading turtles, unfriendly locals and unseen spooks.

I checked the mirror. The back projection was ugly. A big old lorry was coming up fast from behind, filthy with dried mud, bull bars at the front, tarpaulin flapping wildly at the back. It took up most of the road and was obviously in a hurry. There was nowhere to let it pass on this stretch, so I speeded up a bit. The juggernaut was as grey as fear and thirty seconds later it filled the entire rear view.

'We're being monstered by a huge lorry. Where did that come from?'

Annis turned around. 'Bloody maniac, he's dancing around on our rear bumper.'

'I'll try to find a place to let him pass.' We were up in the hills now, either side of the road nothing but ditches and olive trees. The lorry drove so close behind I imagined I could feel its pressure through the metal. At the next bend I checked the mirror before braking. The lorry pulled back a few yards as it needed to get on the brakes earlier than me. For a second I could see two dark faces behind its half-obscured windscreen, but couldn't have recognized them. I hung on the wheel to make the turn while the suspension creaked like a sinking ship. Behind me, the lorry hauled through the bend at suicidal speed. We were going downhill now and within seconds the Scandia badge of the lorry filled our rear window again, the roaring engine of the beast drowning out the scream of our own. This time I felt the bump as the lorry shunted into the back of us.

I accelerated. 'Shit, they're trying to ram us off the road.'

'If this wasn't such a wreck, we could easily outrun them,' Annis said darkly.

'He can't be carrying much of a load if he has this pace.'

'You want me to jump out to lighten the car? They do it all the time in the movies and never hurt themselves.'

'No, just hang on tight. Even a crap car must corner better than a lorry.'

'But this is special French crap.'

'My favourite kind.'

Annis's answer was drowned out in the noise from behind as the lorry shunted into the back of us just as the next corner rushed up. The car snaked first left, then wildly to the right as I overcompensated and the rear stepped out. I screeched sideways through the bend in wholly involuntary rally style, which probably helped to save us.

What really saved us was the gravelled entrance to an old stone quarry opening up to our left. I ran straight into it, then stood on the brakes, sending up clouds of dust and stones. Behind us, our pursuer overcooked the corner. His lorry bounced and bucked with some wheels on tarmac, some on gravel, careened adventurously from side to side, but thundered on without crashing. A blue plastic barrel bounced from under its flapping tarp, flying in our direction like a parting shot. It caromed around the quarry entrance and rolled to a stop near our stalled little Citroën.

'You all right?' I spoke into the sudden silence.

'Terrific.' She rubbed her forehead where she had knocked her head on the door frame. 'I never had this much fun when I was last in Corfu.'

'You went with the wrong crowd, I expect.'

'Still, nice driving, hon. All considered.'

We both got out and had a look around. The lorry had disappeared and, after the rush and noise, everything seemed wonderfully quiet. I lit a cigarette, offered Annis one out of habit and absent-mindedly she accepted. We stood in the spring-fragranced air and smoked like idiots. The quarry behind us was a small effort and seemed to have been abandoned with all its machinery quite a while ago. Since then the locals had added a varied collection of car wrecks, some of them burnt out. I strolled over to the big blue barrel that had been the lorry's parting present and began kicking it towards the quarry mouth to add to the junk when I noticed some writing on the grimy vessel. I let it roll to a stop. Fortunately, the writing wasn't in Greek; it was Turkish, which uses more or less the same script as English.

'Did you see a number plate on the monster truck? His cargo was Turkish; there's writing on this.'

'I didn't see a thing. What's it say, then, you being an expert on all things Byzantine?'

It had been a while since I'd sipped cay in Turkish tea gardens. 'Erm, oh yeah, it says, erm . . . "This way up".'

'*Really?*'

'Give me a chance. There's . . . a lot of stuff about . . . something or other . . . and then it says "Walnut Oil", no, wait, *findik,* it's "Hazelnut Oil".'

'I didn't even know they made hazelnut oil. What's it taste like, I wonder?'

'I don't know but I can find out what it smells like. Hang

on . . .' I righted the barrel and stuck my nose near the gummy two-inch hole in the top. 'Hazelnut oil smells very strongly of absolutely nothing at all.' A theory about our villagers' excess leisure time began to dawn on me. I flipped the barrel on its side and dribbled it towards the quarry, then, with a toe-shattering kick, sent it rolling towards the other junk already there.

I hobbled back to the car, got it started and drove us back to Morva's place, distrusting every side-road and keeping more than an occasional eye on the rear-view mirror. Yet it appeared our adversaries had left the field. I sincerely hoped they were on their way back to Turkey.

EIGHTEEN

'I seem to remember having seen a lorry with blue plastic barrels driving through Neo Makriá when I first got here.' I held out a cup of coffee to Annis who ignored it. She was hunting around our chaotic room for her stuff, throwing things into her suitcase and holdall. 'We slept through breakfast again and there was no one around, so I made us feta cheese and cucumber sandwiches. And coffee. *This* coffee. What are you doing?'

'Just put it down somewhere. I'm packing my bags. And I think you should do the same.'

'Should I get excited? Are we going somewhere?'

'Don't be daft. We should, of course, but, as you said, you can't just walk out. After yesterday's lorry-load of fun, though, I think we should at least be prepared to move at short notice. I have the feeling when we do want to leave we won't be in the mood for folding tee shirts. We'll just want to throw our stuff into the van and go.'

'Ah.'

'*Ah?*'

'I must sort out the battery on the van. At least I think it's the battery.'

'What makes you think it's the battery?'

'Because it's the only car component I can actually name. If it's not the battery, then I'm lost.'

'I'll have a look at it later.'

'I'll get the sandwiches.'

'Don't bother. I'm done, more or less.' She picked up her cup of coffee. 'Let's go eat in the sun.'

We munched our breakfast sitting on the rim of the well in the courtyard. Derringer was asleep in the shade of the fig tree, creating a chicken-free zone around himself. One brown hen was scratching in the dust near our feet, keeping a calculating eye on the crumb potential of our sandwiches. Heat haze was already unfocusing the view of the ruins, but I thought I could glimpse what looked like Helen on the far side, moving about in front of a partially collapsed farmhouse.

'A dollop of mayo would make these perfect,' I observed indelicately through a mouthful of sandwich.

'Conventional wisdom has it that men think of sex every few minutes. How do you find the time, Honeysett? You're so busy thinking of food all day.'

'It's tricky, but I usually manage to squeeze it in somewhere.'

'Not sure I like the sound of that. Well, make space for thinking about this: I don't believe they were playing with us yesterday. I don't believe they were just warning us, either. I think they'd have been quite happy to see us run smack into a tree. And you know what that means?'

'Enlighten me.'

'Remember the Fiesta rolling down the hill and hitting Morva?'

'It's fresh in my mind, thank you.'

'I now think it's much more likely that it was aimed at you and only hit Morva by mistake. You said yourself the Italian bloke with the Merc gave you some kind of veiled warning. Sure, someone – perhaps even the whole village – wants Morva out of here, but I think someone wants *you* out of here even more. With Morva and her students, they're just trying to scare them away, but they seem quite happy to arrange a real accident for you. The highest number of road deaths in Europe, remember?'

I was slowly coming around to her way of thinking. 'In other words, nobody would question it much if I wrapped an old Citroën round an olive tree.'

'No one would bat an eyelid, especially with the police as corrupt as they're supposed to be round here.'

'OK, I'll drive carefully.'

'Going somewhere?'

I was. I had played down any worries about being targeted – much like Morva had, in fact – but secretly I had had enough. What I really wanted now was to wrap this Kyla thing up as soon as possible, so I drove back into town. On my useless tourist map I picked out a different route to Kerkyra, longer, more torturously twisted, but at least it would be unexpected, making it less likely that dirty great big lorries were lying in wait for me en route.

Of course, even once I had found Kyla, there'd still be Morva's spooks to take care of, but at least I'd feel a free agent again. It was pretty obvious to me that firing Margarita would solve many of Morva's sabotage problems, though there was always the chance that it would make the locals even more hostile. And then who would cook for the students who'd been promised an all-in Greek experience? I shuddered at the memory of Morva's evil curry. Where would she find a replacement willing to come to this forsaken place? So, keeping her enemies close, Morva kept Margarita on.

The narrow, twisting route forced me to go even more slowly than usual, allowing me to take in some of the sights and smells I had recently ignored due to obvious distractions. When the view opened up across a steep and narrow valley, I stopped and got out of the car. On the opposite side of the valley sat a red-roofed village. It consisted of no more than thirty-odd houses and seemed to float in a turbulent sea of trees. Looking from here, the continuous swell of green appeared to consist of only two types of tree: the ubiquitous olive and the exclamatory cypress. A strong west wind was today working this forest of olives, making the trees flash the silver underside of their leaves towards the sky, turning the vista into a restless, flickering image. Standing here by the side of the road looking across, I could see no people in the village. The smell of burning charcoal and wild oregano travelled on the wind. A sudden romantic impulse made me imagine this tiny hamlet as my home – past, present and future. I could also smell the sea, a sliver of which flickered not far beyond the roofs. Perhaps once the Kyla thing was sorted, Annis and I could visit the place, rent a room, try for a real holiday. I checked on the map in the car but, try as I might, I could not match what I saw to anything on the map. This could only mean two things: it wasn't marked on the map or else I had managed to get lost in the hills. As I stood by the car looking across, a flash of refracted sunlight caught my eye but was not repeated. It reminded me of the reflection of light from the birdwatcher's binoculars I had seen at Chlomós; it also reminded me that just because I couldn't see anybody didn't mean no one was watching me. I checked all around me and listened, but didn't see a soul and the only thing I heard was the crow of a distant cockerel. But the mood had changed; the romantic bubble had burst. I drove faster now on my way into town.

Corfu Town felt hot and dusty today and I was glad to escape into the coolness of the post office. I called Tim at work.

'No, we don't have to pretend I'm talking about the cat. I came into town to take care of something else. Have you had a chance to check out the names I gave you?'

'I have, with varying success.'

'OK, start at the top.'

'Morton? You can stop being paranoid, or perhaps not. He really is working for your supermarket group, but I can't find a job description for him. He zips all over the world. Sometimes he stays in the background and sometimes he appears as a spokesman. As he did when some baby food in the States had been contaminated with glass, or when a lot of cats and dogs died from their own-brand pet food. He's a sort of troubleshooter and spin doctor.'

'Well, at least he's real. I never checked with anyone that he was who he said he was. I was just dazzled by the wad of fifties and the turbot on the menu. He could have been anyone.'

'He seems to turn up whenever something happens that may taint the company image. I suppose all global brands have people like that.'

'Whole departments of them, I should think. But one employee not returning from holiday . . . how's that going to harm a company like that?'

'That depends what she's been up to, of course.'

'I suspect that's what I'm here to find out.'

'And?'

'I know she's been here before; I found a picture of her in a taverna – a holiday pic. And in the same picture was the guy who ran the taverna having a drink with her. But he denied ever having seen her. The other person in the picture was Gloves.'

'Toyota woman? Is she still following you?'

'Not for a few days. I think she knows pretty well where to find me if she wants to, so perhaps she's packed it in. Got anything else for me?'

'Hang on.' At the other end Tim shuffled paper. 'You've got a joyous bunch of students up there. Your Rob character – Robert Oxley – he was tricky to find. Unremarkable, except for the fact that he lost every penny he had in the recent financial upheaval. He shouldn't have: he's a retired accountant.'

That explained his method of painting at least. Another mystery solved. 'He must have taken his eye off the ball.'

'His wife died of something or other around then too, and soon after that your Robert sold his house in Portsmouth and disappeared.'

'And now he's found. I always find people I've not been looking for. There's no money in it.'

'Says here "relatives are worried about his mental state".'

'They can stop worrying – he's fine. Though I'm not really sure it's our job to tell them that. If he wants to be disappeared, then that's his business. It doesn't say there he's a specialist in reptiles, does it?'

'Reptiles? No. Why? Oh no, don't tell me you've got snakes out there . . . I *hate* snakes.'

'Snakes? In Corfu? No, it's like Ireland here – no snakes at all.'

'That's all right, then. I can't be having with snakes.'

'What else have you got?'

'OK, let's see . . . ah yes, another cheerful character – Sophie Little. Found loads on her. Quite a story. Her son died on a holiday down there and she's refused to leave the island ever since. Her husband stayed with her in Corfu for a while, but then decided enough was enough and went back to work in England. They're from Lincoln. I think she had some sort of breakdown and doesn't want to believe her son's dead.'

'I heard. I know all that.'

'Did you know her son had tried to kill himself before that?'

'No one mentioned that. So it could have been suicide. He could have gone diving and stayed down there on purpose. While his mother was waiting for him in the boat.'

'Cheerful thought.'

'I think mentally she's still sitting in that boat.'

'Well, perhaps she should row ashore sometime soon. She's got a fifteen-year-old daughter back here.'

'Shit – no one mentioned that, either.'

'None of my business, but perhaps someone should remind her?'

'Any more skeletons rattling about?'

'Oh yes, your last student also has an unusual past.'

An image of Helen painting naked among the ruins intruded on my mind. 'Her present isn't exactly standard issue, either. Let's have it.'

'She's got form.'

'The beautiful Helen? Just tell me it wasn't manslaughter.'

'She did a full four-year stretch for embezzlement. She only got out quite recently, too.'

Prison. Perhaps that's what she meant when she said she had lived in a small community and not cared for it much. 'Four years? Isn't that rather a lot? Must have been one hell of an embezzlement.'

'It was. She worked for a big finance company and defrauded her employers for ages.'

'Still – four years? You'd get less for mugging little old ladies.'

'No early release, either. Because she refused to reveal where all the money went. They think she has lots of it stashed away somewhere.'

'And what better way to spend your loot than on perpetual painting holidays in the sun?'

'Oh, one or two spring to my mind. Anything else I can help you with today, sir?'

'Was there another name on the list?'

'Yeah, that Kladders or Kludders bloke – you didn't know how to spell him – but I couldn't find anything on him at all.'

Somehow I hadn't really expected Tim to find Kladders whose name I couldn't spell. There'd been something about him – the extremely self-assured manner, perhaps – that made me suspect he would be difficult to pin down.

I had one other business to take care of in town. It took me a moment to get my bearings but, remembering a few of the left turns I had taken last time, I soon found it again, between the stationer's and the draper's.

Inside, I deeply inhaled the kind of aroma you can only produce by continuously brewing coffee and displaying an awful lot of cake in the same room. The selection behind the glass of the counter was dizzying.

My Greek wasn't quite up to the task so I resorted to pointing. '*Aftó, kaí aftó* and – what the hell – *aftó* as well.'

The table right outside the door was free and I chose a chair facing the street junction to settle down for some people-watching. The architecture still looked Italian to me, but the faces and voices were different. Corfiots dressed far more simply then their Italian counterparts did, though naturally by far the worst-dressed around here were the tourists. To a certain degree, I had to include my lightly crumpled self in this, having long cultivated an allergy to steam irons, but at least I wore the same clothes I would back home, while here I saw many an outfit the owner wouldn't dream of wearing down his own high street.

The waiter unloaded shiny chocolate cake, *kataífi* encrusted with pistachios, baklava glistening with honey syrup, coffee and iced water from his tray, and the little boy inside me – the one that always thinks it's other people having all the fun – stopped whining. As I sunk my fork into the shredded puff pastry of the pistachio-bejewelled *kataífi*, I couldn't help thinking that even being a self-employed, piss-poor private eye did have its moments. At least, I thought, I didn't have to run around in a suit and tie in this heat, like that poor chap coming round the corner just then. Looking straight at me. Coming straight towards me. Pushing his sunglasses more firmly up his nose. Walking right up to my table. My fork froze in mid-pastry-piercing.

'Mr Honeysett.' It wasn't a question. He had spoken my name softly and in a tone of disappointment, as though 'What have I always told you about eating foreign cakes?' could well be his next words.

I quickly forked some pastry in my mouth in case they were. 'It is. Who are you?'

He sat down opposite me without my invitation. He was pale. His hands showed a slight tremor that seemed to run through the entire man. Every inch of him appeared to sweat. Was he ill? Or was he scared?

Neither. When he took off his sunglasses, I could see he was in the grip of one hell of a hangover. 'My name's Fletcher. Mr Morton sends me. Your help is no longer required; the matter has now been resolved. I've been instructed to settle up with you.' With a tragic effort, Fletcher tried for a smile, but he fluffed it and half smirked, then gave up. He fumbled a manila envelope from his pocket and found space for it between the cakes on the tiny table.

'What does "been resolved" mean?' I asked, spearing more pastry. 'Has the woman turned up?'

'All some sort of misunderstanding, I believe. I don't really know much about it.' He nudged the envelope another half-inch towards me.

'She's back in Bath, then? Back at work?'

'I believe so. Though I'm told she's transferring. Abroad. Canada, probably.' Fletcher started to nod reassuringly, but hangover pain flickered across his eyes.

'Canada. Nice big place. I haven't yet worked out how much you lot owe me.'

'There's four thousand there. Mr Morton trusts that will cover it.'

'Does he?' His trust was well founded. Even at the rate I was going, four grand would allow me to stay at this table eating baklava all summer. It was roughly twice the amount I'd have charged and I was sure Morton must have known that. Then, why? People don't usually get paid bonuses for not getting results. *Unless, of course, getting no results was the desired result.* I lifted the fat envelope and popped open the flap. Fifties. Also not the usual way supermarkets paid their employees. Something wasn't right, though in quite an acceptable, carrot-cake sort of way. I stuffed the envelope in my jacket without counting the notes, skewered more pastry and smiled benignly at the sweating Fletcher, who looked as if he was fighting the urge to throw up.

'I expect you'll be driving back to England soon?' he asked weakly.

'Yes, almost immediately. I've had enough of this place.'

'Good, good,' he said, with genuine relief in his voice. 'Well, I'll say goodbye, then.'

'Will you? Back to . . . the office? What's your job description?'

He was already turning away. 'Oh, I just happened to be in the area. Goodbye, Mr Honeysett.' He disappeared into the tourist throng.

I called into the shop for more coffee so they'd know I wasn't doing a runner, then walked to the corner around which Fletcher had disappeared. At first I thought he'd vanished, but then I just managed to catch a glimpse of him getting into the back of a silver Mercedes which drove off the instant he'd pulled shut the door.

Back at my little table I sipped coffee and nibbled through the last of my cakes. So, job over, and for once I'd got paid *and* promptly *and* in cash. No receipts required, I noticed; probably petty cash to them. I breathed in deeply. Here I was, full of cake, on a beautiful Mediterranean island. My lover was here, summer was on its way, I had a few grand in my pocket, the euro was wobbling and the exchange rate was good. So what if the Kyla thing was a bit weird and I never found her – you couldn't win them all, so why worry about it?

I worried about it all the way back to the post office. Dialling Morton's number, I steeled myself to fight my way past his secretary. 'The number you have dialled has not been recognized' was all I got, no matter how carefully I dialled the numbers Morton had given me at the restaurant back in Bath. Eventually, I gave up and called Tim again.

'Next time you have a moment, go to Kyla Biggs's address in Marlborough Buildings. See if there's any sign of life. On the ground floor lives an old lady called Walden. She's friendly with Biggs. Tell her you work for me and ask her if Kyla Biggs has been back.'

What possessed me? I had been paid and told everything was fine, I was free to spend the loot on a sunny island and perhaps even get some painting done, and what did I do? I got in the car and headed for trouble.

NINETEEN

'It is a beautiful island, you have to admit.' I was feeling defensive all of a sudden.

'I never said it wasn't. But there's just too much weirdness going on around here to make for a relaxing holiday. At least now that you've been paid, let's rent a room somewhere. Somewhere less . . . weird.' Annis waved her arms at the abandoned village from her vantage point on top of a low drystone wall.

I was sitting nearby on a bald rock, making rapid sketches of anything that caught my eye – collapsed sheds, broken wells, olive trees, and now grasshoppers . . .

I gave up on the grasshoppers. 'It would feel like we're abandoning Morva.' I felt guilty for secretly having entertained the same thoughts of escape on the drive home while the money was trying to burn a room-with-seaview-shaped hole in my pocket.

'But you did tell her we think Margarita is behind all the weird stuff going on.'

'I did, but . . .'

'But she said she's not sure and, anyway, better the devil you know and who's going to do the cooking?'

'Almost word for word.'

'I know, I was listening at the door. So what do you think we'll be able to do for her by staying on? Apart from making her feel less alone – OK, that's obvious – but we can't hang around for ever.'

Stay the summer. Hang around. Hell, stay.

'Well, if you heard all that, then you must know how she feels. She's sunk all her money and hopes and whatnot into this project.'

'It's the whatnots that worry me. I also heard that you didn't tell her what you really think.'

'What do I really think, I wonder?'

'That buying a house in the back of beyond wasn't such a bright idea, no matter how cheap.'

'I think she's long come to that conclusion herself.'

'Also, that not all amateur painters caught the Van Gogh virus and want to stay in monastic cells with only a DIY communal shower.'

'Well . . .'

'Which produces one minute of hot water in every hour.'

'Perhaps . . .'

'And use a long-drop toilet with enough mosquitoes inside to turn you anaemic.'

'Bit of fly spray . . .'

'And a certain lack of nightlife . . . There's someone coming through the trees.'

Through the deep midday shadows under a group of olive trees stumbled Helen. Stumbling, because she was constantly looking behind her as though afraid of being followed. In her right hand she clutched a rock the size of an orange.

'What's up with her?' Annis sat up on the wall. 'Helen? Over here!'

'Oh, hi, it's you.' She looked behind one more time, then walked towards us.

'Don't they say "Beware of painters bearing stones"?' Annis murmured.

'No.'

'They do now.'

'Hi,' Helen said again as she walked up, looking relieved but still tense. 'Mind if I join you for a bit?'

'Go ahead,' I offered. 'You've been taking your rock for a walk.'

'Oh, that.' She dropped it carelessly into the grass. 'I just felt a bit, I don't know. Sounds stupid, but I was painting over there by a ruined house and I became convinced I wasn't alone. I walked all round it and saw nobody, but the feeling never went away. I kept thinking I could hear someone creeping around just on the other side.'

'Could be a dog, a fat tortoise, even . . .' I offered half-heartedly.

'I know, I know. I told myself that, but every time I went

back to painting I'd hear a rustling or a twig snapping. It just suddenly felt really spooky and I had to get out of there. Left my easel and stuff up there and walked away. I know it's silly, but with all the weird things happening just recently . . .'

'You want us to go back with you? Get your stuff?'

Helen looked in the direction she had come from and hesitated. 'Erm, no, I'll just stay here with you a bit if you don't mind.'

'Tell you what, you stay here with Annis and I'll have a look around. Which house is it?'

'It's right back there at the edge – the one with the bougainvillea. You'll see my easel. Don't look at the painting – it's rubbish. But I bet there's nothing up there, I'm sure it's just me.'

Just her.

I found the place by following the direction from which Helen had appeared. You couldn't miss it. The motif she had chosen for her painting was a large farmhouse, one of the most dilapidated, so much so that I suspected it had been a ruin long before the village was abandoned. The roof had completely disappeared and, on closer inspection, the house consisted of only three walls enclosing some overgrown rubble where the interior floors had collapsed long ago. An old bougainvillea still adorned one corner; the rest was romantically ruinous, which presumably was what had caught Helen's painterly eye. I picked my way through the weeds around the melancholic structure and ended up by the easel again. The painting resting on it was in its early stages, yet her intentions were clear to see. I noted with a certain satisfaction that Helen had taken on board some of what I had told her; the contrasts were less strident, allowing the colour to chime and the composition to work more convincingly.

Then I felt it. It was silent. Deadly quiet. Here the cicadas had stopped and there was no wind. The day had rolled to a standstill. Each object my eyes focused on was sharp-edged and washed in hard, bone-bleaching midday sunlight. I moved my foot and the scraping noise on the dry ground sounded amplified and close. My breath hung in the unmoving heat like a question: *What are you doing here?* Now I could hear what Helen had heard: a crick over there, a rustle closer by, a stony chink in the middle distance. Something nibbled insistently at my rational mind, nudging me, urging me to go away.

Helen's grey plastic art box stood open by the foot of the easel, its stepped tiers pulled apart, inviting inspection. All the art materials inside were French, down to the pencils, erasers and drawing pins, which probably meant she had bought the lot at a French art shop. Perhaps she had been on a painting holiday there in the past. Or was France where Helen had hidden her loot from years of defrauding the finance company? Naturally, being hopeless at finance, I instantly imagined it hidden under the floorboards of an isolated cottage deep in the French countryside.

I straightened up and looked about me. On second thoughts, what better place to hide your ill-gotten treasure than right here in this crumbling corner of Corfu? I left everything in place and turned to go. Helen's past was none of my business. She had, as they say, paid her debt to society, and, according to Tim, in full. Did that morally entitle her to keep the money? And if she returned it now, would they give her back the years she spent in prison for it? I felt tempted to ask her whether she thought it had all been worth it.

As I stepped away from the easel and into the shadows under a large olive tree, I felt it before I heard it – like a huge mouth exhaling in an enormous sigh right behind me. Then came the loud crash and thump of falling masonry. Instinctively, I ran without even looking behind. After the crash, a dust cloud overtook me and I stopped and turned.

The cloud of dust still floated like a ghost where moments before I had mused over Helen's French painting gear. The painting had disappeared. The wall of the ruined house had collapsed outward, now just a line of rubble like a stony arm reaching out towards the point where I had stood a moment ago. The little easel was a bundle of splinters; the painting had been flung several feet into the weeds. Miraculously, the art box stood dusty but otherwise untouched. Annis and Helen came rushing through the trees. 'Oh my god, are you OK, Chris?'

'I'm fine, I'm fine. I was already on my way back when it fell. But only just.'

'You could have been killed,' Annis said.

Helen looked pale. 'And *I* could have been killed. If I had stayed here, painting.'

'Quite. Just before it happened, when I was standing looking at your painting, I was beginning to feel uncomfortable. Just like you did – almost scared to be here.'

'We both had a premonition,' Helen concluded.

'Not really; neither of us thought "Hey, that wall is getting ready to fall down".'

'Well, not all premonitions are that precise. It's obvious, Chris, that you and I have a sixth sense for these things.'

Annis rolled her eyes and walked off to inspect what was left of the house, keeping a respectful distance from the tottering masonry.

'My painting – where's that got to?'

'It's over here.' I pulled it out of the weeds and blew the dust off it.

'Might as well chuck it away.'

'No, it looks OK. I mean, it doesn't look to be damaged.' I handed it to her.

She dropped it back on the ground. 'Well, I'm hardly going to finish it now, am I?' She gestured at the ruin. 'The bloody thing has half disappeared and taken the bougainvillea with it.'

'Yes. Don't you just hate it when your models fidget?'

Annis sank deeper into her multicoloured chair outside the *psistaría* and sipped beer straight from the bottle. 'I'm glad we came out here tonight.'

It was early evening in Neo Makriá and the grill had only just opened its doors to customers. Like everywhere around the Mediterranean, people in Greece ate late, but while the charcoal grill heated we had been furnished with bread, a dish of shiny black olives and bottles of Amstel beer.

'You've had enough of the ghost village?' I asked.

'For today, yes. And I'm probably not the only one. I think Helen has had just about all she can stomach. She seemed quite spooked even before the wall nearly fell on her.'

'Fell on *her*? It nearly flattened *me*! Helen was nowhere near it.'

'Yeah, OK, but if she hadn't walked away when she did . . . and now she can't even finish her painting. Rob had one painting disappear. That never turned up again, did it? Not exactly brilliant for a painting school. It's not like they'll go home at the end of their holiday and recommend the place to friends and family.'

'I don't think any of them want to talk to friends and family much. Where did Morva find that lot? I suppose strange places attract strange people.'

'That includes us, you know.'

'Oh yes.' I had known that for a long time.

'If Helen really has all that money squirrelled away some-where, do you think they're still trying to find out what she's done with it? And try to get it off her?'

'If it's enough money, I'm sure they'll have a go.'

'I wouldn't want to have to look over my shoulder for the rest of my life. Who would come after her – the police?'

'It's possible. But more likely someone like me, a private eye, sent by the insurers or the company she defrauded. She must have wondered when I first got here if I was who I said I was.'

'Actually, I think she quite fancies you.'

'Helen? I doubt it.' I thought back to the drunken night under the olive tree. 'But I think she would like to make sure of me.'

'Oh yes, that she would. Here comes the food.'

Vegetables were predictably not a forte of the local grill. Meat and the ability to pay for it still being a sign of status in the islands, the *psistaría* was where you went to see it cooked quickly over fierce heat and served with a minimum of interference from the plant kingdom, the presence of a few tomatoes and sprigs of parsley being largely symbolic. What it lacked in nutritional balance, it made up in salty savouriness.

'If Tim really does make it out here, he'll try to move in next door,' I predicted when at last I pushed back my empty plate, feeling a stone heavier.

'Yeah, I can see that happen. Getting him to eat anything that isn't brown is hard work. More beer?'

'No, not just yet. Tell you what, let's go for a stroll and come back for another beer afterwards,' I suggested.

We walked west on the tarmac road out of the village, soon leaving the houses, the scent of charcoal grills and the stare of curious eyes behind. Turning down a rutted dirt path at random, we were soon surrounded by well-tended olive groves. Or were they? Here and there, ancient limbs of these massive trees had been expertly propped up to prevent them from breaking under their own weight. Yet I had noticed before that maintenance of the trees and the ground between them appeared to die away only a few yards from the roadside, like window dressing for whoever used the tarmac roads.

These were age-old groves that had been in cultivation for centuries, where each gnarled tree had grown into its own distinct shape. As the wind caught their crowns, they appeared to me like a group of bent old men with wild hair, and they definitely had a neglected look.

Our rutted path joined a broader though no less churned-up dirt road. The sun set behind us. Here the trees looked well pruned again and without tell-tale suckers at their bases. The dusky spaces between them created an atmosphere perfect for private dreams. We walked on quietly in the deepening shadows for a few minutes until a high chain-link fence came into view. The path led straight up to a broad gate which stood ajar.

The place looked familiar. 'I know where we are now. It's the entrance to the Thalassa Organic Oil Co-op.' Yes, it was the exact place where I had encountered the unfriendly convoy of luxury cars. Only this time the gate was unlocked. Something else was different, too. 'There's only one problem with this: it has magically changed its name to the Achillion Organic Olive Oil Co-op.'

'Are you sure?'

'Definitely – same place, same track, same road. Different name. It was Thalassa before; it means "sea" or "ocean".'

'Ocean Olive Oil? We bought a bottle of that once, from your man's supermarket no less. I remember you moaning about the price.'

'With an ocean wave curling round an olive on the label? Yeah, I remember that.'

'There you go; perhaps it changed hands.'

'Perhaps. Perhaps not.' I pushed the gate, just wide enough to squeeze through. 'Getting the name of your estate known and getting it on to supermarket shelves is every grower's dream. Changing the name would be idiotic.'

'Everything else constantly gets renamed,' Annis objected.

'I know, but olive oil isn't like bathroom cleaner or chocolate bars. It's more like whisky or champagne. Everyone I have met so far has something to do with this olive oil co-op. This –' I pushed the gate open another squeaking inch or two – 'is why Kyla Biggs came here, and I'm convinced she came through this gate. I can practically smell her perfume. Let's have a look around inside.' We squeezed through the gate and started down the track which gently curved away to the left.

Annis wasn't convinced of the wisdom of this. 'And if we meet some of the inmates, you are planning to say what, exactly?'

'I'll be saying "Run like hell" or something similar. Unless we meet the guy with the shotgun. Then it's "Run like hell but try to zigzag a bit".'

'Remind me: was it a double-barrelled shotgun?'

We hadn't walked ten yards before we heard a car engine start up and headlights illuminate the trees a hundred yards or so further on. I pulled Annis off the track and we dived for cover in a patch of wild flowers. I was hoping it would be dark enough down here to be quite invisible from the car that came up towards the gate. It was the BMW, still with its top down. Driving it was the same guy as before and in the passenger seat slouched the spiky-haired man with the shotgun. The car stopped level with us; we dug our noses deeper into the flowers. The passenger got out, carrying his shotgun in the crook of his arm, and opened the gate for the driver, who left without him. After he'd closed and locked the gate, Spiky stood a moment in the gathering darkness, then a match flared and briefly illuminated his face as he touched it to a cigarette. He walked back the way he had come.

We waited a while before brushing ourselves down and

getting back on to the track. 'The guy in the car was the one who told me to go away that time just before the crop sprayer arrived.'

'Crop sprayer? Are you sure?'

'Yes, a helicopter – why?'

'You sure it was spraying these trees?'

'Yes, it went back and forth, I could see the stuff wafting down.'

'Not allowed if it's meant to be organic. That's what you pay for – no pesticides, no fungicides, no post-harvest chemicals. Nothing artificial at all.'

'No wonder they didn't want me here when the helicopter arrived. I wasn't thinking of the *organic* bit. If they're flogging ordinary extra virgin as organic, then that's serious fraud. The difference in price is huge. We're not talking a bit of farmgate leg-pulling here.'

'That might explain how struggling olive farmers are driving large Beemers.'

We had been talking very quietly as we walked carefully in the middle of the track, when a bright light lit up the area ahead and loud, carefree voices sounded close by. We dived for cover once more, this time to the right where the light was dimmest. Even so, we had to keep going quite a way before we felt we were safely out of sight again. In the brief moment before we scarpered, the light had revealed a huddle of low, simple buildings and sheds. The male voices called brashly in Greek to each other.

'I don't suppose you understand any of that?' Annis whispered.

'Yes, his hovercraft is full of eels.'

'I thought you learned *loads* on the way down here.'

'I did. And as soon as they ask the way to the post office we're in business.'

After some banging and clanging noises a small engine started up. Moments later a quad bike pulling a trailer came bouncing through the trees. It made straight for us. In the dark, we had managed to take 'cover' right next to a dirt path between the trees, just wide enough to let a bloke with a quad bike demonstrate his racing credentials. We scrambled away behind a large tree trunk just in time. Once it had passed we watched the quad and trailer disappear along the path until it stopped some hundred yards away, near what looked like a shed. Closer to hand, at one-minute intervals, a hollow kind of banging sound came from the direction of the buildings.

'I wonder what's going on there?'

'Sounds like someone's banging a badly tuned drum,' Annis suggested.

'Apart from the chef at the grill twiddling the skewers, it could be the first possible evidence of work around here. I think that needs investigating. Follow me.'

'Just what I had in mind for a night out,' Annis grumbled. 'Crawling on all fours through a dodgy olive estate.'

'Just to the edge of the light; we should be able to see from there.'

What we could see from there was indeed something resembling work. Three low buildings were surrounding a gravelled yard in a loose horseshoe. Two appeared to be large modern sheds associated with olive oil production; the one nearest us looked like a prefab office. In front of it stood a table with chairs and, next to that, a large metal barbecue. The area was only lit by three light bulbs dangling from a cable strung between the buildings and by the light falling through the open door of one of the sheds. Somewhere in the background I could hear the purr of a diesel generator.

At regular intervals spiky-haired shotgun man appeared in the square doorway of the long concrete building on the far side, each time carrying a blue plastic barrel which he flung into the yard where already a collection of twenty or so lay at haphazard angles. He had put his shotgun to rest against the wall beside the door, suggesting that he liked to keep it to hand. He didn't much enjoy his work, judging by the short-tempered grunt he produced each time he flung another barrel towards the growing heap.

'Those barrels look familiar,' Annis observed.

'*Findik*.'

'Speak for yourself.'

'Turkish hazelnut oil, I shouldn't wonder. But I'd like to be sure. Wait here.'

'Are you mad, where are you going?'

'I'm going to go have a quick look, just to make sure.'

'Just to make sure you get caught? I'm just about ready for that beer you offered.'

'I counted and he takes about forty seconds to fetch each one. Plenty of time for me to get to the nearest barrel. Then I'll take cover and come back when he's gone inside for the next. Then we'll get out of here and have that beer.' Spiky went inside and I loped across to the heap of barrels, all the while counting the seconds. I got there in twenty. Hey, I might even make it back in one go before he emerged. I went down on all fours to examine the print around the rim of the closest barrel. All the writing was in French and Arabic. I was so confounded by it that I didn't notice Spiky was back until he flung his next barrel with a loud grunt in my direction. It hit the ones in front of me and bounced straight over my head. I risked a peak at him. He hadn't moved and showed no sign of wanting to go back in. Instead, he sauntered across to a chair by the barbecue where he flounced down and lit a cigarette. He was wearing a black tee shirt tonight with a lurid red inscription across his chest proclaiming 'Have a Stake in the Future – Become a Vampire'. Spiky had left his shotgun leaning against the outside of the long shed. If he did spot me, he would have to get there before he could shoot me full of holes, which might be enough time to dive into the darkness and make my escape. I hoped Annis would take to her heels at the same time.

Some distance behind me, I could hear the engine of the quad bike. The first thing the quad rider would see was me sniffing around in the middle of the yard. Spiky had heard it too, grunted and got to his feet. Now I could hear his footsteps crunch on the gravel as he started to set each container the right way up. It wouldn't take a minute before he saw me lying like an idiot with my nose to one of them. This time my nose didn't say *findik*; it said *definitely olive oil*. Some French isn't that hard; even I understood what *Produit du Maroc* meant. No wonder Spiky kept his shotgun close.

It always works in the movies. I picked up a stone and lobbed it away from me into the trees. The sound was drowned

out by the banging of barrel on gravel. Try the other side. I
aimed at the roof of the office prefab and missed. The stone
pinged on the barbecue. This time it got the man's attention.
He barked a short question at the darkness beyond the pool
of light, then turned and went for his gun. I sprinted off in
the opposite direction, and in the corner of my eye saw Annis
jump up and do the same. I heard a shout behind me and knew
he'd noticed me, but by then I'd moved out of the circle of
light. In the dark between the trees, I zigzagged like a hare.
Only, quite unlike a hare, I had only a vague idea of where I
was going and it didn't take long before my foot caught on
something unseen and I landed flat on my face. Close behind
came the panting Spiky. I lay still and tried not to breathe.
Realizing he could no longer hear me, he stopped to listen.
Far to the left, Annis's fast footfall could be heard. Spiky
didn't waste much time swearing and ran straight past me in
the new direction. I got up and kept on going straight until I
saw the fence appear in the gloom. I shouted, '*Ela tho!*' I had
no idea whether shouting 'Come here' in a dodgy Greek accent
would fool him into thinking I was a local, but I was hoping
it might once more make him follow me instead of Annis.
Then I flung myself at the fence. It seemed to make the loudest
noise I had ever heard. Clawing my way up the links I was
hoping Annis was doing the same further along. The top of
the fence was the worst, swaying this way and that, nearly
pitching me back down until I managed to heave myself over
the top and drop all the way to the ground on the other side.

I might easily have missed Annis in the thin starlight had
she not hissed 'Honeypot' at me as I flew past her. Behind us,
the lights of the quad bike approached and flew through the
gate. We held hands as we ran off at an angle away from
the track for a couple of hundred yards, then stood behind a
tree, panting. The quad bike, still with its trailer bouncing
behind it, rattled away towards the road.

'I hope you've satisfied your olive oil curiosity now,' Annis
whispered.

'I have for tonight. And I'm ready for that beer now.'

TWENTY

'You're lucky you caught me in, mate; I'm off to the airport in about ten minutes.'

'Really?' I hesitated. That meant it was probably a bit late to tell Tim not to bother. Last night, over several post-olive-estate beers, Annis and I had argued long and hard about whether to say farewell to this strange corner of Greece and drop a hint to the police or to stay on Corfu. For the moment I had won – we were staying. But for how long? 'All right, what time do you touch down? I'll pick you up.'

'Don't bother; I've rented a car – part of the package, actually. I'll find you.'

'Won't be easy.'

'You forget – unlike you, I've got an excellent sense of direction.'

'The place is quite hidden away.'

'Rubbish, mate. Never heard of Google Earth? Nothing's all that hidden any more. I'll be there.'

'Did you have a chance to check if Kyla Biggs is back?'

'I did; talked to her neighbour yesterday. Nice old lady – she even made me a cup of tea. According to her, Kyla hasn't been back. Not a sign of her or anyone else. No movement in the flat and her car is still there.'

'I thought so, yet Morton sent someone to pay me off, saying she's back and moving to Canada.'

'Are you going there next?'

'No.'

'Shame. I suppose you know you're out of maple syrup?'

'I think Kyla Biggs stumbled on some huge olive oil swindle down here and it may have cost her. Before you shoot out of the door, could you look something up for me?'

'You're a pest, but yeah, go on.'

'Look up Ocean Olive Oil and Achillion Olive Oil.'

'One tick.' I could hear him hammer away at a keyboard

at lightning speed. 'OK, what d'you want to know? *Ocean* Organic Olive Oil is your current employer's flagship Greek oil. The podgy little TV chef is promoting it for them on telly at the moment. The other one – *Achillion* – is exclusive to the supermarket you *would* shop in if you weren't always broke. That do yer?'

'I think so.'

'Good, gotta go. See you later.'

'Oh, one more thing . . .'

'Yes, Columbo, but make it quick.'

'How long have they been selling Achillion oil?'

'It doesn't say, but this newspaper link is three years old so at least that long, I should think.'

'Interesting . . .'

'Absolutely fascinating, but I'm out of here.'

It was another cricket-sawn afternoon; Corfu was baking under a flawless sky. Morva sent me shopping. 'Your friend arriving here is a good excuse for a feast. And we need to keep the students happy; I want their stay to be memorable.'

'Morv, I don't think any of them are going to forget it in a hurry.'

'*Happy* memories – that's what I want them to take away. And hang the expense; it's their last week, after all.' She pressed some euro notes into my reluctant hand.

'All right. What do you want me to get?'

'No idea; you're the cook.'

'I am? What happened to Margarita?'

'She's stormed off again. I think she's gone for good this time. The mere mention of an extra guest and she made off on her moped.'

'You really don't think she's coming back?'

'I know she's quit before and come back; but not this time, I think. As she was grabbing her stuff, she was saying "I told him it wouldn't work anyway". Whatever that meant.'

'I think it meant she was sent up here, probably by her dad, to sabotage your art school venture. I'm pretty sure that's why she was the only one you could find to work for you.'

'I expect you're right. And she took her lucky cooking pot and spoon with her.'

'Ah, that sounds serious.' I had mixed feelings about Margarita's departure. On the one hand, it might mean fewer accidents up here, but, on the other, it almost certainly meant I was wearing the apron, at least until Morva's students left. Fair enough: it was time to earn my keep.

I rattled round the mountain in the little Citroën, not stopping in Neo Makriá, until I came to a large village called Sinapádes. The contrast to Neo Makriá was instantly noticeable. People were walking around as though they had things to do. There were even a few tourists and a couple of shops catering for them. I left the car near the big village square and went shopping. In a place where most people grew their own vegetables, greengrocers were few and far between, but here I managed to find all I needed. As I was shopping for eight people now, none of whom were vegetarians and one of whom was Tim, I bought the better part of a dead sheep at the village butchers. I spent what money was left on bottles of Henninger and lugged it all back to the car.

Perhaps as I drove off I was preoccupied with how I was going to cook all the food now crowding the boot; otherwise, I'd have noticed Gloves straight away. When I did spot her in the driving mirror, it was only because she was noisily clearing her throat. I stood on the brakes and Gloves shot forward, ending half wedged between the front seats and swearing in unladylike fashion.

Like an idiot, I started apologizing while looking around for something to hit her with. 'Sorry, didn't notice you weren't wearing your seat belt.'

Gloves unwedged herself with a groan. 'You didn't notice anything much,' she said, upright once more. She let herself slump back against the backrest and looked out of the window at some kids who were staring at the car because of the emergency braking. 'Have you given up looking for her, then?' She waved unsmilingly with a leather-gloved hand at the kids who moved away.

'What makes you think I've given up looking?'

'You stopped asking questions. You haven't shown her picture to anyone for ages. You've started behaving like a tourist – nights out, country walks. Pedalo hire next, I suppose.'

Now that I'd got over the initial shock of finding her in my car, this was beginning to get me narked, especially since I already felt guilty enough about not having found her. 'I don't think we've been introduced. I'm Chris Honeysett. Who the hell are you?'

'Louise Mabey.'

'Have you been following me across Europe to *maybe* be Louise in the back of a hire car?'

'You hired this thing? You're stranger than I thought.'

'Stranger than you could imagine. So why?'

'I'm Kyla's girlfriend. Well . . . *ex*-girlfriend now.'

'Ex? You do think she's dead, then?'

'No, I don't think she's dead; she dumped me.'

'Oh no, please don't tell me Kyla's disappearance is about you two splitting up.'

'That's not what I'm saying. And I don't see how it could be since we split up a couple of months back and she did the dumping.'

'Then, what's your theory?'

'I'm not sure. I was hoping you'd have one. She came to this island – I know that much – and I don't think she left again, though I couldn't tell you exactly why I think that. I just feel it. She's here.'

I thought of Sophie who felt that leaving the island would be a betrayal of her son, even though she knew he was dead. How much more impossible, then, to leave the island if you're convinced the object of your love is here, but hidden somewhere, alive. 'How long will you go on looking for her?'

'I took two weeks' holiday and that's running out now. But I'm not sure I care; I'll stay for as long as it takes.'

'No, don't do that or they'll send someone like me down here to find you and the thing goes on for ever.'

'Alive or dead, Kyla is here, and I think nobody is keen for you or me to find her.'

'I had noticed that. Most people I've met so far have been friendly in quite a menacing sort of way. Or maybe menacing in quite a friendly way; I haven't made up my mind yet. You came here on holiday together – when was that?'

'You found that much out, then.'

'Hang on.' I dug the Polaroid I had pinched off the wall in Niko's Taverna from my wallet and held it up for her perusal. 'There. You, *maybe* Louise, Kyla, Niko from the eponymous taverna and another guy. Who is he?'

Gloves took the picture and tilted it against the light. 'Oh yeah, that's us last summer. I don't look too happy there, do I? We had to waste an entire evening being polite to these two. Kyla had had dealings with them when she was here before on business. The other guy is a local olive oil bigwig, and Niko from the taverna is involved in the business, as well. And they both fancied her, too. Boy, was I bored.'

'What kind of business had Kyla been here for? Supermarket business?'

'Yes. Kyla is a buyer – a food buyer. Well, she wasn't then; she was just assisting someone else. She took over from him last year.'

'They bought olive oil for the supermarket?'

'Yes. Posh, single-estate stuff. It's getting rare. There's not that many around – not good ones, anyway. The other guy in the picture is called Sotiris Something-or-other. Talk of things oily.' She handed back the picture. 'Is it just me or is it like an oven in here?'

'It's like an oven in here. We really have to talk about this properly. Why don't you come up to the village and we'll stick our heads together, see what we've got?' I restarted the engine.

'Not in this thing, thanks; I've seen how it drives. I'll follow you in my car.'

'All right. You've had enough practice.'

Back at Ano Makría, Gloves performed a six-point turn by the holly oaks and left the big Toyota parked with the nose aimed downhill. In case of a quick getaway? Just because she claimed to be Kyla's ex-girlfriend didn't mean I had to trust her, but so far she'd been quite convincing.

She stood on the path by the churchyard and took in the sights. 'Looks a lot better in daylight.'

'You've come here at night?'

'Several times. Me and God-knows-who-else. I came up

one night and there were two sets of people crawling about
the village, one spying on you, another spying on them and
me spying on all of you. For a ghost village, the place is
bloody busy.'

'Did you recognize any of them?'

'I had the feeling that one lot may have been local plod.'

'Hard to know just how plodding they are.'

'And I think I recognized the chap who runs the cafe in
Neo Makriá.'

'Dimitris. Talking of spying, how did you know I was going
to Corfu in the first place? I don't remember advertising it.'

'But you did. I was right there on the pavement in
Marlborough Buildings when you said goodbye to Kyla's
downstairs neighbour. You didn't notice me then, either. I was
trying to find Kyla; Mrs Walden said you were going off to
find her, so I followed you. It wasn't difficult. Bloody expensive, but not difficult.'

'Why be so secretive? Why didn't you make yourself
known? We could have pooled resources earlier.'

'Is that what we're doing here, pooling resources?' she said
doubtfully. She stood, arms akimbo, in front of me on the goat
track, looking for something in my eyes. She was still wearing
black leather gloves.

'Take off your gloves.'

She shook her head. 'No.' But she turned and walked in
front of me towards the house now while she talked. 'You
were hired by Morton. I don't trust John Morton, I don't trust
the supermarket. I don't trust, full stop.' She walked along as
though she knew the way.

'You don't trust the supermarket?'

'No. And especially Morton. He's a troubleshooter, a
specialist at burying things. If you ask me, he hired you *not*
to find Kyla. No offence.'

'He hired me to see how well she was hidden. And now
he's paid me off. The question is: did he pay me off because
I got close or because I didn't?'

'There's no telling until you do. But people like Morton
don't usually reward failure. If he paid you, then you did what
he wanted you to.'

'I was told she had turned up, gone back to Bath and was now going to work for the company in Canada.'

'Did you believe it?'

'I didn't. I checked and she's not been back.'

At the entrance to the courtyard, Gloves stopped. When I drew level with her, I could see why. Everybody was there, including Annis, sitting in a wide circle, drawing. They were drawing Charlie who was posing naked by the well with a stoneware pitcher in a mock Greek-urn pose. 'So it really is an art-schooly place.'

'Yes, though when I left, the naked water sprite was still only a half-naked builder. The life-drawing thing is a new development. Bound to happen sooner or later, I suppose.'

Annis noticed us first. She clocked Gloves's gloves and put down her pad and pencil. I nodded my head towards the house and told Gloves to follow me. 'I'll have to get this stuff into the kitchen and start preparing tonight's food. It'll take ages.'

Annis followed us in and I made the introductions. 'This is Annis, my accomplice; this is *maybe* Louise, aka Gloves. Kyla's ex.'

'Welcome to the weirdness.'

A few explanations later and the girls were drinking coffee, while I stood at the kitchen table peeling a kilo and a half of tiny onions for the *stifado* I was cooking. It was agony. 'So Charlie's been promoted to life model? Or is it demoted?' I sniffed.

'Morva thought life drawing was one of the things that was missing on her course. Apparently, she had toyed with the idea of asking you, but thought she knew what you'd be saying.'

'Yeah: not bloody likely.'

'Exactly. Sophie and Helen are certainly drawing with renewed vigour, I noticed, though I'm not so sure Rob is enamoured with the idea of staring at naked builders for hours.'

'It wouldn't do much for me, either,' said Gloves.

I changed the subject. 'Gloves . . . sorry, Louise recognized one of the guys in the Polaroid: he's an olive oil bigwig. I think our excursion to the olive estate may not have been so irrelevant after all.' Only a handful of onions peeled and I'd gone blind with tears. 'Excuse me,' I said snottily and went outside to blow my nose. My jacket still hung on the back of a chair in the courtyard. I liberated the group picture with Kyla that Tim had mailed me from its lining and went back inside. Kyla looked quite different in the two pictures. 'Which one's more typical?' I asked.

'Oh, the holiday one. The managerial face is pure acting. Kyla wasn't like that at all; at home she was more like a kid. Teenage movies and computer games,' she said lightly, then suddenly her face fell. 'Did I say "was"? I said "was", didn't I?'

'Because she's your ex. That's normal,' Annis assured her. 'It doesn't mean anything.'

'I'm hellishly superstitious. Not black-cats-'n'-ladders superstitious. I know it's nonsense, but on some level I always feel that we make things happen, that words make things happen.'

'Words do make things happen. But not magically. Words are real; they can become things. Facts, anyway. It's called civilization.'

They were getting deep quickly over their cups of coffee. 'Any chance of a hand with peeling these onions? There's millions of them.'

'Yeah, all right.' They put down their cups and armed themselves with knives.

'Great, that means I can prepare the lamb.' Words do make things happen. It's called delegation.

Louise still hadn't taken off her soft black leather gloves. As she watched her pick up an onion and begin to peel it, Annis asked, 'Do you ever take those off?'

Louise stopped, sighed. Deliberately, she put down the onion and knife and tugged off one of her gloves. 'Only if I'm lecturing people on what not to do in the event of a chip-pan fire.'

'No wonder . . . no, I mean . . . that looks painful.'

'I was lucky. By a miracle, it somehow missed my face. But it didn't miss much else.'

'Could they do something with plastic surgery?'

'This is *after* plastic surgery.'

'I'm sorry.'

'Easy mistake to make, don't worry. But hey, at least I'm

only "Gloves", not "The girl in the leather mask".' She pulled her glove back on and picked up her knife and onion.

After the meat had been browned, the cinnamon, cloves, onions and tomato added and the big dish shoved in a slow oven, I cleared up the mess. I picked up the photograph to put back in my jacket. *Wait a minute.* So far I had only ever looked at Kyla, the other faces simply filed away as 'other supermarket employees'. I took the photo next door into the studio where I had seen a large magnifying glass on a stand. I took it off the shelf and shoved the picture under it. No doubt about it: the face next to Kyla belonged to the bored-looking man in the back of the BMW. He'd been at the Lord Byron restaurant, too. I took it outside where Annis and Louise were watching the students struggle with Charlie's naked form. Metaphorically speaking. Though I suspected one or two of them also had a more literal interest. I put the picture in front of Louise on the table and tapped the figure next to Kyla. 'Who is he?'

She barely gave it another glance. 'That's Sanders. He was then her boss; she took over from him last year.'

'And what's Mr Sanders do now, do you know?'

'Why are you interested in him? He quit. Left the company. I don't know where he went next.'

'I do. He went here. I saw him leave the olive oil co-op and I saw him again at a restaurant along with a load of shady characters, like your oily Sotiris and Niko from the other photograph.'

'Interesting.'

'More than interesting. I don't know whether Annis has told you, but we paid the oil co-op a visit and one of several curious things we found was—' But I didn't manage to finish the sentence as two things happened at the same time: the drawing session finished and Tim Bigwood turned up.

Woolly of hair, though certainly not of mind, Tim had had no problem finding us, just as he had predicted. 'Finding space to leave the car was the tricky bit. Quite a collection of automotive junk you have up here, to go with the tottering architecture, I presume. Toyotas excluded, naturally,' he said with a nod to Louise, whom he recognized as its driver from my description.

We spent a while bringing Tim up to speed, though he made it quite clear that he had come here for sun, sea and sand. 'The coldest and wettest spring since records began, pretty much everywhere except down here. Expect an invasion round Easter. Is that your cooking I can smell, Chris? I'm starving.'

Naturally, Louise was asked to stay. After another hour bashing around in the kitchen I managed to produce a convincing feast for Morva with the lamb *stifado* as a centrepiece, and just before sunset nine of us sat down to supper at the long table in the courtyard. Margarita, of course, would have thrown a medium-sized fit being asked to cook for this many people. Since I had turned up less than two weeks ago, the population of the ghost village had more than doubled, a fact that couldn't have escaped Morva's enemies at the village. I raised my beer glass in a silent toast to Margarita and wondered when the next ghost-village resident would turn up. As it happened, I didn't have long to wait before I found out.

TWENTY-ONE

'd have preferred Charlie in naked quietude, but it was the din of half-naked cement mixing that made me jump out of bed late next morning, surprisingly unencumbered by any hangover. One look at the groaning dehydrated form I had left behind under the sheets reminded me that, unlike her, I had avoided the local wine that apparently went so well with lamb.

Apart from Charlie toiling at the other end of the courtyard, there was no one to be seen, so, after taking the Desiccated One a glass of orange juice to help with her reconstitution, I prepared Turkish breakfast. Well, there were today no Greeks to offend, who, by their own admission, didn't go in for breakfast much anyway. I had no idea where everyone else was, but I was one hundred per cent certain that Tim was still asleep in the finished room next to ours. I am, of course, quite often one hundred per cent wrong about things, but I could hear Tim snore – and nobody snores like Tim.

'What's Turkish breakfast?' he asked suspiciously, not quite admitting to being awake.

'Tea, orange juice, boiled eggs, olives, feta cheese, sliced tomatoes, butter, honey, jam and, sadly in our case, yesterday's bread.'

He opened one eye. 'Real orange juice?'

'Carton.'

He opened the other eye. 'Still . . .'

Charlie was levelling the cement floor on the last room, two doors down from Tim's. 'Fancy a second breakfast? It's on the table.'

'In a minute. I have to finish this before it sets.'

'You're really getting them done quickly.' In fact, I could have sworn he had only just finished the room Tim was in. I laid a hand on the door handle of the third room. 'Has this one got a bed in it yet? We could have offered it to Louise; save her driving back to her *pensión* last night.'

'No, we couldn't! I mean, no, it hasn't.' Charlie backed out of the room he had been working on. 'I haven't done the floor in that one yet.'

I opened the door on the third room.

'See, still a mess,' Charlie said. 'Breakfast, did you say? Lead me to it.' It was the worst impression of unconcerned-builder talk I had ever heard.

The room was full of junk. Strange junk. A lot more junk than I seemed to remember from when I first looked at the place. Some of it I had definitely seen before, probably by the ruined house with the cistern.

I dropped an octave down to my schoolmaster's voice. 'Charlie . . .?'

'Yes, Chris.'

'This is the most *arty* pile of junk I have ever seen.'

He shrugged apologetically. 'Yes, Chris.'

'It's an amateur-dramatics barricade, Charlie.'

'I know, Chris.'

'Who built it?'

'I had nothing to do with it; Morva did it.' This primary school thing was catching.

'Why?'

'It's only until everybody has left, she said.'

'Why?'

Tim emerged from next door. 'I'm ready for your Turkish breakfast.'

'Go ahead; it's on the table. We'll join you in a minute. I think. You were saying, Charlie?'

He lowered his voice to a murmur. 'I found something. When I started preparing the floor. I thought it was a bag of rubbish at first but it wasn't. It's a body, Chris. There's someone buried in there.'

'And you piled junk . . . What *kind* of a body?'

'A really dead one.'

'*Charlie* . . .'

'It's not her. It's not that woman you were looking for. I'm pretty sure it's a bloke. Definitely a bloke, actually.'

'Let me get this straight: you found a dead body in there,

but you thought it was really *quite* a good place for him? *Best* to just leave him there? *No point* bothering the police with trivial stuff?'

'Hey, first she wanted me to simply put the cement floor over him, but I refused.'

'Heroic stuff.'

'She said she'll call the police once everyone's gone home. Morva doesn't want the police here while her students are around. Bad for business. Too much to explain.'

'I'd say.'

'She hasn't really . . . registered the business as such. Tax-wise. Or the building for business use. Couldn't really, with the sanitary arrangements being what they are . . .'

'Crap. I don't care. Dead bodies don't simply appear; there's usually blunt instruments involved. Or pointy ones. With thoroughly unpleasant people at the other end of them.'

'He must have been there for ages.'

'You're an expert on human decomposition now.'

'Well, it's not a very fresh corpse – like, it didn't smell or anything. Must have been there a few years.'

'He is right, you know.'

I whirled round. Dr Kalogeropoulos was giving me a thoroughly unprofessional look through his bottle-glass spectacles. 'You knew about this?' I just hate it when everyone seems to know more than me. Although I should be used to it by now.

'Not all along. But I have taken an interest lately. For Morva's sake.'

'Who is he? Was he?'

'Petros Grapsas.'

'Ah, well, that explains everything. I'll get some more junk to pile on top of him, shall I?'

'He was a kind of tax inspector. Investigating fraud. Killed by accident. Apparently.'

'By accident.'

'A scuffle. He fell, hit his head on something.'

'Apparently.'

'Indeed. They panicked and hid the body. It happened before I came back here, so he's been in there a while.'

'And, of course, they thought a deserted village was a good

place to stash him. What a disappointment. Why didn't they just stick him in the graveyard?'

'Probably too scared; you know how superstitious people are around here.'

'No wonder they weren't keen on Morva moving in and doing the place up.'

'A couple of villagers came up one night, during the last thunderstorm, to try to move the body, but they couldn't remember where exactly they'd put him in the first place and gave up.'

'I think I saw them as they came past the motorhome,' said Charlie.

'Did you? The villagers were hoping that if they made sure she didn't find a builder willing to do the job, Morva would give up. But then Mr Honeysett here turned up.'

'I knew it would turn out to be my fault.'

'You brought Charlie here.'

Charlie crossed his arms in front of his chest and nodded in agreement: all your fault.

'Well, we can't just forget about him, *even if he was a tax inspector,*' I said loudly for the benefit of Morva who had just entered the courtyard.

She had the decency to put on a sheepish expression. 'It's only until tomorrow; then I'll call the police. Honestly,' she said. 'Did you come up to see me, doctor?'

'No, not you.'

'Oh, OK,' she said and beat a hasty retreat towards the other end of the courtyard to join Tim at the table.

'Well, that's all sorted, then,' Charlie said cheerfully and went the same way.

That left the doctor and me looking at one another for a few heartbeats. 'You've come to see me, then,' I concluded.

He sighed heavily. 'Perhaps we could take a little walk.'

Making Turkish breakfast in Greece had, of course, been tempting fate. Reluctantly, I followed the doctor out of the courtyard. He struck out at a surprising pace into the heart of the ruined village. We passed Helen who was sketching another ruin from a respectful distance. The doctor squinted in the direction of my wave. 'Is there somebody?'

'Helen, over there, in the shade under the walnut.'

'I'll have to take your word for it.'

'Your eyesight is really quite bad, isn't it? I noticed that before.'

'Failing. Failing fast, in fact. A year or two and I'll be practically blind.'

'I'm sorry to hear that. Can't they . . . operate or something?'

'No. It's congenital; there's no way of stopping it. I shouldn't be driving, really; I only get away with it because I've known the roads around here all my life.'

'What will you do when . . . you know? Can you go on practising? As a doctor?'

'Of course not.'

'Anything I can do?'

We had reached a squat deserted farm building and its skeleton crew of outbuildings. He halted by a convoluted fig tree. 'Is there anyone close by?'

'Not that I can see.'

'Well, there *is* something you can do. Go away. If you don't, the local police will soon find a way to get you off the island, anyway.'

'Has this to do with Kyla Biggs?'

'You've been sniffing around the olive oil co-op.'

'The one that mysteriously changes its name?'

'The village has a lot invested in that business. *My mother* has. *I* have – everything I had. I wasn't entirely sure what I let myself in for then, but it's too late now. The income will be important once my eyesight goes completely. Not just for me and my mother; many people in the village rely on the co-op.'

'Where is Kyla?'

'I'm not sure.'

'She's alive?'

'I think so. Yes. Yes, she is. Look, they are not bad people, but they've got themselves mixed up with mafia types and they are quite ruthless, I assure you. Kyla suspected something was not right and decided to do a bit of investigating. And got caught doing it. They were supposed to get rid of her, but they didn't. They're not murderers.'

'Tell that to Mr Junkman down at Morva's place. So where is she?'

'They've pretended to the mafia lot that they got rid of her. They didn't want to harm her, but they couldn't just let her go, so they're keeping her hidden somewhere. She's fine. But unless they find a way to make sure she doesn't expose the scheme, they can't really let her go home. No one knows what to do about it.'

'Have you seen her?'

'No, I'm not that involved. It's best not to get too . . . close.'

'So there's obviously fraud involved. How does it work?'

'It all started quite small, the usual thing – EU subsidies. There's never been a real survey of who owns which trees. So, to get maximum EU subsidies, everyone registered the same huge number of trees. From the aerial pictures, one tree looks much like another. No one bothered to count them, so everyone got subsidies for the same trees. Then the subsidies got phased out. So the co-op was formed. A few oil samples were faked and the supermarket deal came.'

'It's not really organic, then?'

'Oh no, far from it. That would mean real work. No, they get sprayed a lot. For Dacus fly and other pests.'

'And the name changing?'

'It worked once; so why not twice? Another name, another supermarket, another exclusive deal.'

'So that's where the Moroccan oil comes in.'

'Moroccan oil is good oil and still quite cheap. In a bottle with a label from an organic Greek estate, it suddenly becomes very expensive.'

'I know, I bought some of it. And the supermarkets – don't they know this is going on? Don't they visit sometimes to see how it's all going?'

'The supermarkets try not to know. They all want the business. Were you sent to find out about the oil or to find the woman?'

'I think I was sent to see how well the secret was kept.'

'Then finding out might well put you in danger. You *and* your friends . . .'

'Is that why you are telling me? To make it too dangerous for me?'

A faint smile, a waggle of the head. 'If you've been inside the plantation, then you already know.' He avoided my eyes, looking vaguely across the narrow valley. 'My eyesight may be going, but I still know every stone in this village. We used to play here a lot as children. There was only one old couple left up here then, eking out an existence. Keeping a goat, growing some vegetables, keeping chickens. Some winters, they must have been near starvation. Yet they couldn't bear to leave this place. You don't belong here, Mr Honeysett. None of you does. You can easily leave and go back to your life in England. This is a poor country and the supermarkets are very rich.' I opened my mouth to protest, but he cut across me. 'Have you tried the oil?'

'I bought some in England.'

'And did you like it? Of course you did. Perhaps you think you are a connoisseur but really you know very little about olive oil. And so it was good enough for you.'

'How about Turkish hazelnut oil, then?'

'You found that out, too? Then you really must go home, Mr Honeysett.'

'What about it?'

He looked at me for a moment, shrugged: what the hell. 'That's a separate venture. Hazelnut oil doesn't taste of much. With a bit of deodorizing and mixing with strong cheap extra virgin, it makes a passable olive oil. Everyone does it; the Italians did it first. Everyone knows they're exporting twice as much oil as they produce. It has to come from somewhere, you know.'

'So it's all rubbish? None of it is real? Where do you go for real olive oil?'

He pushed himself off from the tree he'd been leaning against and walked off without looking back. 'Your olive trees. *Your own* olive trees. Go home and plant some, Mr Honeysett. And take your friends with you. Soon?'

I watched him walk away until he disappeared behind a building near the church.

When I returned to the long table in the courtyard, I found Annis in a less than chatty mood. Louise chased the last olive round her plate with a morsel of bread. 'Nice lunch; every bit as good as last night's supper.'

'It was breakfast.'

'You have lavish breakfasts.'

'Trying to.' There was stale bread and some honey left. I drowned the former in the latter and stuffed it in my mouth before Tim could snaffle it. Everyone except the students was here.

'Are your students likely to come in at any moment?'

Morva checked her watch. 'Not for half an hour or so.'

It seemed somehow proper to make my report to Louise, perhaps to convince her that I wasn't completely useless. 'Kyla is alive and she's on the island.'

'Where? At the co-op?'

'Quite likely. Remember the quad biker driving out to the shed?' I asked Annis.

'Uh-huh.'

'I think that's where they keep her. To stop her from exposing the fact that the place exports fake olive oil.'

'And the supermarket is selling it? Last year half their organic vegetables were found to have pesticides on them. No wonder they don't want this to come out. Kyla must have got wind of it somehow.'

'So why don't we just call the police right now?' Charlie asked.

'Because we're pretty certain they're in on it.'

Louise was getting agitated. 'I can't believe we're sitting round here discussing it. Let's go there and get her out. Now!'

'There's Vampire Boy,' Annis warned.

'Who's Vampire Boy?'

'They've got someone guarding the place with a shotgun. He was wearing some vampire tee shirt when we saw him,' I explained.

'What kind of tee shirt?'

'It had some sort of joke . . .'

Annis helped me out. 'It said "Have a Stake in the Future, Become a Vampire".'

'*What?* That's *my* tee shirt. I mean, it's Kyla's. I had it printed for her because of the teen vampire stuff she likes to watch. I invented that slogan; you can't buy them. She's definitely there. We must get her out.' Louise shot up from her seat.

I pulled her down again. 'We will.'

'When?'

'As soon as it's dark.'

'And the vampire shotgun?' Annis asked, not unreasonably.

I had no plan at all but Morva came to my rescue. 'We'll all go. Not the students, I mean, but us lot here. They're not mad; they can't kidnap or shoot all of us.'

'Oh, quite,' Annis agreed. 'Not all of us. Remind me, Chris: was it a double-barrelled shotgun?'

I ignored her. 'Tim, you can get us in through the gate, surely?'

'No probs.'

'There you are,' I said to Louise. 'We'll set off as soon as it gets dark.'

Sophie's eyes shone. 'I'm gonna come, too. The more the better. Surely.'

We had managed to persuade the students to go for a meal in Corfu Town, but Sophie had changed her mind at the last minute and stayed behind.

'You shouldn't have told her,' I said to Charlie, who was unsuccessfully trying to get Sophie to relinquish her wine bottle.

'Let her come with us.'

'She's pissed.'

'She'll be fine. I'll look after her,' he promised.

'On your head be it.'

At dusk, we set off in the two cars, with Charlie and Sophie, who was still stubbornly clutching her bottle, in the back of my rented wreck. As agreed, we drove in convoy through the village, waved at anyone who was looking as though we were off on an adventure.

Which we were. At the turn-off to the olive grove, I slowed. No one appeared to be around and I gave the OK signal to turn on to the narrow track. After a hundred yards and out of sight of the road, we turned off the track and cut the engines.

It was darker here than I had anticipated, but this was my third visit and I remembered it well enough to lead the troops, all but Sophie, who had passed out in the back of the car, clutching her bottle. We decided it was safer to leave her there, and after a short march and stumble we reached the front gate.

We stood back in the darkness, breathing in the faint scent of charcoal burning, while Tim magicked the lock open. It took him all of one minute to defeat it. We left the gate ajar for a swifter exit and moved quietly along the lane. I took point with Annis behind me, while Charlie brought up the rear.

We had had a short argument about whether or not we should arm ourselves, and he was still unhappy that he had not been allowed to bring clubs, knives, billhooks and pitchforks on the raid. He remained unconvinced by my argument that if you went equipped for an uprising, then that's what you were likely to get. Now, as we padded softly down the track towards an electric nimbus of light, I was ready to admit that some sort of weapon would have given me a little more confidence than I was feeling.

The yard was lit by its three feeble lamps. Where I had last seen Vampire Boy and a pile of empty barrels stood the BMW, the quad bike and trailer and Margarita's battered moped. The lights were on in the Portakabin office and the barbecue was sending up thin wisps of smoke. As arranged, we stuck together – based on Morva's assumption that they wouldn't shoot a whole crowd of people – and stuck to the paths, thinking that it would be a lot quieter than six people stumbling in the dark through the undergrowth. This meant cutting across the right-hand corner of the yard, within sight of the Portakabin window, behind which I could see shadows move.

Never had three light bulbs appeared so bright. I halted my squad at the edge of the light and murmured to Annis, 'Keep low and slow, past the quad bike and down the path on the right. Pass the word.' I waited until the Chinese whispers had died down, then set off on a ridiculous duck walk across the yard. To my ears, we sounded less like ducks, more like a trampling line of rhino. At every step I expected an eruption of shouts or shots, and when we had all made it on to the path and out of the immediate pool of light, I could hardly believe it. We straightened up gratefully in the relative safety of the trees among which the path disappeared into the dark.

'I can't see it, but the hut is somewhere back there.'

'What if she's not in there?' asked Tim, not unreasonably.

Standing in the dark, I conjured up the image of the quad bike rumbling past towards the hut that evening. Crockery is what I heard clink on the trailer. Quadman was taking food to the hut. 'She's there.'

'Then let's go,' Louise hissed.

The path curved gently as the darkness under the trees closed in around us. Not daring to use even the tiny torch I had brought, I was reduced to walking at a snail's pace with both arms outstretched, the blind leading the blind. Of course, it could be anyone inside that hut, I realized now – a sick person perhaps, an elderly relative who needed looking after, a wounded man with a gun under his pillow . . . I had trouble keeping the worst case scenarios from popping into my mind.

'There.' Visible at first only as a dark outline, the stone hut took reluctant shape.

Tim appeared by my side. 'What kind of lock does the door have?' he murmured.

'No idea; never been here. You go look.'

'Oh, ta.'

'All right, I'll come with you.'

As we got within eight or ten feet of the front, we could hear small noises, occasional muffled thumps. And perhaps a voice. Tim had heard it too and laid a hand on my arm. The noises continued. Together, we approached another couple of feet on tiptoe, then stopped when we heard what was clearly a human voice, talking in a quiet, desultory way on the other side of the door in between the other muffled sounds. I held my breath as Tim and I closed the final distance between us and the door.

There were two voices. One male, one female. It was impossible to make out what they were saying. I pulled Tim back from the door to where the others were waiting. I found Louise in the darkness. 'Go and listen at the door. See if you recognize her voice.'

Without a word, Louise slipped away to the front of the hut. After only a few seconds of listening, Louise tapped on the door. 'Kyl, it's me, it's me; we're getting you out.'

Tim was there in an instant and I followed behind. Everyone seemed to be talking at once: the voices behind the door, Tim complaining that the lock was too stiff, Louise chattering soothingly that we'd have her out in no time at all – and me telling them all to shut up. And then Tim finally got the door open with a squawk of the hinges that sounded to my ears like a scream. A man and a woman tumbled out, the woman flying straight into Louise's arms. One – perhaps both of them – crying now. We were out of sight of the yard, and there were so many of us now it felt quite safe to turn on my torch. I shone it into the face of the man. It was Kladders, the man from the boat. His face was bruised and there was dried blood around his mouth.

'What are you doing here?' I whispered, not ready to trust anyone quite yet.

'I'm a journalist. Undercover. Well, I was until they found my mobile. I'd dropped it in the shed.'

At last I had a look at Kyla. Life in the hut had not been good for her: her skin was pale and her hair wild. But she looked very alive and happy to be standing under the stars. Gloves introduced us. 'You've no idea how glad I am you found us,' Kyla said.

'Team effort. How long have you been stuck in there?'

'Weeks. Dimitris and his friends were supposed to get rid of me but couldn't bring themselves to do it. They told their mafia chums I was dead and buried in the groves somewhere. How long they thought I could survive in that hut I have no idea. I think I was meant to grow old in there.'

'Is this what you came here for? The olive oil scam?'

'Yes. I had seen some suspicious emails as far back as two years ago but had been told not to worry about it.'

'But you did.'

'They were going to ignore it all. They knew they were selling bog-standard olive oil as their flagship organic oil. But they had just spent nearly a million on an advertising campaign with the nation's favourite fat chef endorsing the stuff. Last year half of their organic veg was found to have pesticides on them, and not long before that lots of their so called "freedom food" was proven to come from intensive farms.

They couldn't afford another scandal or middle-class shoppers would have walked out on them. Ask Kladders here; he was investigating the lot of them.'

'Yes. Shame we could not have met earlier. Much as I have enjoyed your company these past few days. I think Morton hired Mr Honeysett here to find out whether you were safely out of the way or could suddenly reappear to become a huge embarrassment.'

'I'm going to take great pleasure in becoming embarrassing,' Kyla said. 'I'll also sue the pants off him and the company.'

'I'll be glad to help,' promised Kladders. 'But right now we should really get out of here. These guys are jittery as hell since Mr Honeysett's last visit and we're all making too much noise.'

He was right. We'd been standing and chatting as though it was all over. I shushed everyone and took the lead again. Our easy success seemed to have lightened everyone's spirit just a little too much: our footsteps were heavier, our breathing louder and, behind me, everyone still whispered and murmured.

Kladders walked beside me. 'If it wasn't so dark, I'd say we'd strike across through the trees, but it would make even more noise. We've really got to get out of here quickly. Their lords and masters are due any minute and they're not from peasant stock, I can tell you. We were trying to dig our way out of the hut with a soup spoon when you came.'

We had reached the edge of the yard. 'Have you got cars nearby?' Kladders murmured.

'Just outside the gate. We left the gate open.'

'Then I suggest we run for it.'

But it was too late. The headlights of the BMW flared up and two men stepped into our path. One of them was Vampire Boy. He levelled his shotgun at us and swept it from side to side, keeping everyone covered. The man next to him was the friendly cafe owner, Dimitris. He held a baseball bat and didn't look so friendly now. Vampire Boy started shouting. 'One person move, I shoot everybody! No you move!'

The third man from the car joined the line-up. He was carrying no weapon but moved nervously, and looked light on his feet like a boxer. Behind them all, at the window of the

Portakabin, the unmistakable shape of Margarita. Morva bravely stepped forward and instantly the shotgun was levelled at her. She started a fierce exchange in Greek with Dimitris. He didn't meet her gaze but kept a close eye on the males in the company, whom he perceived as the greater threat.

He was wrong, of course. Behind enemy lines, into the pool of light, slanted the less than steady figure of Sophie. Every few steps she stopped to fortify herself with a swig from her bottle before advancing further. Morva turned up the volume to keep the Greeks focused on her. At the window, Margarita, despite having a grandstand view, stood unmoving as Sophie staggered up to our adversaries. Having first satisfied herself that the bottle was really empty, Sophie changed her grip on it, swung it high and hit Vampire Boy over the head. The bottle didn't break. The man staggered and the gun slid from his hand. Sophie swung again, overbalanced and stumbled back. Dimitris reached for the shotgun, but Morva jumped on him like a wildcat before he could get his hands on it. Now Margarita came flying out of the Portakabin and for a few seconds the fight turned into a free-for-all until three cars, headlights blazing, came down the track, fanned out and began shedding men, some in police uniform, some in mufti. They descended on us in a frenetic rush, not bothering to establish who was who, everyone shouting in Greek or English.

Behind them, at a leisurely pace, strode up Superintendent Michael Needham with the officer from Athens. 'That's right – we'll sort the wheat from the chaff later; for the moment, arrest all of them.' Needham pointed a chubby finger at me. 'But especially that one.'

EPILOGUE

The body of Petros Grapsas, the tax inspector the police had been looking for, was only later 'rediscovered' during restoration work at the farmhouse, since we all thought there was already enough to explain and the air conditioning at police headquarters had been turned off to save money. Needham and his incorruptible counterpart from Athens had been investigating all around us right from the start, which explained why, in Corfu, even the tails had tails.

No one congratulated us on freeing Kyla and Kladders. Apparently, the Greek police really do not like foreign PIs working in their country without a licence. After interminable questioning, they booked me a seat on the next plane back to Blighty. I explained to them that I never flew. They were very understanding and gave me a window seat.

Helen and Rob mysteriously vanished. They and their luggage disappeared while everyone was busy being grilled by the police.

Sophie, who had drunkenly saved the day, sobered up and went back to Lincoln to look after the living and bring up her daughter. But she kept on the flat with sea view, north of Corfu Town.

Tim and Annis, who could both produce return tickets, were allowed to stay for another week of sunbathing and kebab snaffling. Derringer, a real villain without a passport, took to the hills behind Ano Makriá until everyone had gone, then returned to Morva's place where he's being spoiled rotten by her new batch of painting students. Because Morva *did* stay on, running her freshly registered painting school and feeling much safer now with Charlie there to lend a hand. Apart from being a good life model, he turned out to be an excellent cook, which none of us had realized before, since, as he rightly pointed out, no one had ever asked.

It was later in the same year that I received a large envelope with unintelligible French postmark and no return address. Inside was a small watercolour sketch of an eighteenth- or nineteenth-century French farmhouse, seen against a backdrop of olive trees. In the foreground, near an empty easel, stood two deckchairs. On one of them lay a paint-spattered straw hat.